THE ONE THAT I WANT

SCORNED WOMEN'S SOCIETY BOOK #3

PIPER SHELDON

WWW.SMARTYPANTSROMANCE.COM

COPYRIGHT

DEDICATION

To J.R., always

And to my readers, so glad to find you here

CHAPTER 1

ROXY

*T*onight I could be nobody. I had no worries waiting for me. I was just a woman looking to get her dance on. And I was damn happy about that.

The club music pumped all around me, taking over my mind, drowning out the responsibilities that waited for me back in Green Valley, Tennessee. Lights flashed in a pleasing and disorienting way. Bodies all around me moved to the heavy bass and electronic beats; some faced the stage, dancing solo, others paired up, groups of girls clumped together to form that invisible, creep-repellent forcefield any clubbing regular immediately recognizes.

Blissfully in my own world, my arms reached for the sky and I rocked my hips to a sexy blend of hip-hop and Latin that had me flexing newly learned dance moves. Despite how my sweaty face probably looked, I was happy. One dance club in a foreign city, and I could take a full breath for the first time in years. Six years ago, I was given a second chance to change my life. I vowed I would never let down those who saved me.

But maybe just one night off to dance was okay too.

I danced until I forgot about what waited for me back home. The chaos that Diane Donner's sudden disappearance left, the worry about the promotion I was desperate to earn, or the new manager that was in charge of that decision. I hopped up and down to the music, shaking off the thoughts that threatened to ground me.

An awareness of being watched had me twirl to scan the crowd. Something across the room snagged my attention. Rather, someone. A man stood at the bar, leaning casually despite intense eye contact that zipped through me. Or at least I thought he was looking at me. It was hard to tell among the flashing lights and jumping bodies. A group of girls jostled me and I lost sight of him. I turned in time to the music, trying to spot him again, wondering if I imagined that initial jolt of energy.

There had been something about his look. It wasn't that scary, stomach-hurting focus that some men triggered. Instead, there was an intense interest to it that felt like more than just a passing glance. It was rare for me to make eye contact with someone and react so physically. His gaze had been piercing but his light coloring surprised me the most. Light hair, light eyes, even across the dark bar I could tell that much. He required more time to study. For science.

Sadly, I would never know because he had disappeared.

It wasn't long before a deeply satisfying sweat broke out on my brow. I was getting overheated in my favorite leather jacket over a loose tank top and tight jean skirt. When the band took a break, I pushed through the crowd of people toward the bathroom. I missed this in some ways, the electricity of bodies and music and being free. I didn't really let myself go in Green Valley unless it was from within the safety net of the Scorned Women's Society, SWS for short. They were my gravity when the world spun out around me.

I didn't have the same startling beauty that Suzie Samuels had. I didn't charm easy like Kim Dae. I couldn't say whatever came to mind like

Gretchen LaRoe. I only had the protection of looking completely unapproachable.

I patted my face with a damp paper towel to cool off, careful to not blur my eyeliner. My fingertips shook my bangs back in place. I tilted my head and squinted at my reflection. Gretchen once said she envied my resting bitch face, RBF for short. (A term I resented but, unfortunately, universally acknowledged.) She told me it was my superpower. She was right. I did not exist to make sure people felt comfortable when they looked at me.

My full lips and freakishly long lashes gave me a perpetually pouty face. People always asked me if I was cosmetically altered. It didn't help that I was naturally thin and covered in tattoos. I always drew looks. Typically, I just gave them one of my winning glares and they scurried away. Smiles came as easy for me as catching a greased-up pig and stayed half as long. My blunt-cut bangs and thick eyeliner completed my badass look.

As I washed my hands, a younger girl—or maybe I was getting ancient at twenty-eight but she looked like a baby—stepped up next to me to wash her own. I felt more than saw her look me up and down. I kept my focus on my reflection.

She was just about to leave the bathroom, when I said, "Hey, you. Stop."

She froze and turned around. She looked around and back to me, before gripping her clutch tighter. "Uh, yeah?"

I rolled my eyes. Even when happy, apparently I looked meaner than a wet panther. I needed a T-shirt that said "nicer than my face looks." My RBF was a good thing when I still rode with a scary motorcycle club called the Iron Wraiths, but since leaving, I overanalyzed every interaction I had with "normals." It helped to think, *What would the SWS do?* Kim would become her best friend. Suzie would give her makeup tips. Gretchen would probably find out what she needed in five minutes and figure out how to get it for her in another five. Me? I didn't bring anything to the table, but I could get better.

I pointed to the toilet paper stuck to her shoe. "You've got a clinger," I said dryly.

She followed my gaze and let out a nervous giggle. "Oh. Thanks," she said and scraped it off.

I turned back to dry my hands as she left, making sure to take my time so I wouldn't have to make small talk with her. I was making changes but it wasn't time to start expecting miracles. After I double-checked my eyeliner was in place, I made my way down to the dance floor.

Carillo's was a hipster gastropub turned nightclub in downtown Denver. It was recommended to me by one of the vendors I had hit it off with earlier at the hospitality convention. I'd spent the last two days representing Donner Lodge, trying to gain new business and potential vendors: corporate suits, fake smiles, small talk, blah. I was beyond exhausted but certainly earned a promotion when I got back. The vendor with the most potential was a corporate adventure company called Outside the Box. Before today I'd never even heard of outdoors activities used to bond coworkers, but after a long conversation with the co-owner, William, not only did I understand the popularity but could easily see how they'd fit in at the Lodge. It was actually William who told me to use his name to bypass the line to get into the club tonight.

Now I could let the weight of responsibility melt off me like humidity on a glass of sweet tea. I was going to dance until my thighs shook or my feet gave up.

The walls of Carillo's were draped with gold pressed-velvet curtains interspersed with a wide range of mixed media art—or random junk from garage sales—it was hard to tell in the dim lighting. Crystal-beaded chandeliers dropped from the ceiling. Couches made of jewel-toned velvet were tucked away in deep alcoves that lined the dance floor and the upper level. Burly bearded bartenders scrambled to keep up with shouted orders.

I went to the bar and chugged a water. I definitely didn't scan the room for that man that watched me earlier. What I felt was a one-off. I didn't care about men in bars anymore. Especially not tonight.

Though I had just told myself how content I was to dance alone, I couldn't help a hint of disappointment. I had cooled off considerably but wasn't done dancing yet. The band was getting ready to go back onstage for their next set. I took off my jacket and folded it gently and placed it on a barstool. It felt like taking off a protective shield.

I backed up, ready to get back to the dance floor when I smacked into a solid body.

"Watch it," I mumbled as I was steadied by strong hands on my shoulders. Then I remembered to be nice and tried to scoot to the side.

The arms held me gently in place. When I looked up, glaring pointedly, he dropped them. It was Mr. Eye Contact from across the room. A little thrill tickled the back of my knees. He was damn fine this close up. Not my taste, but definitely a certain appeal. Like, if I wanted to know someone with a yacht to "summer on," he'd be my type.

His eyes were startlingly blue. His hair was this dark shade of blond, thick waves swept back with lighter tips that looked as though it had been bleached naturally by the sun. A smile quirked his mouth and my focus moved there. He had soft crinkles around the corners of his eyes and a natural tan that spoke of time outside.

He said something with the tilt of his head and a soft smile on his lips. I blinked away, wondering if my mouth had been hanging open catching flies as I took him in.

"What?" I yelled and pointed to my ear. The band had just started back up.

His smile grew to expose that two front teeth protruded just a little. It was a disarmingly charming flaw, like a puppy with just one floppy ear. His gaze moved over the exposed skin of my neck and shoulders under my tank top, seemingly studying the tattoos.

I wasn't knocking my edgy looks, but I typically didn't attract men who could have been plucked straight from an Ivy League fraternity mixer. At least the collar of his black button-up wasn't popped. And he wore nice sneakers and jeans, not boat shoes and pink shorts. Okay, so he wasn't preppy per se, but squeaky? Like he'd hurt my teeth to take a bite out of. He didn't even have a beard, for crying out loud. Not to box this guy in, but guys like this did not go for girls like me. Then again, sometimes there were the guys who liked to "slum it" with the easy small-town girls from Green Valley.

Mr. Eye Contact leaned closer. He smelled like a shower after a hard workout. It was like the cleansing smell of a spring morning after working all night at the Dragon Bar. My jaw was clenched tight, thinking about taking a bite out of him again.

"Dance?" he asked. His voice had a rich and deep timbre that sent a tiny shudder down my spine.

His confidence was sexy without being overwhelming. He tucked his hands deep into his pockets and waited patiently as I took him in, studying him head to toe. There was no pressure in his question. I suspected if I said no, he'd walk away without another word. I told myself I wanted to dance alone but suddenly I wasn't so sure. Wouldn't it be nice to have hands on me? Wouldn't it be an escape to just be a woman dancing with a man to good music?

Shocking myself, I realized I was interested. So I felt a zing for this man? It didn't mean anything. It meant that my warning system wasn't going off. It meant that I was a person who wanted to dance. It didn't have to *mean* anything.

He extended his hand. I bit my lip. I was here to celebrate my hard work. It was one night before an early flight home tomorrow.

"What the hell?" I said unheard in the club.

I slid my hand into his. His hand was not the buttery-soft warmth of an Ivy Leaguer. His hand was calloused and hot. What might it feel like to have those rough palms gripping the tender skin of my hips?

He pulled me only long enough to let me pass, then he let me lead the way to the floor. As I made my way to the other dancers, I felt his gaze on my backside like the vibration of a motorcycle. I risked a glance over my shoulder. His focus returned to mine as he licked his bottom lip.

"Lord, help me," I mumbled to myself.

Good thing it was just one night and just one dance. This guy would be way too easy to fall for. But what could one dance with a stranger hurt?

CHAPTER 2

SANDERS

*W*hen the universe gave me a sign, I listened.

I'd come to Carillo's to find the team and apologize. I'd planned to tell them how I would make things right. They knew I would. They knew my head hadn't been right, not since …

No. I wasn't thinking about that tonight. I was here to start to fix the terrible day I'd caused. The conference, the biggest hospitality convention of the year. The one we'd been preparing for the last three months. The one that could help save our business. And I missed it. I owed Skip a kidney for stepping in last minute.

At least the day *had* been terrible. Until she danced into my line of sight, a sign that even I was worth saving. Now it was quite possibly about to be the best day of my life. Recently I'd felt like I could do nothing right, but maybe coming here tonight was turning the tide back in my favor. The bouncer Ty had waved me right in as he always did when Skip and I sometimes met the team here.

When I first spotted her about an hour ago, I felt the whole energy of the day finally shift. It was like driving with the emergency brake on and not understanding why I couldn't move forward. Or what that burning smell was.

She had been dancing alone, as though she didn't have a care in the world. No, that wasn't right. She danced as though this moment could put all the cares of the world on hold. She moved with languid confidence. She was fully present. Didn't care about any of the people around her.

Our eyes had met across the bar for only an instant before she vanished into the crowd. I found her again at the bar, taking off her leather jacket, revealing a beautiful long neck, smooth shoulders, and an array of tattoos, covering her arms and peeking out from under her short skirt and flimsy blouse.

As soon as she reappeared, I couldn't risk losing her again. There was no thought. My feet carried me until I stood in front of her. It was obvious she didn't want a dance partner; many men had tried to move up to her but she ignored them. But if I left this bar without at least asking her, it would stick in my brain and I'd regret everything about this day.

Second chances in life were rare. You had to take what you could, when you could. Though it was crazy, watching her dance made me think that she understood that. She was so taken aback when I asked her to dance, I thought for sure she'd say no. And yet here we were. Moving in perfect tandem on the dance floor.

I had no idea what I was doing but I had learned early on that you just had to pretend that you knew and soon you would. Fake it until you make it.

We faced each other and moved without speaking. She was almost as tall as me and I liked that along with her broody fashion-model vibe. The flashing lights would occasionally catch her face, highlighting full, beautiful lips and dark eyes shadowed by long lashes. Her long brown hair with fringe emphasized her intense focus that kept flicking over me, like she didn't know what to think of me. The more I smiled at her, the more her frown grew. She was so open and free with her movements but at the same time her expression remained distant. I wanted to talk to her and learn everything about her.

We faced each other and danced without touching. I fixed that as the music changed to a tango-style tempo. I pulled her closer, my hands on her hips. She wrapped her arms around my neck, occasionally she'd run a hand down my arms, back, and shoulders, like she couldn't help herself. Fuck if that didn't make me feel like a king.

The key to dancing with a woman? Spinning them. If they couldn't get orientated, then they couldn't tell you actually had no idea what you were doing. As I twirled her away and back, she tossed her head with a laugh before hiding her face in my neck. Her hair smelled fruity and sweet, a surprising contrast to her dark edges. I liked how she ran her fingers through it as she danced, how she threw it around her as she spun. It was as part of her dancing as her hips were.

I brought her back so I could keep studying her face. I couldn't get enough of it. She was gorgeous and hypnotic. Pouty and dark, and completely intriguing. My arm was wrapped tight around her core, her breasts pushed up against me as the tempo changed to more of a samba. Her arms wrapped around my neck and her scent engulfed me.

"What's your name?" I shouted close to her ear but her head shook without understanding. Now wasn't the time for talking anyway.

I slid my thigh in between hers and hefted her up onto me. I was lost in the way we were dirty dancing. The bass pumped with the rhythm of our bodies. Her shirt stuck to her damp skin. As I pulled her higher up my leg, her skirt rode up. Her skin was smooth and soft under my palm.

My hands splayed out across her rib cage. The edge of my thumb grazed the bottom of her breast and she shivered, dropping her head back. Her arms lifted to run through my certainly sweaty hair but she didn't seem to care. Her eyes burned as she brought me closer so that our faces were almost touching. The heat of her gaze was unbearable and amazing.

Her arms gripped my biceps, maybe for balance, but maybe not. Her gaze followed to where I had been memorizing where she rode my leg. Her blink seemed to slow down as she bit down on her lip.

I took a risk. My mouth lowered to hers while our bodies still rocked. It wasn't a deep kiss, more a grazing of lips. To test the waters. To see if she felt everything I was. There was no trace of alcohol and there was no haziness in her gaze save the heavy-lidded blink of longing after I pulled back to study her.

I felt more than heard her gasp of pleasure. The flare of interest in her big brown eyes told me this definitely wasn't one-sided. Our mouths met again. There was no hesitation this time. I kissed her, she kissed me back. I pushed forward and she pushed back. Every action, she met me fully. Our bodies stopped dancing, still entangled.

I couldn't believe we were making out like this on the dance floor like teenagers at a high school dance. Maybe I should be worried about it but all I could think was … well, I couldn't think and that's what made it so fucking fantastic.

When we pulled apart, I took a steadying breath in. If the cost of this perfect kiss was my shitty day, then I'd pay it every day for the rest of my life. She was looking at me with eyes wide and her mouth slightly parted. I wanted to lick those lips until she moaned my name. But first, I'd probably have to tell her my name.

Dancing was no longer enough. I glanced around to see if there were any open booths but she must have had the same idea. I found myself being dragged toward the hallway, next to the bar, that led to the kitchen. There was a small alcove that looked like it might have held a pay phone years ago. We tucked into it as a server passed.

My mouth was on hers again as soon as we stopped. This time I delved deeper, exploring her with my tongue and she opened up for me, exploring in return. I held her waist, thumbs grazing up and down, greedy for more but recognizing that we were still very much in public. She gripped my arms, pulling me closer. I pressed her against the wall and my need for her brushed her thigh. We pulled apart, both panting and sweating.

"Holy shit." She blinked up at me.

"You're amazing," I said with a laugh at her bluntness. "I've never done this before." I wasn't sure why I said that. It was the first thing that popped out of my mouth. I needed her to understand I'd never felt such extreme and immediate electricity from a touch. Kissing someone had never felt this frustrating and rewarding at the same time.

Her eyes grew wide. Maybe I had been too forward.

"What?" I asked.

"You have an accent. Australian?" she asked in a thick accent of her own. I'd lived in the US long enough to know it was Southern but not able to pinpoint it exactly.

I nodded with a cheeky grin. "So do you."

Her eyes narrowed. "Fair point."

"Though usually people know this about me before we reach this point."

"You just said you've never done this before?" she asked, with a hint of teasing behind her sarcasm.

"No," I said. I forced the seriousness into the word. I lowered my head close to her. "It's never felt like this." There must have been an unspoken message to my tone, because the furrow in her brow melted away.

Her chest heaved. Her long eyelashes almost touched her eyebrows. Her lips shone as her mouth formed an O. Those lips were handcrafted to drive me crazy.

"Me neither," she whispered.

My hands cupped her head and I brought her to me again. This time when we kissed, it was less fevered and more luxurious.

A small part of me was already worrying about what came next. I needed more. I didn't want to come on too strong but I couldn't let this go. What if I couldn't ever let this go? This was something. I broke our kiss. My thumb brushed along her bottom lip. Her eyes fluttered and her body shivered.

"You want to get out of here?" I asked.

But where could we go? I wasn't ready to go home and face reality. This perfect moment was like an umbrella, soon reality would come pouring down. Soaking me to the bones. Making me icy.

"I'm at the hotel. Across the street." After she said it, she made a face like she couldn't believe herself.

Her gaze flickered over my own stare. Were we doing this?

She misinterpreted my delay in responding. She shook her head. "Shit, er, sorry. We just said we never do this—"

"I want to." I searched her face for any sign that she may not want it but everything about her languid lean against the wall, the flush in her cheeks, and the heaving of her chest told me she was right there with me.

"Let me just go to the bathroom," she said. "And then we can go."

I dropped my head to kiss her again. It was absurd but my chest already ached at the thought of her walking away. I gripped her hands in mine, intertwining our fingers as we kissed once more. I could deal with the worst of what life had to offer. Because whenever there was darkness, there were also bits of sunshine like this to balance it out.

I pulled back and she straightened. She smoothed her skirt and touched her lips in a daze. "Give me two shakes," she said and I loved the twang of her sweet voice.

I watched her the whole time as she crossed the bar and moved toward the bathrooms. She turned around to glance back at me. I grinned and she bit back a smile.

I definitely didn't deserve this woman, but I wasn't about to let her go without getting to know her more.

CHAPTER 3

ROXY

I took a steadying breath as I pushed into the bathroom unable to help the smile that pulled at the side of my mouth. My goodness. Who was I? Who was this man?

I halted. Wait. Seriously, who? I hadn't gotten his name yet.

"Lord, help me." I looked to the ceiling. I'd lost my damn mind and I didn't care. I was giddy with lust. I hadn't wanted anybody like that … well, I honestly don't know that I ever had wanted somebody so bad. So instantly. I thought that was a made-up thing, but the second we started dancing, I felt it. Hormones? Pheromones? Whatever it was called, I was all for it.

I did my business and replayed some of my favorite memories of the night. So far. I wanted to burn them into my brain, so I could pull them up at any time like a slideshow for my lady spankbank. His calloused hand sliding up my thigh. His hip as it pushed and pulled mine on the dance floor. His grumbly hum as my booty shoved against his arousal.

My goodness, I was hotter than a jalapeño on a campfire. I was in over my head and I needed a second opinion.

I opened my group conversation with the SWS. My thumbs hesitated over the screen. What's the best way to ask what to do when you meet a crazy hot Australian that makes you feel like you tripped and fell in ecstasy and that you want to take him back to the hotel and do bad things with him that feel very, very good?

Roxy: Met a hot guy. Brain is broke.

Roxy: Tell me to pump the brakes.

I waited for a response, unsure who I'd hear from. Blithe had all but stopped hanging out with the SWS for reasons unknown. Kim was off all the time with some new mysterious conductor guy. I met him once when he invited us to his house. That part was cool and his house was amazing. Who was I to hate on a moody masked man, but I knew he was hiding himself from Kim and that was not cool. Even Suzie was with Ford more often than not. That left Gretchen, who was always there at least. Everything else was changing.

Kim responded immediately.

Kim: What's his name?

Suzie: Drive faster!

Gretchen: SEND A PIC

I shook my head at my friends but felt some of the tension relax out of me. I wouldn't be doing anything I might regret later.

Roxy: Don't know his name. He's HOT and sweet. Not pushy.

I chewed on my lip and thought more.

Roxy: I'm not taking a pic, you freak.

Gretchen: It was worth a shot.

Gretchen: You don't know his name, you ho! ;)

We teased each other mercilessly but this was exactly why I had texted them. What was I doing? I didn't know his name. I didn't know anything about him.

Not entirely true. I knew that his scent grew intoxicating when he sweat, pumped full of some sort of magic that shot straight to my ovaries. I knew that when creeps started to move up on me, he gently danced me away without making a scene but clearly marking me as taken. I knew that his accent was sexy as fuck. Oh, and most importantly I *knew* that he kissed like he was giving life. That his hands stayed respectful but hot enough to know he was as close to losing control as I was. I knew that he was well endowed. Sorry, but I am *so* not sorry. I knew when he focused on me, I felt like I was the most interesting person in a club full of attractive people. That was heady stuff.

My phone pinged.

Kim: If you want us to talk you out of going home with him, we will. Have you been drinking?

Roxy: No.

I responded instantly. Kim didn't mess around with drinking anymore because of her short time with the Wraiths. I didn't blame her at all. I saved my drinking for special occasions.

Suzie: Leave if you aren't comfortable.

I frowned. I was very comfortable with him. That was part of the problem. He made me feel so good. I was ready to jump in headfirst like I used to, before I had been saved from the Iron Wraiths.

Roxy: I leave in the morning. I should cut this short.

Gretchen: You can always just talk.

Her words surprised me. I thought she'd be the first to tell me to get away from him without looking back. She had trust issues with men.

Honestly, most of the SWS did. My gaze snagged on my reflection in the full-length mirror.

My shirt had come untucked during my encounter with the mysterious stranger, revealing a hint of one of the tattoos on my hip. As I tucked the material in again and smoothed my skirt down, I shivered. All the delicious heat generated by our short encounter swiftly left my body in an inexplicable draft of icy dread.

"What am I doing?" I asked the woman staring back at me in the mirror.

Like two lenses trying to focus down to one image, a mixed-up sight wobbled in front of me. The Roxy I was now overlay the Roxy of my past. Bleary eyes from drinking too much, too fast. Hair wild with curls and added volume. Eyeliner smeared. Lips swollen and smudged from making out. That Old Roxy stacked on top of the image of who I was now. Roxy who had gotten her life in order. Who had a good job and good friends. My mind flashed back to nights at the Dragon Bar when I'd drunkenly check myself out in the mirror. I remembered how it felt as a wave of depression crashed over me. How I swallowed it down, before going back out to dance with another biker I didn't like.

My breaths came shallow and fast, but in that chest-seizing way that made me feel like I might die.

All the work I'd done these last few years to change my life and what was I doing? What would the new manager of Donner Lodge think if he saw me now? I'd been sent to Denver to attend a hospitality convention and, after one night alone, I'd slipped right back into old habits. My goal tonight was only to go out and have fun with myself. Men were never on the schedule. I let myself get so caught up in one charming man.

I was supposed to be a professional. William from Outside the Box told me earlier that a lot of people from his company came to this bar. That he might even stop by. This wasn't Green Valley, but the industry was still small. Too small. I had cut it too close.

18

"Oh my God," I wheezed out and tried to steady my breath. I'd been such an idiot.

My phone vibrated again but I didn't check it. I had to leave. I didn't like myself like this. I had to be better than what I used to be: out of control. It would be okay. This was a blip in the radar. A relapse. I was still on track.

I'd sneak out of here and I'd never see him again.

The mature thing would be to go and tell him I changed my mind. Recalling the way he'd asked me to dance, my gut told me he wouldn't pressure me or make me feel guilty. He wasn't a man that felt that his attraction to me meant I owed him something.

But it wasn't him I was worried about. It was me. What if the second I saw him again or smelled him, or touched or tasted him, I'd be lost to my initial desire for him? All of my senses were out to get me. I have always been too good at making excuses to do bad things.

With a final bracing breath, I pushed out the door and beelined it to the side exit just past the kitchen. I pushed out into the dry, summer night, making it all the way across the street, almost to the hotel, when my feet stopped.

I couldn't leave like that. There was no way I'd ever see him again, but I could picture his face, frowning as he waited for me. The hurt he would feel with each passing second. No. I couldn't leave it like that. I had to woman up. I turned back to the club.

I smacked into him. Again.

"Oof," he grunted as I said, "Oh shit, sorry."

He steadied me again but quickly dropped his hands, making me feel even worse about glaring at him the first time.

He took a step back on the sidewalk. He couldn't quite meet my gaze, the hurt was written all over his puppy dog face. "You forgot your coat. It's nice. I thought you'd miss it."

"Thanks," was all I could manage, the words catching in my throat. He was too kind and sweet.

He ran a hand over his mouth, as though debating what to do next.

"I'm sorry if I came on too strong. I didn't mean to imply anything," he said.

With his head down and bathed in the soft halo of light from the street-light above, he looked up at me with scrunched-up eyebrows. Good Lord, this man was the emotional equivalent of a fireman holding a puppy. My body couldn't handle it.

I like you too much; it freaked me out. I come with a ton of baggage. This was just one night ...

"No," I said. "I have an early flight and lost track of time."

He looked me up and down quickly. He nodded once but I got the impression he hadn't fallen for my bullshit excuse.

I shrugged into my coat, the cool mountain air chilled me. Or my shitty behavior. I fixed my bangs back in place.

"Well, have a safe flight." He turned to go.

I gnawed my thumbnail as he retreated. Panic grew with every step he took away from me.

"Wait," I called completely surprising myself.

He was back in front of me in less than a second. "Yes?" His expression was open wide and a smile teased his mouth.

"It doesn't leave until six a.m.," I said.

I had hurt him. I didn't deserve another shot but I just wasn't ready to end this night. I fought to keep still as his smile grew.

"Plenty of time to get ice cream, hey?" he suggested.

I loved his accent even more every time her spoke. "Ice cream?"

"A sweet treat couldn't hurt? Maybe chat a bit and get to know each other."

I smiled at the ground and let my hair fall to cover my face. He didn't insist on my hotel room. He didn't ask for more explanations. He just wanted to go get ice cream. With me. The innocence of it made my heart swell. Had a man ever wanted to just *talk* with me? Sure, I had to leave in a few hours and would never talk to him again. But I could have tonight. We could have a few hours of talking. *Talking.* I could handle this.

I looked left and right, not sure what I had expected. "Ice cream actually sounds really good."

CHAPTER 4

SANDERS

I fought to keep from punching the air in victory. It was just ice cream but it felt like so much more. Another chance to explore why meeting this woman felt so right. I'd never felt a physical connection so strong, so fast. If touching her felt like a gift from the universe, imagine what good conversation would be like.

I laced my fingers through hers, desperate for contact again but keeping my touch light like capturing a baby bird. "Is this okay?" I asked.

Blush pinkened her cheeks as she glanced around the busy sidewalk. "Um, yeah." She lightly squeezed my hand back.

Not to put the horse before the cart, but I wracked my brain for things to ask her. I wanted to know anything and everything she'd share with me. And the way she called me back after returning her jacket, told me she wasn't ready to end the night yet either.

"I was thinking," I started as we maneuvered through the nighttime crowds, toward the 16th Street Mall area, "it's going to be difficult to have a conversation with you without knowing your name. I can't keep referring to you as The Beautiful Woman Who Stole My Heart On the Dance Floor."

She scoffed loudly. I was laying it on a little thick but I liked making her blush. You'd think she'd never been praised for her astounding beauty before.

"You're too much." She glanced away.

"I'm just looking out for you. It'll be easier to remember than Good-Looking Stranger With The Sweet Dance Moves."

She snickered again. Making her laugh was beginning to feel more valuable than the thrill of adrenaline. "Actually I've just been referring to you as Smooth Talker, not too bad."

"It's Sanders. I'm Sanders."

She stopped and her gaze narrowed before she tossed out her hands to the side. "Fine. I'm Roxanne."

"See, that wasn't too hard," I teased and then immediately started singing the famous song by The Police that shared her name. She gasped and covered my mouth with her hands after a few people stopped to stare at me.

"Stop. Oh my God!" She was laughing though and I continued through her fingers. "Shh. Stop," she pleaded with a grin, casting looks from side to side.

I pulled her closer. Her laughter stopped as her hands fell to her sides. Her gaze grew heavy as it dropped to my lips. I'd pay money to know if she was replaying our earlier kissing like I was.

She cleared her throat and stepped back. I gave her space but kept her hands grasped in mine.

"You know that song is about a hooker, right?" she asked with one arched eyebrow.

I frowned in thought before saying, "Actually, I think it's about a man who's fallen in love with a woman and is telling her she can forget about her dark past and just focus on their love."

Her mouth parted slightly and she studied my face like she was just seeing it for the first time. A moment later, she cleared her throat and the cool mask she wore was back in place.

"Most people call me Roxy anyway," she said in a soft voice and pulled me to start walking again.

I hoped I hadn't accidentally offended her as she grew quiet again. But at least I had her name. A name that suited her perfectly and now I couldn't see her as anyone else but beautiful Roxy. "Roxy, The Beautiful Woman Who Stole My Heart On the Dance Floor. But I suppose I could shorten it to just Roxy. Roxy and Sanders. Has a nice ring to it, don't you think?"

I snuck a glance to find her shaking her head with a quiet smile. "You're one of those painfully optimistic people, aren't you?" she asked.

"I just know how fast life can change. I prefer to live in the moment."

She went quiet again and I could almost see her digesting those words as her brow furrowed and lips pursed. "Life can change in an instant. We agree on that." Her free hand fiddled with the edge of her jacket as we walked.

"My best friend deals with that by trying to control every aspect of his life," I said. "I go the other route."

"What do you mean?"

"I like adventures. Skydiving, bungee jumping, base jumping. Really anything that involves a waiver and a free fall."

"Oh, okay. So you're a crazy person." She softened her jibe by poking me in the ribs.

"Nah. Just an adrenaline junky."

It had always been like that. The moment the darkness started to creep in the edges of my mind, I pushed myself to some new limit to clear the fog. I had just been about to explain that many of my adventures were part of my job so I didn't seem as flaky but she spoke up first.

"I think I'm more like your buddy," she said.

"Ah, a control freak." I kept my tone light so she knew I teased.

"I never thought about it like that," she said. Again her voice got that airiness to it, like her thoughts were far away. "I guess, like you, I know things can be taken away without a moment's notice, so it's best to be prepared."

Her words rang so true. My life had changed in a moment more than once and seeing her so guarded made me understand that she had experienced darkness too. Where I spun out, she held on tighter.

"It must be exhausting to try and prepare for every situation. Plus, where's the fun in that?"

"You and I are very different people." She said it with a forced smile that made me feel sad but I couldn't identify why.

I struggled for what to say next. I wanted to learn everything about her but sensed the more I pushed, the more she'd clam up. As we walked, her head was on a swivel as she took in the tall buildings and shops of downtown Denver. Even this late in the evening the streets were still fairly crowded and the warm summer night held that magic of endless possibilities.

"Are you from a big city?" I asked her when she stopped to study a colorful mural painted on the side of a brick building.

She shook her head without taking her eyes off the street art.

"Medium sized?"

Finally, she turned to narrow her eyes at me.

"Small town?" I ventured again.

She hesitated to debate her answer, then said, "Small town. Am I gawking?"

Yes. And it was adorable. "Nah, just curious. You're hard to get info out of, you know that?"

When she turned toward me, her brows were furrowed and she fidgeted with the cuffs of her leather jacket again.

"Sanders." I didn't like how she said my name with such finality. "I'm leaving in just a few hours. It would probably be better if we both understood that tonight can't go past this." She gestured to the city around us. "Let's just keep things light, and no more significant details about our normal lives. Just be in this moment, like you said, okay?"

My gaze roamed over her face, taking in the serious squint to her eyes and her full lips, slightly turned down. She must have felt this connection too. There was no way this was one-sided. But she was holding back, as though afraid to reveal too much. I would respect her wishes, even if I felt an ache start to burn in my chest.

"Fair enough," I said lightly. "But we're still getting ice cream."

"Oh. You had better provide. Never tease a woman with treats unless you plan to deliver."

"I would never." I linked my arm back through hers.

"Yeah, you're way too smooth. I knew a guy like you once," she said. "A real Romeo."

"I guarantee you've never met anyone like me, baby." I said it with over-the-top swagger.

She shoved me and rolled her eyes. "You really are too much."

"So this guy you knew—"

She held up her hand. "Nice try," she said. "But we won't ruin such a nice time by bringing up the past."

"You're a tough cookie, aren't you?" I asked her and squeezed her hand.

"Just ask the guy who told me to smile once," she said. "You'll have trouble though because his jaw is still wired shut."

She said it so casually I almost missed the joke. I threw my head back and laughed. When I was done, she was focused on the ground, her hair hiding her face. She reminded me of Skip, in that she didn't say much, but when she did, it was usually perfectly on point.

"Ah, nuts," I said as we came to a stop in front of the closed ice cream shop. "I didn't think this through."

Little did she know that not thinking things all the way through was very much my MO. Maybe there was some freedom in keeping things light tonight after all. I didn't have to tell her about how I almost ruined my business this weekend and she could keep looking at me like I was a dessert she rarely let herself indulge in.

She studied the closed storefront. "You're a terrible tour guide."

I guffawed. "Okay. Challenge accepted. I know where we can try next. How are your feet?"

She glanced to her shoes. "My feet?"

"Are you good to keep walking?" I asked, she wasn't wearing heels though, just Chucks.

Her mouth opened and closed with a shake of her head. "Lord, they don't make them like you where I'm from," she said.

"Considerate?"

"Something like that," she mumbled and then added, "I've got hours of walking in these bad boys."

We walked for a while passing storefronts closed for the day and bars with people spilling out. We found a food truck that served fried ice cream and spilt a paper dish under strung lights. We stood close, faces near and she told me about her best friend and a book club she was in. Or at least it sounded like some sort of book club, she was hazy on the details. I told her about Skip and growing up together in a suburb of Denver. Her dry, caustic humor had me cackling more than once. She wasn't quick to smile but that made it all the more rewarding when she did.

There was something about the way she listened to me that told me she understood me inherently, on some base level. She intrigued me. She kept so much hidden it only drove me to want more.

"My throat is raw," she said. "I can't remember the last time I talked this much."

I took the empty dish and tossed it in a nearby trash can. Our time together was coming to an end.

"No?" I asked. I felt my nerves taking my words.

"I'm not usually a big talker," she said.

"I am."

"I gathered that." She smiled at me. "You'd think not being able to share many details we'd have run out of things to say." She yawned widely.

But we never stopped talking the whole night. Not once, sometimes we talked over each other, two separate conversations seeming to happen at the same time, back and forth, weaved like intricate knitting. I was so close to telling her I needed to know more. A phone number. A freaking social media account, I'd take anything.

"My flight is in three hours," she said. "I still have to pack my suitcase and get to the airport."

My heart constricted. Despite my best attempts all night long, she wouldn't share more than surface-level details. Skip once told me I could charm Sasquatch into buying a winter coat, but she didn't crack at all.

"Where's that flight to again?" I asked, carefully not looking at her.

She tsked. "Nice try."

"Not even a last name?" Panic made my voice shaky. Fear gripped me like a jumper three sizes too small. This couldn't be the end. I leaned forward and grabbed her hands. "We can't end like this. Tell me we'll see each other again."

Her face shuttered, emotion slipping into a cool mask.

"You don't know me." Her head shook solemnly. "The truth is, I'm never so open. I never … I'm not normally like this," she finished.

"We cannot let this be the last time we talk to each other."

"We're from different worlds," she said sadly.

This was more than just dancing and kissing. This felt like the most important thing. I couldn't let her go without hope. There had to be more for us.

We walked in silence back to the front of her hotel.

"Thank you for a wonderful night, Sanders. I'll never forget it."

When I looked up at her, my sadness must have shown clear. She reached out and brushed a thumb over my cheek.

"I'm not ready for it to end," I said.

"It's not meant to be," she said firmly but her voice shook.

I stood up straighter. My heart started to race with hope.

"My dad told me he knew the moment he met my mom she was the one. He was in Australia for a work trip and happened to pass her on

29

the street. He literally stopped her just to talk to her." Her eyes widened slightly at my words. "At first she told him it wasn't meant to be. He always insisted luck brought them together because they happened to be at that exact place at that moment."

"You make your luck in life," she said.

"That's what she told him!" I hadn't meant to shout it but I was too excited to keep this locked down. How couldn't she see that this connection was so real? I calmed my voice. "And so he stayed. Left his entire life for her. He showed up at her house every day for a month to help her dad on his farm. She called him 'Farmer Charmer.'"

My voice tightened talking about my parents. They weren't a topic I ever brought up, but if I didn't try everything, I would regret it.

"That's very sweet. They sound lovely. They really do." She smiled softly.

"He never gave up and eventually they got married. They *were* meant to be."

"But life isn't destiny or magic." As she spoke, she looked just past my shoulder, thinking about something that waited for her back home. "Life is about showing up and working hard."

I grabbed her hands and squeezed them. "You feel this." It wasn't a question.

She let out a soft sigh before she met my eyes. "I feel a connection too. But look, our lives are totally different. We live worlds apart," she said.

"I can't believe our paths would cross like this only for this to be it." I brought her closer to me. Her gaze flicked over my face and she dropped her head to my shoulder.

"I'm not one for blind leaps of faith. There's a lot about me you don't know." Her voice was muffled and her body trembled against me.

I wrapped my arms tight around her. That tiny sign of emotion gave me hope that this was her fear talking. That she wanted more.

"Roxy," I said. "Can't we at least try?"

She straightened off me abruptly and stepped back. "I'm sorry."

"I'll get on my knees and beg."

"Please, no. I don't doubt that you would but this hurts me too. I'm just trying to be smart about this. If you believe it's meant to be, then hold on to that. Okay? Maybe I'm wrong." She fixed her fringe and spoke one last sentence. "I hope I'm wrong."

I ran a hand over my mouth. I couldn't speak, my emotions were too close to the edge. What else could I do? She needed to go. I wasn't going to make her feel bad. Was this karma for my screwups?

"I'm going to go." I closed my eyes against the pain as she spoke. "Thank you. You have no idea what this night meant to me. You're amazing." She pressed a palm to my cheek.

I leaned into the touch unable to watch her leave. When I opened my eyes again, she was in the lobby of the hotel. She looked back and her eyes shone as she gave me one last sad wave.

I stood there staring after her for longer than I cared to admit, hoping she'd come running out. But she never did. Whatever held her back was bigger than our instant connection.

I stumbled back across the street to the bar where my car was parked. My heart ached in my chest and I wondered how many hits it could take before it gave out.

Carillo's was shut down for the night, the parking lot mostly empty. I was so lost in my head that I didn't see Ty, the bouncer, until we practically bumped into each other.

"Sanders. What's up, my brother from down under?" He pronounced under as "undah."

31

"Hey, Ty," I mumbled, getting my keys from my pocket.

"What's wrong, man? I've never seen you frown before."

"I met someone."

"The girl from your work? I saw you talking." He pointed to where I returned the jacket to Roxy. "I take it that things didn't go so well."

"Not so much." I turned to go to my car when his words hit me. "What do you mean, from work? I just met her here tonight," I said.

"Really? I assumed she was part of your crew since she gave me William's name to get in."

My head shot up. "She did?"

He looked around, my sudden shift in mood had him suspicious. "Yeah, she said she was with Outside the Box, or maybe she just said she knew him. Sorry, man, I see a lot of people in one night, I can't remember exactly what she said."

"I could kiss you!" I grabbed the big man's shoulders and shook him.

He chuckled but backed away wearily. "Check with William. I'm sure that she said she knew him."

My heart raced with hope. I hadn't lost this day after all. I'd call Skip, AKA William—my best friend and co-owner of Outside the Box—first thing in the morning. There was still a chance.

Roxy may not believe in destiny, but I did. And the universe just smacked me in the head with the mother of all signs.

CHAPTER 5

ROXY

*T*he axe went flying out of my hand and the handle hit the target. It flopped to the ground with a sad thump. Instead of our usually scheduled meetup, we'd decided on this outing last minute. Even though Kim was at rehearsal, Suzie, Gretchen, and I took the SWS on the road and headed out to Knoxville for a change. They'd been hammering me for details ever since I got back yesterday afternoon. I slept the rest of Saturday instead of preparing for my meeting with Vincent this week to discuss my promotion. They let me be, but now on Sunday they were done waiting patiently.

Tons of students milled about the surprisingly packed hipster hangout, making us feel ancient. There was a bar with a few local brews on tap and lanes designated for throwing axes. Beer and weapons seemed like a risky business venture, but even I had to admit it was fun. Us scorned women typically have a lot of energy to burn. Though tonight I wasn't feeling very scorned, more sorry.

"And then I packed my bag and left for the airport." The next axe flew out of my hand and hit the target but didn't stick. "This is stupid," I mumbled. I shook out my arm not at all surprised at my total lack of athletic ability.

Gretchen walked forward in the lane next to mine. "You just left? Without even getting his number?" Her axe flipped smoothly in the air and glided down the lane as though guided.

THUNK.

Hers hit the center of the target and stuck with the satisfying thunk I had been hoping for. Of course.

"Ugh," I growled.

"You warmed it up for me." She winked and fixed the oversized sunglasses propped in her fiery red hair.

"But no. I didn't even get a last name," I explained. My stomach soured remembering his face as I walked away.

There had been a magic to the night that I couldn't wrap my mind around, let alone explain. It would sound hokey if I tried to. But when he spoke about the song Roxanne, I felt like he could see right into my past. When he held my hand for every person to see, I felt proud. And when he spoke about his parents, I felt … like I would disappoint him. He was so hopeful but I couldn't be enough for him when I had a whole life here to maintain.

We had only just met. It didn't make sense.

I wasn't sure how we'd even fit together. And that was getting ahead of myself. These two seemed perfectly comfortable with who they were meant to be. Ever since I left the Iron Wraiths, it was like I was trying to find my place. All I knew was that I couldn't screw up the life that I had built up. I wouldn't go back to my old life.

"It sounded like you had a connection?" Suzie asked on my left. Hers went flying next and hit so hard a chunk of the target flew off. Gretchen and I exchanged a look. "I used to do this behind the trailer park for fun." She shrugged.

"Remind me not to mess with you," Gretchen teased to my right.

"You wouldn't dream of it." Suzie winked. Her short hair had grown into a chic bob that only made her electric green eyes pop more.

"Come on. Tell us more, tell us more." Gretchen flicked out her hand, gesturing me to go on.

If I was honest about the connection I felt with these two, they might push me to do something I just wasn't ready for. I loved them but I didn't have time for anything else in my life. Not when I had to work so hard to show Green Valley and the Lodge that I was no longer a biker chick. Getting involved with anyone sounded about as fun as chasing headless chickens. But I knew Gretch and so I had to give her something.

"He had this amazingly sexy accent," I said.

"Oh, what sort of accent?" Suzie asked.

"New York? I've always found New Yorkers sort of sexy," Gretchen said.

"No. Australian," I said.

The other two women made a sound of awe.

"That's all you know about him? He's Australian? Maybe he's a Hemsworth or like a cousin," Suzie said excitedly.

"He was damn good looking enough to be," I said. "He's fit. A confident dancer. A gentleman. Hotter than a summer day with no AC. He had sun-bleached dark-blond hair and blue eyes like I've never seen. And his front teeth stuck out which shouldn't be adorable but was. Nothing about him was my type. But damn, he was a fantastic kisser."

I squished up my face when I realized what I said. They were both looking at me like I *was* a headless chicken.

"You made out?" Suzie nodded and fist-bumped me. "Nice."

"A little," I said coyly. More like our mouths introduced our souls to each other but I was definitely not about to say that.

"Did you get very far?" Gretchen asked with a grin.

Suzie shimmied her shoulders sexily.

"We only made out for a minute while we danced. And then the rest you know."

I held back how much we learned without knowing anything at all. His love for his best friend and his parents was written all over his open face. His emotions were always right out there. He was earnest and had no shame. I almost flushed when I thought of him singing to me. He was charming and thoughtful. But he was like a secret treasure I found that I wanted to keep just for me. I wanted to turn it over and play with it at night when I was free to think about him.

"You don't have to explain." Suzie put her hand on my shoulder. "Not to him. Not to us. If you wanted to leave, then you had that right. You owed him nothing."

Gretchen nodded. I agreed wholeheartedly with the sentiment. But it wasn't like that. I felt too much too soon. Life wasn't a freaking fairy tale. And nobody would ever cast me as the leading lady. Twenty-four hours had gone by since I'd left him and I still hadn't stopped thinking about the way he kissed me. He shouldn't be allowed to kiss like that. It messed with my brain. I shook my head and picked up the next axe.

"I met a guy in a bar before. All these years later and I'm still recovering," I said.

I had intended it as a joke but a shadow passed over Gretchen's face. We had all dated Jethro Winston at some point, some of us longer than others, that's what formed the Scorned Women's Society. It was never a point of contention between us, more a sisterhood in bad choices. But Gretchen knew more about my life with the Iron Wraiths and we never talked about it.

I quickly added, "I just didn't want to make something more of one summer night. It happened so fast and it's over now."

THE ONE THAT I WANT

And there was the truth of it. Even if I had met an incredible man, the timing wasn't right. Neither was the distance. He didn't see me as I really was.

Or did he see the most real version of myself?

I squashed that voice right back down.

Gretchen looked at me closely. I felt her brain spinning, could see her making plans and I didn't like it. "Is there any way you could track him down?" she asked.

I knew Gretch better than I knew myself. She would push for whatever she thought was best for people. Her heart was in the right place but sometimes it bulldozed over everything else.

"I don't want to look him up," I said.

"You work so hard at the Lodge. You deserve to have a little fun too," Gretchen said.

I'd been digging my nail into the woodgrain of the table, studying the different names people had carved. When I glanced up again, Gretchen's eyes were glued to my face like she was trying to peer into my soul.

I knew that look. That was *the look*. "Gretchen, don't. It just wasn't meant to be."

"I didn't say anything." She held her hands up innocently.

"You're scheming," I said. Turning to Suzie, I added, "Note this look, Suze. This is when she's about to meddle."

"I've seen it before." Suzie laughed, then added, "I think growing up together gave you two mind reading powers. How long have y'all known each other?"

"Inseparable since the third grade," I said hoping the conversation change would derail Gretchen from her train of thought. "She socked

Ben McClure in the arm when he called me a giraffe on the playground. She got held after school for it."

"She picked me flowers and waited to walk me home so I wasn't alone," Gretchen finished.

Gretchen smiled at me and the anxiety I'd felt about leaving Sanders eased a bit.

"Y'all make me jealous. I never had a friendship like that," Suzie said.

"You do now," Gretchen said and slung an arm over Suzie's shoulder.

"No ex left behind." Suzie held up her beer.

"No ex left behind," Gretch and I repeated and tapped our plastic cups.

This was what mattered. The thought solidified all the unsteadiness I'd been feeling. Like riding a mechanical bull and trying to walk afterwards, I'd been wobbling since I got home from Denver. Sanders had been a lovely distraction, but being back here with my girls, remembering all the good in my life, focused me on what I wanted now. I had the stability of a good job and good friends. That was enough. Next week I'd demand the promotion that I deserved and prove to this town that I had been worth saving.

"Enough about me," I said, more than ready to be done talking about myself. "What the heck is going on with Kim?"

CHAPTER 6

SANDERS

I stood outside the arrivals area of the Knoxville airport, the swampy Tennessee humidity a far cry from Denver's clear, mountain air. I held the phone close to my ear and braced myself for Skip's backlash.

"Tennessee, I am in you," I announced into the phone.

"Tell me why you felt the need to fly out there?" he asked in his usual quiet tone.

If I was the bright and shiny packaging of Outside the Box with my award-winning charm, then Skip was the internal machinery that made it run. I typically attracted clientele and Skip made them stay. When we first started our corporate adventure company together, the idea was new and it took our power duo to get to where we were. Now companies all over the world sent their employees into nature in hopes of innovation and team building. And I had come close to ruining it all. I was going to fix it all.

"I'm getting us more business. You said this Donner Lodge was looking into OTB. Green Valley is an up-and-comer. It was named one of the top-growing small-town communities in Small Town USA magazine."

Skip made a soft sound almost like a sigh. "And this has nothing to do with your sudden interest in Roxy Kincaid?"

"If this meeting goes well, we could get some more clientele," I side-stepped.

"I was going to go myself," he said. Even through the phone I could picture his hairy face twisted with concern. That was his role though. He was the thoughtful, tentative one, I was the impulsive, fun one.

"Now you don't have to. I know you don't love the face-to-face stuff. I'm going to fix everything, Skippo. Don't you worry. I know I made a bit of a mess of things but I have a plan. Donner Lodge is looking to draw business. We are looking to get business. I have an idea that's a win-win for everyone. And if Roxy and I hit it off, even better."

"You sound very enthusiastic," he said. He sighed again and then added, "I've never seen you so interested in a woman."

"I just have a feeling about her and Green Valley." Skip was far too level-headed to hear anything about destiny.

"I just hope this isn't like the time you woke me up to go swimming in the lake because the moon was full," he said.

I cleared my throat. "It was a super blood moon lunar eclipse. You're welcome for that once-in-a-lifetime experience. You make me sound so impulsive."

"Or that time you went to Norway to jump The Troll Wall," he went on.

That was on my parents' anniversary two years ago. The darkness had gotten so heavy I needed to do something big. I didn't care for this stroll down memory lane, so I got us back on task. "Listen, I should have been there that day when you met with Donner Lodge. This is me making up."

"We still need to talk about things. You're still grieving. Don't you think—"

My heartbeat quickened and my esophagus spasmed. "Anyway, mate. I just wanted to let you know my plan."

He let out a defeated sigh. "Okay. Keep me up to date."

"You know I will."

"And then we should really talk about—"

"Gotta go, mate. Ride's here." I hung up the call.

The ride share car rolled to a stop in front of me, the sticker in the window announcing itself.

The passenger window rolled down. "Sanders Olsson?" a knockout of a redhead asked.

My eyebrows rose. "Yeah, that's me."

"I'm Gretchen LaRoe, I'm your ride into Green Valley. Need help with your bags?"

She moved to unbuckle herself but stopped when I held up a hand.

"No, thanks. Just this." I gestured to the military canvas bag over my shoulder.

After I was situated and we were on an interstate, I took in my driver. She was wearing a miniskirt with suspenders over a half shirt. Her red hair was long and flowing, topped with a jaunty beret. She was candy for the eyes but not to my particular taste. I was deep into a brunette with a pouty mouth and crackling sass these days.

An image of Roxy popped into my brain and her short skirt riding up a smooth thigh. I envisioned her big brown eyes blinking up at me after we kissed.

"So Green Valley. Not a very big town, yeah? I imagine you know just about everybody," I said.

Gretchen LaRoe glanced over at me, her cat eyes narrowed in suspicion. "Where are you from?"

The small town looked out for its own. I respected that.

"Australia. Perth specifically."

"You know Hugh Jackman?" she asked.

"Oh sure. All us Australians know each other."

She cast another quick look at me. Her face was unreadable but "friendly" was not a word to describe it. "Funny," she said.

I gave her my biggest, flashiest grin when she looked over at me again. Her eyes widened ever so slightly and she sucked in her lips. It was almost like she was trying to bite back a smile.

"Have I got something stuck in my teeth?" I pulled down the passenger mirror to examine my teeth. "These little bastards up front tend to catch things."

I felt her look at me again as I examined my smile.

"No, nothing." She reached over and pushed up the mirror. "Honestly, it's not you, doll. You're fine."

"Okay." I gave her a weary look.

All of a sudden, her cool demeanor melted into that famous Southern hospitality. "You were asking about Green Valley. Anybody in particular you looking for?" she asked sweetly. "I know everybody and their mamas."

"I believe it. Nobody in particular." Suddenly, I felt shy about delving into the truth of why I was here. Or one of the truths. She seemed a little too eager for information. If I could have done it subtly, maybe. But now I felt a bit cringy outright asking after Roxy.

I mean what were the chances this Gretchen LaRoe even knew my Roxy Kincaid anyway?

"Did you come all the way from Australia?" She snapped her gum loudly, causing me to flinch slightly. The woman scared me, if I was being honest.

"Ah, no. I've been in the States for some time. I'm from Denver."

If I wasn't crazy, I swore her hands gripped the steering wheel imperceptibly tighter.

"Here for business or pleasure?" she asked.

"Business." I dug into my pocket and pulled out a card. "Looking to grow our company."

She grabbed the card and looked it over. "Corporate adventure, huh?" She definitely seemed excited now. "Here." She reached across my body to shuffle through her glove box. My eyes widened when I saw the gun. Americans.

"Ah, pretend you didn't see that," she said with a wink.

"See what?"

"Attaboy." She handed me a card. "Feel free to call if you need anything while you are here. I'm a bit of a concierge for the town."

The card read "Gretchen LaRoe - Fashion Consultant, Driver, Landlord, and all-around badass," and handwritten on the bottom was added, "matchmaker - by appointment only."

"Bit of a Jackie-of-all-trades, I see," I said.

"You know it."

"Thank you." I slid her card into my wallet. "I'll hold on to this."

"I see you're heading to Donner Lodge. Staying there?" she asked.

"Sure am. But also hoping to do business with them."

"Corporate adventuring? Like trust falls in suits?" she asked.

"Sort of. The goal is team building. You really learn to trust your peers when they're in charge of your ropes as you climb a mountain."

"Yikes," she said.

"This area seem good for corporate adventuring?" I asked.

"Sure. Green Valley can hardly contain itself with all the new growth," she said. "You should definitely meet some locals. There's tons of businesses that might like to partner with you."

I felt the growing excitement that came when I was on a roll. I knew I screwed things up in Denver but I did have a nose for this stuff, a gut instinct for a new market in need.

"The Smokies are beautiful," I said to fill the silence.

We shared a moment to appreciate the majestic beauty as the car pulled up to Donner Lodge. To be honest, it was a lot nicer than I expected. Skip mentioned that they were in the process of renovating. Gretchen pulled up the long driveway surrounded by a lush manicured lawn leading to a large main building painted a fresh farmhouse white. The driveway looped around and a few golf carts were parked waiting to take visitors to their getaway homes.

She put the car in park and turned to me with a dazzling smile. "Listen. Not sure how long you're gonna be in town, but the Lodge is hosting a movie this Friday at the drive-in. It's not as exciting as the nightlife in Denver, I'm sure. But it'll be fun. A bunch of locals. Movie, food, beer. It'll be fun if you're looking for a good place to network. I'd be happy to introduce you to some of the bigwigs in town."

"That'd be great, thanks," I said and I meant it.

"See ya around." She winked, but the sneaky smile on her face as she drove away had me wondering.

I wouldn't worry about that though. Worry was a pointless emotion unless it drove change. I'd learned years ago to not overthink and question everything. Obsessing over facts you couldn't change was a hamster on a wheel. Best to take life one day at a time. Today, I had a business to save.

* * *

Roxy

ALONG WITH A FULL-LENGTH SELFIE, I sent the following message to the SWS group text:

Roxy: Corporate Roxanne asks for her promotion.

In the picture, I looked the complete opposite of the woman I'd been that night in Denver. Every tattoo was covered by my simple black business suit that went to my knees. Even my long hair was twisted into a bun so tight it made my eyes water. I wasn't exactly comfortable but at least I looked the part. There wasn't a hint of the Roxy that rode with a motorcycle gang.

Kim: The promotion she earned.

Suzie: Looks great. U got this.

Gretchen: Very corporate, Roxanne.

I frowned at the text, hating how it caused a little twist of nerves in my already nervous belly. Luckily, my friends knew me well and sent a follow-up to boost my confidence.

Gretchen: Knock 'em dead.

I smoothed my plain black skirt and let out a long breath. Hell yes, I deserved this promotion to events coordinator. I'd spent the week trying to get on Vincent Debono's calendar. Now, almost the end of Friday, he was able to see me.

My hands shook as I slid my phone into my purse. After dropping my bag in my work cubby, I made my way to his temporary office next door to what was formerly Diane Donner's office. The Dragon Lady—

a well-deserved term she'd been dubbed secretly by most of the staff—had originally hired Vincent as a renovation consultant. Since her sudden disappearance, Monsieur Auclair volunteered Vincent into the lead role on the events side of the house. I had hardly interacted with Vincent since he'd been brought in to transform the Lodge into a "Historical Experience Boutique Lodge," but I hoped to change that today. After the trip to Denver, I'd proven I wanted the best for the Lodge.

I tapped on Vincent's door immediately wishing that I had knocked with more confidence. *Come on, Roxy, you didn't leave the Wraiths just to be a chicken-livered sissy.* I straightened my shoulders and lifted my chin.

"Come in," Vincent said.

I pushed open the door to find the small office was strewn with papers and half-open boxes stacked haphazardly in the corner.

"Hello, Mr. Debono. We had an appointment," I said from the doorway.

He pushed my request to meet back all week. We were to discuss the potential networking opportunities I secured during the hospitality conference. I don't know that he even had a chance to look at the presentation from my trip, highlighting the most promising prospects.

"Please come in," he said.

Vincent stood next to a tall cabinet rifling through some folders. He was an inch or two shorter than me, especially in my heels, but his presence was commanding. He was an attractive man, maybe mid-forties, with short cropped hair and thick black-framed glasses. His crisp white shirt was rolled up revealing pretty defined forearms. The gray vest over his shirt was as perfectly tailored as his pants. His dark eyebrows always seemed full of judgment, but I was the last person to blame someone for the impressions their face made. He was from New York and money leaked off him like sap on bark.

"Roxanne Kincaid. I'm sorry we haven't had much time to meet yet," he said with a strong Yankee accent as he made his way to his desk. Reaching out to shake my hand, he asked, "What can I do for you?" then gestured for me to sit.

Now, I wasn't one for a ton of small talk, but this was the South, you didn't just jump right into things. I had a plan of how this talk was going to go. First I'd made small talk and then oh so casually remind him of all the good I did at the conference, before pitching my ideas for bringing in more business, like this weekend's drive-in event. Finally, I'd get to the meat-and-potatoes part of the conversation and suggest my promotion to the events coordinator, a new and official position filled by yours truly. I was prepared but his direct question had me feeling like I was weeble wobblin'.

But I wouldn't fall down.

I cleared my throat, crossed my ankles, and clasped my hands in my lap. If he wanted direct, I could be direct.

"I want to be promoted to the position of events coordinator."

His thick eyebrows shot up behind his glasses before they smoothed back down, the rest of his face expressionless. He glanced to the stacks of paper on the desk, looking for something. "Events coordinator?"

"It would be a new title and position for the Lodge but a needed one," I explained.

"Remind me of your qualifications," he said flatly.

"I've been working at the Lodge over four years. I started in house-keeping, was promoted to the front desk within the year. Diane Donner encouraged me to get a degree online for hospitality management."

Or as I called it, hostility management. I wasn't about to tell him that it was an online degree from the local Merryville community college. I could only imagine what Ivy League university he went to. Fighting to keep my hands from fidgeting and maintaining eye contact, I continued. "I've been unofficially running all the weddings and graduation parties, even as I continued to be the front desk lead. But I-I think—" I clenched my fists and took a deep breath. "My talent would be more beneficial running the events full-time."

It was the speech I rehearsed all week. No weak verbs, no hesitation. I was the best candidate for this position.

"I don't disagree that event coordination is more than one person's full-time job." He leaned back in the leather office chair and it squeaked. "Probably an entire team if we get it to the point where Diane wants it." He frowned. "Wanted it."

Hope started to loosen the tightness in my chest.

"But, unfortunately, with the way things are right now, I can't make any major decisions. I need to talk with Auclair when he's not tied up in cow business." He said the last part quietly like he couldn't believe the small-town antics he had to deal with. "Let me run it by some people. See how you work with the staff, things like that."

The collar of my knockoff suit itched my throat. This close he could probably tell that my Burberry suit jacket was actually a Burdberry that I bought out of the back of a van a year ago. It was a hair too snug, but as long as I didn't slouch or breathe too deep, I was fine. I was just used to people disappointing me, and preferred to plan events by myself. That was why I wanted to do it full-time. Solo.

"I've been running events for a while now," I said. "I coordinated tonight's event at the drive-in not only to show hotel guests to the charm of Green Valley, but to interact with the community and generate more local business."

I couldn't believe the words came out so smoothly.

Mr. Debono studied me closely. I wondered if I should try to smile. People tended to like that but Gretchen told me once my forced smiles looked like a snarl and that it was better to embrace my neutral expression.

"I appreciate your directness, Ms. Kincaid. Many people down here tend to talk in circles before getting to the point and I'm never sure where I stand," he said evenly, not smiling either.

He was as hard to read as a French dictionary, but at least we had that in common.

"So I'll be direct with you," he said. "I have no doubt that Diane trusted you. You wouldn't be doing all this if she hadn't. But I'm not comfortable giving you a promotion even one that you may very well deserve. I'm in a tricky spot with the new responsibilities thrust upon me. I can't make any major decisions without the temporary board's approval."

Perhaps my face played out the dread coiling in me because he softened his features and added, "I'll make you a deal. I'll observe you over the next few weeks, see how you work with the clients and the staff and then reconsider your promotion. I'm slowly making my way through years of emails in the Lodge's main account. I'll search your name and see what Diane had to say about you."

I felt my chest rising and falling quickly, hoping it didn't give me away. I could easily prove myself. I'd handled mothers of the brides with food poisoning and raucous bachelorette parties at two a.m. I could handle whatever life threw at me. I was a professional, dammit. I was worthy. I'd worked my ass off. I wanted to scream but I was a professional now. We only screamed internally.

"That sounds fair," I said coolly.

"Starting with tonight. I'll accompany you to the movie event. See how you handle things. It would be good for me to meet more of the locals anyway. I have no idea how long I'll be here." He pushed up his thick frames to pinch the area between his eyes.

"Tonight," I repeated, finding my bearings but feeling like a baboon on roller skates.

An icy sort of dread tingled at the base of my spine though I couldn't be sure why. Maybe the prospect of having every single one of my actions scrutinized. I already felt uncomfortable in my skin half the time, too afraid to talk to strangers and expose my country background. But I did have one advantage in this situation: Vincent Debono knew me only as Roxanne Kincaid. He had no idea of my past, all I had to do was show him the professional that I was and everything would be fine. What was another few weeks?

He blinked at me expectantly.

"The shuttle will be leaving here to take the guests at eight p.m.," I said.

"Perfect. Then we can discuss more about how the conference went on the way over. I skimmed your presentation and found it very informative. A lot of potential for growth."

"Thank you," I said.

"That reminds me …" he started and then sifted the mess of papers on his desk.

Wherever Diane Donner was, she was shuddering at the chaos.

"One of the companies you mentioned in the presentation reached out for a meeting with us," he said, "but the timing hasn't worked out. The corporate adventure company."

My heart skipped a beat—that was one of the companies from Denver I had been most excited about. But then like a damn bursting after a spring storm, all the other thoughts I'd been pushing down from that weekend flooded through me. Sanders with his blue eyes and smiles that made my knees tingle. The dancing. The talking. The feeling.

I shoved them deep into a closet in my mind and slammed the lid.

"Outside the Box?" I asked tentatively.

He held up a finger. "Yes, that's the one."

This conversation was not going at all like I planned. I'd rehearsed every possible way it could go but nothing had gone right since I entered Vincent's office. Why had they been talking? Was this a man-to-man thing? Was I not good enough? Quickly, I shut those thoughts down. I had spent hours talking to William. He wouldn't go over my head.

"You talked with William Goin?" I asked.

"No." Vincent pressed a finger to his lips as he thought. "That doesn't sound right. I wrote it down somewhere."

I fought to keep a frown from screwing up my features. His glasses dropped back in place as he continued to search through the mess on his desk.

"They want to talk on the phone?" I felt my tongue grow thick with frustration, my drawl slurring my words.

"No. He's here," he said.

"Here? In Green Valley?" I asked. That didn't make any sense. William and I had planned to speak next week, when I thought I would be in my new role.

He nodded distractedly, still searching the papers on his desk. "Though he didn't say why," he mumbled lost in thought.

I shook my head, not understanding. "But it wasn't William? Soft-spoken, nice guy?"

"Soft-spoken? Hardly." Vincent cocked his head. "This guy was definitely—"

Vincent's desk phone rang. He exhaled sharply with frustration and held up a finger. "This thing rings nonstop. Sorry, hang on."

As he picked up the phone, I felt the world spinning out around me. If not William, then who? And why was he here in Green Valley? I tried not to think the worst but my mind was already sprinting toward the danger zone. Maybe William had shown up to Carillo's that night. Maybe he had seen me dancing like a ho on some guy and decided I wasn't worth talking to.

No. I pushed the thoughts away.

He covered the mouthpiece. "Listen, I have to take this. I'll schedule a meeting for us next week to talk more. And I look forward to tonight," he said and flashed a quick, polite smile.

I nodded numbly as I got to my feet. I snuck quietly out of his office as he spoke in brisk bluntness to whoever was on the phone.

There was no need to panic. He probably got the companies mixed up after reading through my presentation. There was no need to assume the worst. But assuming the worst was my favorite pastime. You can't be blindsided by disappointment if you prepared for all the worst-possible scenarios.

I had been so sure I'd walk out with a new title and my very own office. I'd been so close, worked so hard these past years. I fought the burning in my eyes, fought that voice that told me I was starting all over from square one by clenching my fists until my nails dug into my palms.

No, I repeated to myself. I could do this. I'd handled Wraiths, I'd rebounded from painful rejection resulting from a lifetime of bad decisions. The new Roxy had something to prove. I would show Vincent Debono that I was worthy of that promotion and nothing would stop me. Nothing.

CHAPTER 7

SANDERS

I hadn't planned to go out. I was content to stay in and catch up on work, but after wandering the Lodge and three different employees mentioned the movie night at the old drive-in, I figured this must be some sort of historic event in Green Valley. It would give me a chance to get out and meet the locals. And I was always up for some research.

There was a shuttle taking Lodge guests up but I decided the two-mile walk would be good for all my chaotic energy I needed to burn. I was too wound up. My skin felt too tight, and if I sat still for too long, my brain started to dwell on things I didn't want to think about.

I hadn't found Roxy yet. I'd talked to a manager a bit about the Lodge cooperating with Outside the Box, but he seemed a bit distracted. Skip told me Roxy was handling the events side of things and I didn't want to seem like I was going over her head. I suggested to Vincent that all three of us should meet but I also didn't want that to be the first time I saw her. This wasn't an ambush, it was a reunion. I needed to handle this whole situation with tact as I had acted without an actual plan. I suspected that Skip would never equate me with tact, but alas, I was trying to turn over a new leaf. The fresh Tennessee air was inspiring me.

I all but kicked my heels as I sent Gretchen a text asking for details about the movie night. She responded almost immediately with explicit instructions on how to get there, what weather to expect, and the best place to park to see the screen. I dressed in my usual uniform of khaki cargos, hiking boots, and a Henley—blue to make my eyes pop—having decided anything more would look like I was trying too hard. I might have messed with my hair a solid ten minutes so that it looked tousled but un-styled.

The single-lane highway leading to the drive-in wasn't conducive to walking I soon discovered. I balanced along a thin strip of dirt at the edge of the asphalt surrounded by a dense forest on either side. Some corners didn't even allow for a shoulder and I had to walk on the road. I kept my ears pricked for the sound of motors so I could jump to the side as needed. The sun was just setting and I contemplated the journey home when it would be pitch-black—because who needed streetlights on windy backroads? I would have to see if I could hitch a ride or risk becoming roadkill.

The night was warm and sticky, such a far cry from the dry air of the mountains back in Denver. The sweet, earthy smell was intoxicating. These mountains didn't have the grandeur of the Rockies, but there was something heady and mysterious about them. These were the mountains that held ghosts and secrets.

Also, mozzies. Mozzies everywhere. Only five minutes into my walk and already the little bloodsuckers were eating me alive. Walking may have been a poor decision and I was beginning to understand why there were no footpaths anywhere. I thought I left the worst of nature's creatures behind in Australia. The worst I'd found in Denver were unironic hipsters.

The map made it look like the theater was just up the road, but the darker it grew and the more the mosquitoes tried to eat me, it felt like miles and hours had passed. Maybe I should have taken the shuttle with the others.

Breaks squeaked as a car slowed to idle alongside me. "Hey. You tryna get run over?" Gretchen LaRoe called out to me from her window.

I grinned. "In some countries, call me crazy, they have these things called footpaths so people can walk places."

"Crazy." She popped the locks. "Get in."

Noting the passenger seat was already taken by a dark-haired woman, I climbed into the seat behind Gretchen and said, "I'm not supposed to get in the car with strangers."

"Your mother tell you that?" she asked.

"She did. She also said redheads were trouble."

"Your mother sounds wise," the dark-haired woman said.

The typical jolt at the mention of my mum struck a chord but I had learned to hide the reaction over the years. I had also definitely learned not to bring her death up unless I wanted to face the awkward pitying faces. I forced a grin and extended my hand. "She was."

The passenger was strikingly beautiful with emerald eyes and short jet-black hair. She turned around to shake my proffered hand. "I'm Suzie Samuels."

"Sanders Olsson. Pleasure to meet you."

"I like your accent," she said.

"I like yours too." My typical response.

Suzie turned to Gretchen. "Old friends?"

"Nah, we just met the other day when I drove him into town. He's gonna be here for a bit for work. I thought he should get to know the locals."

Suzie said, "Ah," and gave her friend a look that could only be described as *What exactly are you up to?* Which was exactly the look I'd felt myself giving during my own brief interactions with the redhead. I was starting to understand that Gretchen LaRoe didn't do anything without thinking four steps ahead.

After only another two minutes of driving, we slowed onto a turnoff I would have never thought was an actual road. Just a less dense area of forest. I probably would have made the walk but was not so secretly glad for the rescue.

"I don't suppose I could hitch a lift back later?" I asked with no shame at all. "These roads are treacherous at night, I imagine."

"I'm sure we can work something out," Gretchen said.

Her friend shot her another suspicious look.

"This movie isn't some deviant thing is it? It's starting to feel like the start to a bad slasher flick. Two way too beautiful women. Scary back-road in the middle of nowhere. I better check my phone for signal. The second I hear banjo music, I'm running for it." I teased but, honestly, what had I gotten myself into?

The two women threw their heads back and laughed.

Not encouraging to say the least.

The pseudo-road opened up to a field filled with about fifty cars. On the farthest edge, backed up against the dense forest, was a large screen propped up on wooden stilts that were peeling paint. A few food trucks lined the perimeter and people near the front picnicked on blankets or out of the back of their cars. The families on blankets relieved me of any weird stress I'd been feeling.

"See, we're here. No masked murderers," Gretchen said.

"Not yet," I mumbled.

"Why don't we get out and walk around a little. Oh, Patty is here. I wanna see if they're still doing open mic night."

"I'm not getting out of this car." I scratched at a new bump on my neck. "The mozzies are eating me alive out there."

"Mozzies?" Suzie asked.

"Mosquitoes," I explained. "I'm too sweet. I can't help it."

Gretchen rolled her eyes and Suzie raised an eyebrow. My usual charm fell a little flat on these two. Maybe I was off my game. I so desperately wanted to ask if they knew Roxy Kincaid but worried about showing my hand. I glanced around the field for the shuttle bus that carted over the Lodge guests. If she was running this event …

"Looking for someone?" Gretchen turned to face me, arm braced on the passenger seat.

"Nope. Just checking out the sights."

"Make you a deal," she said. "You go get us some snacks, then you can hide out in here the rest of the night."

"That sounds fair."

"And I'll drive you home later."

"Deal," I said.

Suzie watched this exchange with narrowing eyes. "I'm gonna go find Ford. Whatever this is I don't want to be a part of it."

"No snacks?" I asked.

"I'm good, doll. You two go crazy." She was out of the car but bent and gave Gretchen one last look. "Whatever is up your sleeve … be careful."

"Go find your man and come back later for the show," the redhead responded.

Suzie shook her head and was gone.

I asked, "Anything in particular you'd like, madame? My treat for the lift, of course."

"Such a gent. I think the Lodge is handing out popcorn to the kiddies. That sounds good," she said.

With the windows down, the smell of popcorn and fried food wafted through the air. I got out of the car and stretched, observing the area. The crowd hummed with excited chatter and laughter. Children ran around chasing each other, screaming with glee. Something about small-town living made all of this seem charming without being kitschy.

Gretchen got out of the car too. Today she was dressed as a fifties pinup cowgirl. I had to admit, the lady had style. "I gotta go talk to some people. See ya in a few." She pointed to the table set up a few yards away next to the black charter bus from the Lodge. "You'll be wanting to head that way."

She fluffed her red hair and sauntered away. Did she somehow know that my eyes searched the crowd for Roxy? It didn't seem likely …

A small queue waited in front of the table. And then all at once, just like that night at the club, the crowd parted to reveal a path to my true north.

Standing behind the table, handing out bags of popcorn, there she was. Roxy.

My Roxy.

I'd never felt instant possession like this. Not ownership of her, nothing close to that. She owned *me*. She could bring me to my knees with the crook of one finger. It hadn't all been in my head. Those feelings of destiny were as strong as the night we met.

She glanced up and looked around, as though someone had called her name. I tucked myself behind a truck to avoid being seen. I needed a minute to collect myself. I felt like I'd waited a lifetime for this moment. I had to play it just right. Like an accident? No. Best to be straightforward. We were destined to meet again. I was just expediting the universe's machinations.

I peeked out to see her again. Take my fill. Her beauty was like a halo around her. How was it possible that the crowd had not stopped to just stare at her? Gone was her short skirt and leather jacket. Her body art was hidden under a business suit and her hair was up, fringe perfectly edged. Seeing her again inflamed the thousand thoughts I'd had on repeat since we parted. My fingers twitched at my sides, desperate to pull down the length of her hair as I brought her mouth to mine. I wanted to peel that suit off of her and kiss the sweet skin underneath.

But mostly I just wanted to talk to her more. I wanted to learn about her career at the Lodge. How she spent her days and who her friends were? I was desperate to know everything about every moment that led up to our paths crossing. I needed to understand the magic of the stars aligning.

Taking a deep breath in, I made my way to her table.

CHAPTER 8

ROXY

"We're low on the artisanal nuts," I said to Vincent.

I made a mental inventory of what snacks were left. We'd been working the event for over an hour, and the line had remained steady with about five to ten people at all times. My initial nerves started to settle as the crowds kept coming. This was the first event Vincent had watched me plan and host, so every detail had to be perfect. I hadn't taken into account how much people loved free food and we were running low. It felt like most of Green Valley had shown up to have a relaxing evening under the summer night. This evening was an opportunity for the people of Green Valley to enjoy a fun night out all the while promoting the many activities at the Lodge.

So far, so good.

I'd even begun to relax around Vincent a little. He wasn't exactly chatty but neither was I, so we worked side by side only talking when we needed to. And that was A-OK with me.

"People love their nuts," Vincent said as he handed the last bag to a bearded hulk of a man.

I think it was Everett Monroe. Talk about a family with good genes. He took the bag, opened his mouth to say something, then thought better of it, walking away with a shake of his head. What's in the water here? Between those Monroe brothers and the Winstons, Green Valley had more good-looking men per capita than any other city, I was sure of it. I'd have to bring that up at the next SWS meeting.

I shot a look to Vincent to see if he'd been joking but his face remained serene, so I kept my raunchy response at bay. "That they do," I said neutrally.

"I'll start more popcorn." Vincent reached for the next bag of kernels. "You know, I started out at the front desk too," he said as he dumped the kernels into the little pot.

"Oh?" I asked.

"I think it's very impressive not only what you've done here tonight but for the Lodge. I can tell your career means a lot to you."

I hid my face, hating how my cheeks heated at the compliment. "Thank you, sir," I said, then cringed at my use of the honorific. Where was this man in the hierarchy of the Lodge? I wondered if he even knew with all the sudden changes. I respected that he didn't want to give me a promotion without knowing me. Even though it sucked. At least he was making an effort to get to know me. Maybe he was starting to see me as something close to a peer.

I had to be careful. If he learned about my past, he wouldn't be so eager to promote me up the ranks. As I helped person after person, checking in on local families, interacting with the visitors staying at the Lodge, I maintained a professional persona. Nobody said anything about me being *that* Roxy Kincaid. However at one point, Scotia Simmons made a comment about how glad she was "I turned my life around." Thankfully, Vincent had been busy helping out and didn't hear her. Soon, I started to relax and just get lost in the transactions. Hand out popcorn, pimp Lodge. I could do that.

"This has been a really great event, Roxanne," Vincent said when the movie started and the line finally stopped.

It was so weird to hear him call me anything but Roxy after spending the last few hours chatting with him. But he'd finally stopped calling me "Miss Kincaid" and so it was still progress.

"Thank you," I said. "It's a good little town."

"Hmm," he said looking out at the crowd. His face was unreadable as he looked back at me. "Excuse me, I have to see a man about a horse. Is that what you all say?"

As always, my face spoke for me.

"I'll work on it," he said with a hint of a smile before walking away.

I took a deep breath, finally alone for the first time in hours. And yet, being alone with my thoughts, the inevitable crept in. The "I made a terrible mistake leaving Sanders" thoughts. It had seemed so important to me to maintain boundaries that night in Denver. But my mind kept drifting back to him. Like the pair of shoes I talked myself out of buying only to obsess over how often I would've actually worn them. But a thousand times worse. Because now my heart was constantly aching over might-have-beens.

I searched for something to do behind the table to distract me. I folded brochures, restocked the water, fluffed the popcorn. I was just bending down to open a new case of water when a voice said my name. A voice I never thought I'd hear again.

"Roxy?" the smooth Australian accent asked. "Is that you?"

I straightened and turned around slowly. I'm sure my eyes were as wide open as my mouth. There he stood. Sanders. Sexier, taller, and even more stunning than the memories that had played on a loop this last week. Like he'd been manifested straight from my recurring dreams, there he stood with his head tilted, brows pushed up together with hesitation and a soft smile playing on his lips.

It would be damn corny to say that my heart exploded into a thousand little butterflies and took flight into the air around me. So I'd just keep that feeling to myself.

I was around the table without thinking. My arms wrapped around his shoulders. His deep rumbling laughter filled my ears as he squeezed me back, lifting me off the ground. My feet kicked up. I was laughing. I was actually laughing. Or crying, I couldn't tell. The relief was immediate.

I was still floating off the ground, held in his strong bracing grasp, when I pulled back to look at his face. My gaze moved all over from his laughing grin with his silly teeth to his dark blond brows lifted high with humor.

"It's you," was all I could say.

"Hi," he said back.

For who knows how long, we seemed to just stand there memorizing each other's faces. I never thought I'd seen him again. Truly never. And now that he stood here in front of me, I understood so clearly how that thought depressed me. I'd been telling myself it was for the best but my instant joy told me otherwise. Eventually, he slowly dropped me to the ground.

The second my feet touched the field, reality sunk back in. Where we were. What I was doing. I stepped back with a heavy heart. I was here for work, this wasn't the time or place to have a reunion. After feeling like that night in Denver had been a weird and wonderful dream, I couldn't seem to slide Sanders into my real life. He didn't fit in this world, like wearing a life vest to a funeral.

"What are you doing here?" I asked.

He opened his mouth but from behind me, Vincent said, "Hello. Who's this?"

As I scrambled back around the table, he extended his hand to Vincent.

"I'm Sanders Olsson," he said. His face was still bright with a huge smile. I managed to smooth my features into neutrality but my heart was pounding.

"Sanders," Vincent said, flatly. "We spoke on the phone earlier.

"You two know each other?" Vincent asked, looking between the two of us in a way that made my stomach twist.

"I met Roxy in Denver. My corporate adventure company was at the hospitality convention," Sanders explained.

It was all facts but thankfully excluded the more intimate details.

Vincent turned to me with a question in his brow. "Roxy? Is that what you prefer to be called?" he asked.

"Or Roxanne. It doesn't matter." I wasn't sure why I said that. It didn't actually matter but no, nobody else called me Roxanne despite what my name tag read. It was flustering to stand here between these two men and find my footing. Sanders had almost reached fantasy levels in my brain, and to see him as real as my manager, it was all too much.

Sanders watched me the entire time, barely flicking a glance to Vincent. God, he was saying too much looking at me like that. I must have frowned because his smile finally turned down a few notches and the absence made me feel awful.

Vincent asked Sanders, "Is Roxanne why you're in Green Valley? I didn't get the impression you knew her when we spoke on the phone. Or are you here because of Outside the Box?" His face remained coolly blank but I felt like whatever was said next would mean everything for my career.

Heat burned my cheeks at his tone as realization settled in. Everything Sanders said connected at once.

Sanders. Outside the Box. The convention.

Everything had been so full of color and hope when Sanders appeared. In a moment, the world fell away. I was sure of it. The poles reversed or gravity suddenly stopped working because everything definitely shifted sideways. I had to grip the table to keep from falling over.

A hand went to my mouth, as if to keep me from gasping, before I realized what I was doing and tried to look casual. I couldn't believe my luck only a moment ago, but now … now I couldn't believe my fucking luck. William had mentioned his partner that couldn't make it at the convention …

How much had Vincent seen? What did he assume right now?

"Yes, Roxy met with my business partner, Skip, in Denver. I would have been there …" Distantly, I heard Sanders explain how we met up later. But I couldn't focus for the blood rushing in my ears.

"Skip?" I asked. The best friend he mentioned several times? No. That wasn't right. None of this made sense. Maybe this was still just a misunderstanding. "I spoke with William." My voice sounded far away.

Sanders grinned. "Oh, well, for work he usually uses his real name, William, but all his friends call him Skip."

I nodded but needed a minute to think. To regroup.

The two men talked back and forth but it was like listening through water. I needed to get away. I needed to think. The scene I just made … My reaction to seeing him.

"I-I'll be right back," I said, already backing away.

"Are you okay?" Vincent asked.

"Can we talk?" Sanders asked at the same time.

Sanders. Him. He. The man who threatened to sweep me off my feet in Denver, he was the potential business partner. Oh my God, what if I had slept with him that night?

I couldn't seem to think or focus. I knew myself enough to know that if I talked now, I'd only fuck up this insane situation more.

"Just—I need to go get something from the bus," I said and walked away.

Keep it together, keep it together. What would the SWS do?

I pressed a hand to my stomach as I stumbled toward the bus, the suit suffocating me.

After ten steps, I spotted Gretchen. She stuck out as always in a cream leather skirt with fringe and cowboy boots. Her vintage collared shirt was white with red swirled designs and shiny opal buttons. A red cowgirl hat was propped on her barrel curls.

"Hey, girl! Glad I caught you, who's that hottie working the table with you?" she asked. "Is it—" She stopped short when she was close enough to see my face. I shook my head once, feeling too dizzy to speak. She was at my side in an instant. "What's wrong?"

"I think I fucked up." My voice was shaky.

"Okay, okay. I gotcha." She glanced around before wrapping her arms around my shoulders and leading me to the trees and out of sight. "What's going on?"

"Sanders. From Denver." All the words tried to come out at once. My whole body was shaking now. Anxiety was closing in on me, I couldn't catch my breath and my hands went icy.

Her hands gripped my shoulders. "Just breathe, hon. Slow down. Try again."

"Sanders is here. He's a potential business partner for the Lodge."

"Oh. Well, that's good, right? To see him again?"

"Not here. Not while I'm working. Not to find out like this," I explained.

"I thought you'd be happy ..." she said, trailing off.

Anxiety slithered in my gut. "You knew? How?" I shook my head. "You knew he was here and you didn't warn me?"

This wasn't happening. I knew she wouldn't set me up to be cruel but it all felt like too much to process. My carefully contained worlds were colliding.

"I wanted to surprise you. I thought you'd be happy." The fringe of her shirt flared as she crossed her arms.

"You're behind this? You brought him?" I tried to keep my voice calm.

"Well, it's not like I brought him to Green Valley, he obviously came to see you."

"No," I snapped. It cracked off the trees around us and her eyes widened before narrowing. "He's here for business. And you—you can't just do stuff like this. I asked you not to get involved."

"You need some fun, girl. You two obviously had a connection."

"Gretchen, stop."

I held up a hand and then pressed it to my forehead under my bangs. She shut her mouth immediately, her jaw jutting out.

"I didn't want to see him again," I said.

"I don't understand why. Plenty of people who hook up still work together—"

But it wasn't about hooking up. It wasn't about a quick fling. It was so much more than that but all my thoughts were jumbled up and I wasn't explaining myself well. I was too upset.

"You always do this," I cut her off. My anger grew as I freaked out. Didn't she understand why I pushed him away? Couldn't she see that I needed to keep things the same? She knew how loose my hold was on this new life. But how could I explain all that without her feeling guilty and hurt for her role in my past?

"What? Help people who are too afraid to admit what they want?"

"Stick your nose in other people's business!" I snapped and then lowered my voice after a few people looked toward us. "This isn't a game."

She chewed her lip before saying, "I really think you're overreacting."

If she had looked even remotely remorseful, if she had looked even slightly apologetic or ashamed, maybe I wouldn't have lost my cool and unloaded. But she stood there like she didn't regret a thing and I was the one acting crazy. I couldn't keep a lid on my thoughts any longer.

"I know you think I'm being bitchy. I know in your head, I'm being irrational. But Gretchen, I'm angry. I didn't want to see him like this." My fingertips pressed to my hot cheeks. "I'm humiliated," I added weakly.

She was speechless. Her hands dropped to her sides, and she backed up.

I glanced around to make sure nobody could see us fighting. "You accuse Green Valley of treating the SWS like the side characters in Jethro and Sienna's story. It pisses you off so much and then you go and do the same thing to us. We're real, breathing, fleshed-out people. Not little pieces on your game board," I finished.

She blinked rapidly and shook her head, continuing to back up. "Okay." She started nodding. "Good to know how you feel."

She was retreating. I'd hurt her and she was retreating. Classic Gretchen. Guilt twisted at me. I didn't want to hurt her. But this was all too much. This night. Seeing him. Being in charge of one of my first work events, trying to prove my worth to Vincent, and then to act like a schoolgirl seeing her crush. I would have to go smooth things over. I had to prove my worth to Vincent. Gretchen would understand that. Once we all calmed down.

"Look, I just wished you had talked to me first. I have to get back to work. I'll call you later," I said.

She held up her arms. "Sure. You do what you gotta do."

"You took the choice away from me, Gretchen, can you understand that?" I asked defeated.

She held my gaze for another moment, then sauntered away without another word. I waited until the urge to cry passed and went back to the table. Sanders was gone. No surprise. I didn't look for him. We could talk next week. At work. Work we would be working together.

I kept my focus on helping people and packing up as the movie ended. Feeling eyes on me, I glanced up once to see Sanders with Gretch and Suzie, Ford, and his friend Jack. Quickly I averted my gaze, pushing down the hurt.

I still couldn't believe Sanders was here. And he worked for Outside the Box. I couldn't quite wrap my mind around all of it. As though he could hear me thinking about him, Sanders looked up at me with worry. I swore I could hear his thoughts.

Can we talk?

Not right now. I looked away. I wasn't ready. I just had to get through the rest of the night.

"I see your wheels spinning," Vincent said as we loaded guests back on to the shuttle at the end of the night. He looked concerned. "Whatever is going on, I promise it's going to be okay."

I nodded. It would be. I had cooled off some. Maybe I had overreacted in the moment. I was just so freaked out and overwhelmed. But I would talk to Gretchen and explain how important this night was for

69

my career. I would focus on making sure I did my job and I did it well. And I definitely wouldn't think about destiny and the chances of seeing Sanders again. After all, I knew better than that.

CHAPTER 9

SANDERS

*I*t was two a.m. If I were any more wound up, I'd have enough force to shoot into space and orbit the earth a few times. I paced my room at the Lodge so many times I was covered in a sheen of sweat. A jolt of energy pulsed through me every time a thought of Roxy flashed across my mind. The insane relief at being able to see her again. The absolute solace that I hadn't lost a chance to just talk to her again. I hadn't realized until I saw her how scared I was. Our professional connection had to be a gift from the universe. A chance to fix whatever I had messed up.

But then, she had transformed in an instant. Holding her felt like everything in the universe had finally lined up but then, a moment later, she retreated into a shell of protection. A hard shell covering the gooey insides I had seen glimpses of. She turned quiet. Changed. Wouldn't even look at me. Wouldn't talk to me.

Despite the change, she was still as breathtaking as I remembered. No. More so. The image in my mind was a screenshot of a screenshot, reposted too many times. It did no justice to her breathtaking beauty. Her gaze that pierced to my chest. Those lips that begged to be sucked on.

Fuck.

I groaned out loud and turned to pace in the other direction.

But tonight she was so shut down. In Denver, she gifted me with her attention and conversation. It was like having a butterfly land on me. She danced without a care in the world. She spoke without doubting herself. Tonight her jaw was locked, her shoulders set with ever-present tension.

If I could have just gotten her alone and explained … I tried to get more information from Gretchen. But after her own talk with Roxy, Gretchen was a different person from the chatty redhead that had picked me up. Her arms were crossed across her body the rest of the night, and when she spoke, it was only in clipped words. Saying quote: "It wasn't her business," end quote. I wondered if I had done something, but when I shot a questioning look to Suzie, she just shrugged sadly.

If only I could have talked to her a bit more. That hug had been amazing. To hold her so close only to lose her again …

"This is not going to be good," I groaned to the ceiling. I knew what I needed to do if I ever had a hope of sleeping again.

I turned the phone over and over with my fingers.

"Fuck. No. Okay." I stopped pacing and let out a breath I'd trapped in my chest.

I unlocked the screen and dialed my best friend. It was only after several rings that I considered the time.

"Hello?" the groggy voice answered.

"Skip. Skippo. My man."

"What time is it?" he asked.

"I messed up." I chewed on my thumb, bracing for his reaction.

There was a moment of silence and then, "Okay. Hold on. Waking up. Just give me a second."

My foot tapped rapidly. Shuffling sounds and then the click of a lamp.

"You messed up? You've been gone barely one day," Skip said.

"Yup."

"Okay. Back up." More shuffling and the sounds of his steps on the wood floor of the hallway. I imagined him going to the kitchen, flipping on the light as he rubbed his eyes awake. There was the sound of the kettle turning on, right on cue. "Start from the beginning."

I ended up talking until my voice cracked. Opening with Gretchen picking me up from the airport to the high of seeing Roxy followed by her abrupt dismissal, I told him everything.

"I thought she'd be so happy to see me." I took a gulp of water from the bottle next to my bed. "Now I'm remembering how she left that night in Denver. Saying it had to be like this. What was I thinking?"

"You assumed that something took her away. Something that was outside of her control. You assumed the best," Skip said simply.

A weird pain tightened my chest. "Yeah. I did."

"You always assume the best in people," my at-home philosopher said.

"Why does it not feel like a good thing when you say it?"

"Good is relative. Things are what they are."

"Well, now what am I thinking?" I asked.

"And now you're thinking that maybe she left of her own choice."

The pain sharpened. I couldn't seem to take in a full breath. "Yes."

"It sounds like you need clarification. But it also sounds like she might need some time to process."

"How so?"

"Don't forget I met her. We actually spent a lot of time together. She was highly organized and focused. To be honest, she reminded me of myself."

I sat on the bed. "Huh." Wasn't sure how I felt about that.

"Yes. And she and I have similar business aesthetics," he explained. "We collectively geeked out over the use of color-coded highlighters in our planners."

"Nerds."

He laughed softly. "Yeah, yeah. Just remember that I don't like surprises. Unlike you, I find sudden change very upsetting and I need time to readjust."

"I know, Skippo."

"So give her some space. She might need to process things. Just don't bombard her."

"You're right. I should go talk to her. I wonder if she's awake now? How can I figure out where she lives?"

"Sanders," his tone warned.

Skip was soft-spoken with a very slight speech impediment on some of his words. He told me once he had therapy as a kid but it still sometimes came out. He'd always been self-conscious about it and I wondered if that was why he hardly spoke. Or maybe it was because I was always the one talking when we were together. But when he had something important to say, he was firm. He was firm with me now.

I flopped back on the bed and studied the wooden beams that crossed the ceiling. "Fine. I'll be patient."

There was a sound of a deep breath.

"Hey, I can be patient," I repeated.

"Like the time you said you would wait for me and then ran to the beach before I even had my sunscreen on?" I started to speak but he cut me off to finish. "And then you ended up getting stung by a jelly-fish. Need more examples? I have plenty."

The memory made me wince. "Point taken. Moving on."

"You're many wonderful things," he explained, "but patience is a virtue that skipped you. Sometimes, this is an awesome thing, your tenacity is unmatched. Sometimes, it leads to intense talks in the middle of the night and flights to small towns in the middle of nowhere."

"I can do this," I said out loud mostly to myself. I felt a change happening within me. I wanted her to take me seriously.

"Make sure when you talk again, it's on neutral ground. Somewhere she feels comfortable," he said.

I closed my eyes and imagined Roxy's face. Her soft, full lips. I recalled her body rocking against mine. My palms burned to touch her skin. "With her, I can be patient."

The silence lasted so long on the other side of the line that I pulled the phone away to check that we hadn't disconnected.

"What's wrong?" I asked. "If you're worried about the business stuff, don't be. I met another perspective client tonight. His name is Ford. He's got this amazing charity that gives teens somewhere to put all their angst. We're already planning to take them camping."

"Despite your impulsiveness, I know you always intend to put OTB first," he said.

"You're not saying something."

"I'm not worried about the business, man. Not really. I'm worried about you," he said. "Don't you think we should talk about things? If this is just a big distraction from—"

"No," I said, firmly. "It's not a distraction."

For a split second, I wanted to tell him everything. I felt like I could crack my chest open and share with him all my worries. I could share about Dad and Roxy's rejection and my fears about business and how I just kept managing to fuck things up when I only want to be the best …

I waited a beat too long.

"You know, I was planning on going out there anyway. I'd been looking at flights," Skip said. I could practically hear him reaching for his laptop and logging on.

"What? No, mate, you know I'm fine," I said with an easy laugh. I was the easygoing one. I wouldn't burden him with my shit. He had his own worries.

"You're sure?"

"Of course. I always am. I'll clear this up. And I will nail this account. Getting more business by the day. All good things."

I closed my eyes again. My hand rubbed circles on my chest. I reached for the half-empty bottle of antacids.

"It'll be fine," I said. My eyelids felt heavy. Sleep was finally taking over.

"Okay, Sanders. Just be careful."

CHAPTER 10

SANDERS

J took Skip's advice to heart. I spent the rest of Saturday and Sunday completely focused on OTB and hardly thought of Roxy at all. I went into town and schmoozed with local business owners, including a nice lunch at a place called Daisy's Nuthouse with Ford and Jack. I avoided areas where I thought Roxy might be, which was easy enough given the size of the sprawling Donner Lodge. I wandered through the winding footpaths, and mostly did my best to focus on work and respecting her space.

Well, that wasn't to say that I wasn't constantly thinking of Roxy but I wasn't *doing* anything about those thoughts, which was serious progress. Forty-eight whole hours of not actively pursuing her challenged me. Hard as I was trying, the inaction had taken its toll and by Monday morning I was a carbonated drink that had spent the weekend on a paint shaker.

It wasn't my fault that the very first person I saw upon leaving my room that morning was Roxy. How could I not think the universe was rewarding my patience? I'd come down to the main lobby and found her bent over, struggling to pick up a box half her height. Her hair was pulled into a tight bun and professional gray trousers clung tightly to legs I had memorized by now.

I looked to the ceiling and threw out a silent cry, *Come on. You're killing me.*

The box was slightly larger than her arm span and she couldn't get enough of a grip to leverage the size. The lobby was deserted at the early hour, so I spent twenty seconds enjoying the view. It was wrong of me. I would never let anybody else ogle her like that. But other people hadn't known her body intimately while dancing. Hadn't held her hand for hours. Eventually, I did move to help her. I stepped quietly until I was right behind her.

"Can I help?" I bent forward to ask in her ear.

She shot up immediately and I stepped back just in time to avoid a bloody nose.

"Sanders." Her gaze roamed over my face, pupils dilating. For a flash she almost looked as though she were happy to see me. But then her focus flicked to check the room around us. "Hello. Good morning. Ah, no. Nope. I'm fine." She patted the box.

"Are you sure?" I smiled and leaned in. She smelled amazing. Her scent was different each time I'd been with her, the base the same but with different accents, like a series of wines made from the same grapes but with slightly different tones. Today her underlying scent was accented by flowery notes of … gardenias?

She leaned back. "How has your stay been so far? Your accommodations are good, er satisfactory?"

"The beds are fantastic." I smiled.

Her eyes widened a fraction and flicked around the lobby. "Good." She nodded.

Color rose to her cheeks and I felt myself preen. But then I realized what I was doing. I was doing the literal exact opposite of what Skip told me to do. My normal, albeit overwhelming charm, would not be wise. A wave of guilt had me straightening and taking two steps back.

She smoothed her cream-colored silk blouse. I was slightly disappointed to note that I couldn't see any of the art decorating her body that had been visible the night we met. I would love to spend hours memorizing each once. Tracing my fingers over the patterns ... seeing where they led.

I cleared my throat. How long had we been standing there just staring at each other?

"Well, if you got it handled. I won't bother you." I turned to leave.

"Ah, actually." She hesitated. "This delivery was supposed to go to the back entrance but somehow there was a mix-up. I was trying to move it out of the way."

She was fixing her fringe when I turned back around. "Bit of an eyesore," I hedged cautiously. *Patience*, I reminded myself.

Her hand dropped quickly. "I wanted to move it to the back office before any guests came down. It's for a wedding this weekend."

"Happy to help." I hefted the box into my arms in one smooth movement. Showing off slightly. The bugger was heavy. I was sufficiently rewarded when her eyes flicked to my biceps. I flexed them as the box slipped and I readjusted to grab the bottom. She sucked in her lips and looked away. Thankfully, the box hid my cocky grin.

"Follow me," she said.

Unfortunately, the box also blocked most of my view. The soft sounds of her heels clipping along the floor guided me. I risked my balance by looking around my burden to glimpse her retreating backside. My knuckles smashed on the corner as we turned and I almost dropped the box.

"Shit," I swore. Served me right for not paying attention.

"Are you okay?" She helped me set the box down in a back room.

"I'm fine. Karma." I mumbled the last part to myself.

She grabbed my hands and winced at my knuckles. It wasn't anything bad but the skin was peeled back and there were little dots of blood along each knuckle.

"'Tis but a flesh wound," I joked.

"Come here." She didn't drop my hand as we walked a few more feet to a small janitor's closet. She set me down on an overturned bucket and opened a first aid kit on the wall.

"It's fine. I'll just rinse it off," I half-heartedly said. To be honest, there was nothing sexier than her nursing me in that little suit.

She ignored me as she took out a few things, reading the backs and reaching for the next package.

"Some help I am." I kept talking because, boy, it was quiet in that little room. "Now, I'm keeping you from your work."

She ripped open a square packet and shook out a damp sheet. She crouched down, balancing on her heels and gestured for my injured hand.

"Really, if you need to get back to work. I'm fine—oh, ouch!" My hand shot back but she didn't release it.

"It's an alcohol wipe," she said.

"It burns like the dickens," I said.

Her eyebrows shot up behind her fringe. Her mouth was a flat line but a little light teased her eyes. "Like the dickens?" she repeated, staying focused on her work.

I sniffed haughtily. "Nah. This is fine. I'm totally fine." My arm tried to pull out of her grip again when the next wipe burned even more.

Now she was definitely trying not to smile.

"I'm glad my pain brings you joy."

"No, it doesn't," she said lightly.

I leaned in closer and just about died when her mouth pursed and she blew a soft stream of air on my fingers. She may as well have been blowing on my cock for how hard I became in that second. I swallowed and began to mentally list all the states in America, a nearly impossible and terribly unsexy task. *Don't misinterpret things again.* Just because I found her every single action sexy as all hell didn't mean she was making a pass.

I was stock-still, too afraid to breathe or move for fear of pulling her onto my lap.

She looked up at me through her luxurious lashes. Her face was unreadable. But she wasn't pulling back either, was she? Her gaze flicked between my eyes, dropped to my lips and then quickly shot back up. Our faces were only inches apart. My mind screamed a thousand reasons why it would be a great idea to close the distance between us. But then Skip's dour expression popped into my head. Arms crossed over his flannel shirt and his face turned in a frown. Talk about a bucket of ice water dumped on my head.

My focus moved back to my knuckles. I cleared my throat and asked, "Why is it these shallow little cuts always burn more?"

"It's because they're not deep enough to trigger the pain receptors like a deeper wound does. That's why paper cuts never seem to stop hurting," she explained matter-of-factly as she placed little Band-Aids on each knuckle. A tiny frown formed between her eyebrows as she worked.

"Huh. Interesting."

She was placing the last Band-Aid on when she added, "And because you're a big baby." She flicked a playful glance up at me through her lashes. That look did little to calm my heated blood.

My hand remained in hers as she went down the line and checked each bandage was properly stuck to each finger. "Nice hands," she mumbled and I hardly heard her.

"What was that?" I asked. Had she just complimented my hands? I would need her to say that louder. I needed that recorded actually.

She shook her head and stood up and away from me.

She took a deep breath, and before she could speak, I said, "Look. I want to apologize for Friday night ..."

"We should talk about it," she said, seeming to choose her words carefully. "I'm the one who needs to apologize. I was just caught off guard. When I learned that you were William's partner—"

"Skip's business partner," I inserted.

"Right. It just threw me off. I was in work mode. I'm trying for a promotion and there is a lot at stake. Still. I'm sorry."

She leaned back on a shelf, looking down on me with sincere regret. I was still crouched on the bucket covered in tiny bandages. I wasn't feeling my most masculine at the moment but again Skip's words played in my head. She needed to feel comfortable to open up. So I hugged my knees planted almost to my chest, feeling like a giant man-child. I'd endure far worse to see that light returning to her that I first saw in Denver.

"I didn't mean to bombard you. My plan was to tell you who I was before the meeting with Vincent," I said. I tried to cross my leg but almost tipped over, so I uncrossed it and tried to look serious. "And I didn't know who you were the night we met in Denver, I promise."

She nodded like she believed me. "I think I'd—"

Just then the little door to the janitor closet opened and light spilled in. Roxy stood up straighter. Vincent stood framed in light.

"Roxanne. I was just looking for you." His gaze then found me sitting like the naughty kid wearing a dunce cap. "Mr. Olsson." One sharp eyebrow cocked. "Everything okay?"

Roxy stepped forward. "Minor mishap. He was helping me move a box. I'll fill out an incident report for the supplies," she said in a brisk business tone I was growing accustomed to. Unfortunately.

The well-dressed man nodded. His sharp eyes looked to Roxy and back to me. Then back to her again. "I was looking for both of you," he said. "Let's go back to my office to chat."

Roxy wouldn't look at me. Instead, she nodded and followed his retreating figure. I would have been more hurt but getting off that bucket with my ass half asleep required my full attention.

* * *

Roxy

AFTER THE FIASCO at the drive-in, I spent the weekend preparing for my next encounter with Sanders. I replayed the relief and disbelief of seeing him again, only to have it dashed by my own selfish worries about my career. I knew I had hurt him but damn, I could have used a warning that night. A weekend of talking myself up all thrown out the window as soon as I saw him. I had a whole speech prepared about a professional working relationship and how important it was for me to focus on my work. And then the second I heard that voice, smelled his soapy man smell, I was a goner. He was catnip and I was a pussy.

And now here I sat between Vincent and Sanders, trying to get my bearings.

I checked back into the conversation when Vincent addressed me. "… But what I'm hoping for, Roxy"—I didn't miss how he emphasized my name—"is that you two will work closely with MooreTek. They're a big client for both of us. Based out of California. They're coming next week for a corporate retreat, and if they're happy, it could mean a lot of potential future business. It will be good to see how you handle an event of this size," he finished to me.

He clasped well-manicured fingers on the desk which looked marginally more tidy since the last time I had been in there. Based on the fact that his phone hardly stopped buzzing during our entire conversation, he still had a lot on his plate. Vincent proposed to Sanders that Outside the Box work directly with the Lodge for the visiting corporate account. It would be a chance to see what corporate adventuring was all about and how it could integrate with the Lodge. When I glanced to the side, Sanders was grinning ear to ear. I fought the instinct to roll my eyes at him.

"This is fantastic," he said. I felt him look to me but I stayed focused on Vincent. "Of course I'll have to check with my co-owner," he finished in a more serious tone.

"William?" I asked, finally turning to him.

"Skip, yeah. He only had great things to say about his meeting with Roxy," Sanders said pointedly to Vincent.

The other man nodded. "That's what I hear." Vincent held my gaze until I was worried there was something on my face. I fixed my bangs and looked away. What else had he heard about me? I swallowed down my fears and stayed focused.

"I thought Skip was supposed to come out here?" I asked, keeping my tone light.

Sanders nodded seriously. "Ah, yeah. He really wanted to. But some stuff came up at the corporate office, so I took one for the team."

The more Sanders spoke, the more I felt like he wasn't exactly telling the truth. His sexy Aussie accent flared up more on the ends of his sentences, growing more pronounced as he spoke. Southerners do this thing where sometimes their statements sound like questions. Apparently so did Australians.

Vincent continued, "The group will arrive next Monday. They'll be here for one week with about ten members from their upper-management team. From what I understand they are struggling to innovate and cooperate with each other. They're hoping some fresh air and the Smokies magic will invigorate the team." Vincent picked up his phone and began to scroll as he spoke. "I can do my best to help out, but to be frank I'm drowning in other responsibilities and would like to leave the heavy lifting on this to you two."

I shifted in my seat. Us work together? I had already done most of the planning for this event. Rooms were booked. Continental breakfast provided by Donner Bakery was included and they'd paid for lunch in advance too. They'll be on their own for dinners but there was always the restaurant in the Lodge or they could go into town—

"We'll take them camping," Sanders interrupted my internal list making.

"What?" My head snapped to him.

"What's a better way to bring people together than camping?" His blue eyes were wide and bright. He was like a puppy that caught its first ball.

"I don't really camp," I started.

"It'll be great. We'll teach them to fish and to clean and grill it. How to start fires."

"I don't think the rangers of the national park forest would like that …"

"Maybe even a little rock climbing."

"Whoa. Whoa—" I said, holding up my hands. "The liability alone, that's just not feasible." I turned to Vincent, eyes wide and with horror at Sanders' ideas.

Vincent looked back at me pointedly. "I trust that you two will work together on everything. Roxy, can you help Sanders with whatever

Outside the Box needs, since I can't help? I want the Lodge to support this idea fully and see if it works out for us all."

I blinked at Vincent. Stuck together? Well, shit. I didn't even know how Sanders and Outside the Box worked. I needed schedules. I needed to know every single detail of every day. What was Sanders thinking? That we'd go hiking and camping and just figure out the rest with the client? This wasn't a campfire and we weren't singing kumbaya. Sanders flinched slightly when I turned to him in shock. I didn't need a mood ring with this face. Not that I could help it, just like he couldn't help his own goofy little smile.

Vincent watched our interaction closely. I swallowed. I was supposed to be the professional, show him I could handle this position. No biggie. I could do this.

I wanted to scream but instead I smiled and said through gritted teeth, "I'm sure whatever we decide as a team will be great."

Vincent leaned forward, eyes looking between the two of us. "That won't be a problem, right? There's no reason you two can't work together?" he asked.

"No," I said instantly.

At the same time, Sanders said, "Nope."

Vincent nodded once, a hint of doubt in his gaze. "I'll let you all handle the details. This is important. I trust you will do what is best."

I sat rigid, while next to me, Sanders practically vibrated with barely contained energy.

Vincent smiled briskly, glancing at his watch to signify the end of the meeting.

"Thank you," I said.

Sanders and I walked in silence until we were outside. He wasn't following me exactly and I hadn't dismissed him. We walked to where a light dirt trail skirted the path between the main lodge and the forest behind it.

Sanders and I together all week? This wouldn't work. Oh, I had said what I needed to say for Vincent. But I didn't need this lovely man and his distracting smiles muddling up my focus. Bless his heart.

What would the SWS do?

They would do what they needed to get the job done.

So could I.

I came to a stop and took a deep breath. It was fine. Tall pines swayed in the summer breeze. There was only the sound of our breaths and the creaking of the trees in the wind.

"It's beautiful out here," Sanders said, breaking me from my thoughts.

When I looked to Sanders, he was studying me with soft eyes before he quickly looked away. It sent a shudder of longing through me.

All at once I understood with complete certainty that this partnership wasn't going to work without some ground rules. I respected Vincent's wishes to work with Sanders, but there were too many complications between us. I couldn't stand here and pretend that working together would be easy. We needed strict boundaries and a set path.

"Listen, Sanders. I think we should make things clear."

"Good idea." He watched me so eagerly, so openly. Too openly. His earnestness left him vulnerable. Someday someone was going to shatter his rose-colored glasses and it wouldn't be me.

"Friday night, I didn't react well," I started carefully choosing my words. "Like I said earlier, I was caught off guard by you being here in Green Valley. I didn't expect to ever see you again."

"You didn't want to see me again?" he asked.

I hesitated. "I just—" I struggled to find a thread of the speech I prepared. "If I had known that you were the other half of Outside the Box, Skip's partner, I would never have … I don't want you to think that my behavior that night was in any way an attempt to persuade you to do business with the Lodge."

Sanders blinked, his eyebrows rose in genuine surprise. "I never thought that. Not even for a second."

He stepped closer. I didn't retreat though every inch of me wanted to run away. "I didn't know who you were either. I just needed to see you again. It felt *important*."

I frowned at the ground.

"Tell me you didn't feel that too," he said.

"You flew across the country …"

"Just a few states, really."

"For a connection?" I finished.

"For destiny. And I notice you haven't denied it."

"Sanders, you can't talk like that," I said. I held up a hand and took a step back. Boundaries. Plans. "The way I acted that night was out of character, that isn't who I am." It was though, wasn't it? That was the real problem.

"We would have met again eventually because of work. I just took Skip's place temporarily. It's not as dramatic as all that. Think about it. We would have met again." When he put it that way, the anxiety eased up a bit in my chest.

"This is all just too much," I said honestly.

"Why did you want to leave things that night? Why so final?" he asked boldly. He wouldn't let me look away.

I couldn't look into those blue eyes without wanting to pour everything out. "I...I—"

"Tell me. Did I do something?" He looked so open and vulnerable again. *Gah.* He had to stop doing that.

"Please." His hands reached for me but then dropped and stuffed deep into his pockets. "You can be honest. Was it me? Did I push too hard?"

"No. It wasn't that." Didn't he remember that it was my idea to go back to the hotel? A fresh wave of shame burned my cheeks.

I couldn't handle his puppy dog eyes.

"Roxy?" he pleaded and moved closer. If his eyes were catnip, then his masculine scent and the heat of his body was straight heroin to my system. I was powerless. He continued, "I know your career is important to you. My career is important to me too. Let's leave all that back there." He gestured to the Lodge. "Right now we're just two people standing in the forest. We're a man and a woman that met in a club. Tell me what's going through your head and then back to business. I just want to understand."

I glanced around and then forced myself to focus on his face. Tentatively, I explained, "That night, things were moving too fast. I'm not in a place to think about anything other than my career."

There were a million other things I wanted to explain but I couldn't even have this conversation with my best friend, let alone a business associate.

"It's best if we move forward as coworkers. Maybe even friends. And that's it," I finished.

Something shuttered behind his smile. A hand rubbed his chest. "Thank you for being honest with me."

I chewed my lip and nodded once.

"I'm so sorry I bombarded you Friday. I was just really excited to see you again." Hear that? That was the sound of my charcoal black heart cracking open. "About the Lodge," he said, "Outside the Box could pull out. If I messed this up. I'll talk to Vincent and explain. We don't have to do this if you think it'll be too weird."

I didn't know this version of him. He seemed distant, professional, probably trying to mimic how I had acted toward him. He actually seemed a little worried. Dammit if it didn't make me want to hug him. This was what being around him did to my brain. It made me all touchy-feely.

"No. Don't. It really would be fantastic for the Lodge. And for Outside the Box."

"Right. Yeah." He nodded looking at the ground.

"You have a life and family in Colorado, I'm sure. A completely professional relationship would be for the best," I emphasized again.

"Of course."

I kept myself very still, my face purposely blank. I knew this was for the best. I knew I couldn't risk being around him, not when he spoke so openly and sweetly. It was like asking a kleptomaniac to house-sit, I couldn't be tempted like that.

"For this MooreTek business. I have everything planned. There are a few afternoons free where you can schedule in your activities." I shifted from foot to foot. "I will email you the itinerary and you can go from there," I said.

"Wait, what? Vincent just told us to stick together like glue."

"I know what he said. But I work better alone. Plus, it's better for you. Think of this as a group project and all you have to do is show up and get the grade." I fixed my bangs when a breeze blew through them.

As I spoke, his smile slipped off his face. I steeled myself. This was all for the greater good. *WWSWSD?*

90

He ran his hands through his hair, looking like he was debating on saying something.

Finally, making up his mind, he said, "Sure. I understand. See ya around." He turned and headed back to the Lodge.

When he was out of sight, I leaned against a tree to catch my breath. I pressed my hand to my chest hoping to calm my racing heart. I hadn't expected it to be so hard to set this line in the sand. I wanted to do the right thing for both of us, so why did it feel so wrong?

CHAPTER 11

SANDERS

*M*y hands shook with unidentifiable emotion as I walked away from Roxy but my smile remained carefully in place. Roxy was struggling with something and needed time. So while I wanted to go back and wrap her in a hug, the smartest thing was to show her I could be patient and respect her wish for boundaries.

Stupid boundaries.

I hated that she was pushing me away. My appearance had not been the happy reunion I'd been hoping for, but Vincent had told us to work together. To tell me she worked better alone was a flimsy excuse to not be around me. I understood it but I didn't like it.

All joking with Skip aside, I would and could be patient. I would never push myself on her. If friendship was what she needed, then that's what I would offer. Better to be in her life as a friend than not at all.

Acid churned in my stomach and up my esophagus. What had I eaten? I'd not had anything but eggs and avocado this morning and yet my insides rioted like I'd gone crazy at a six-dollar buffet. I was feeling restless, talking with Roxy had done little to quell the energy. And in fact I was feeling … frustrated? And maybe hurt. I needed to burn off some energy. I needed to get out and clear my head. I hated feeling pointless emotions. Just push that shit aside and move on.

What I needed was to go for an invigorating hike and brainstorm some ideas for MooreTek. I'd present a thorough list to Roxy when we met; I'd be the most professional business partner she'd ever worked with. I wouldn't try to touch her every possible second. I wouldn't find ways to get close enough to breathe her in. I would be the best fucking mate she didn't know she needed.

I hurried back to my room to quickly change into hiking boots because the sky was blanketed in heavy gray clouds and my weather app warned of a storm later.

"Argh," I yelled into the room as soon as I shut the door behind me.

"Everything okay?" a voice from the corner asked.

"Shit!" I yelled, jumping and clutching my heart. "Skip!"

He laughed. "Sorry." He was opening a suitcase on the second bed. "Didn't think my face was that scary."

"It really is." I grinned and stepped toward him. I opened my arms. "But boy am I glad to see that ugly mug."

He embraced me and I smacked his back before we broke apart. "What are you doing here?" I asked.

He shrugged and looked at the ground. "I just wanted to see what all the fuss was about in Green Valley."

Maybe I hadn't sounded as put together as I had thought when we talked. At 2 a.m. Where I had called him in a manic state. Okay, so he was clearly concerned for my ability to handle things for OTB when my heart was in knots.

"You really didn't have to come all the way down here."

He gave me a look. "I thought maybe you'd like company."

I scratched at the back of my head. "Everything's okay. I just talked to Roxy. And we have our first official client."

He stuffed his hands in his pockets and jutted his chin toward the door. "It sounded like things were great when you came in."

I laughed. "Oh that?" I didn't know how to explain my behavior to myself so I certainly couldn't explain it to him. I searched around quickly for an excuse. I glimpsed my bandaged fingers. "I just hit my hand on the door as I was coming in." I held up my knuckles.

He studied my face too closely. He had freaky best mate X-ray vision, so I knocked my smile up a notch and busied myself by grabbing my hiking boots.

"Feel like a hike? Are you tired?" I asked him.

"Nah. That sounds good. By the way, I'm actually not rooming with you." He gestured to his stuff.

"You can crash here. I don't mind."

He hesitated a split second before saying, "Just waiting to check in. The person at the front desk gave me a key to your room. I'm not trying to tell them how to run their business but they may want a little better security." He grabbed the poncho he packed. Then he reached back into his suitcase and tossed one to me. Probably a good idea. Skip always had my back.

"What would I do without you, Skippo?" I swung an arm around his shoulders as we made our way out to the hall.

"I shudder to think."

"I'm glad to see you, mate. Really, I am," I said seriously. I hadn't realized how lonely I was feeling until I saw him. For him to drop everything ... I really was lucky to have a friend like him.

He cleared his throat and pushed the button for the lift. "What's this about our first client?"

I explained to him about the meeting with Vincent.

"Sounds like a big deal. And you're working with Roxy?" We'd just made it to the trailhead as a drop of rain hit my nose.

"Yep," I said.

We slid our ponchos over our heads as we walked.

"Would it be better if I took the lead on this one?" he asked coolly.

Yes. I thought immediately but I couldn't say it. I couldn't lose an opportunity to be with her as much as possible for the brief time I was in Green Valley.

"Nah. She and I are good. We talked today actually. Completely on the same page now."

"Good. She's a straight shooter."

"That she is," I said more than a little forlorn.

"She's okay?" he asked.

"Yeah. Wants us to be coworkers only. Keep things simple while I'm in town," I explained.

"Sounds reasonable." He shot me a skeptical glance.

"Very much. We could even become friends." I rubbed my chest, the mystery heartburn returning.

"You'd be okay just being friends?" he asked as we crossed a small wooden bridge over a stream.

"Better than nothing at all," I said.

Rain started to fall harder. "Maybe we should head back," he said.

"Just a little more."

He looked back toward the Lodge. "Only another few minutes. I don't want to die out here."

We walked on as the rain relented into a mist and then stopped. "Seems to be clearing up." We'd been walking about twenty minutes. My muscles were working, blood flowed. I felt better already. So I flew across the States to see a girl who only wanted to be friends. That was fine. I was fine. Eventually, she'd come around and see that our connection was more than just fleeting.

"Just me and my best mate out in nature. What else do I need?" I stopped and held out my arms wide. Just then lightning flashed and thunder cracked. We both ducked instinctually.

"Shit," Skip swore.

"Okay. You may have been right. Let's head back."

Without any more discussion, we began a slow jog back toward the Lodge. We were used to bad summer storms in Denver. One second it'd be perfectly sunny, the next a torrential downpour was washing out the ditches. I guess I'd been expecting more of a soft misting rain all day.

We made it to the little bridge that had marked the start of the trail only to find the trickling stream transformed into a full river, almost completely submerging the bridge. It was barely passable.

"We're gonna just have to go for it," Skip shouted over the raindrops pelting our ponchos.

He leapt onto the bridge. Skip was about my height, tall, lean, athletic. He smashed five steps and made it across despite the torrential downpour. To be honest, he made it look stupid easy and my fragile male ego felt challenged. Before I could overthink it, I launched myself forward.

I copied him exactly, but after my first three steps, I hit a snag. Literally. A large stick, some might say a log, came rushing down the stream, some might say river. The heavy log smashed into my ankle just as my poncho caught the edge of the railing.

The moment happened fast but I processed it in slow motion. Like how the world spins out of control only to slow back down to a narrow focus in a car wreck. My upper body was tugged back and my legs slipped forward. I slammed onto my back. Unable to catch my breath. Vaguely, distantly, I was aware that this may have been a good thing because I was completely submerged.

My lungs burned to take in a breath. Icy water gushed over my entire body, into my ears and mouth. Instinct had me remembering my training, reminding me that I needed to get up. I needed to move. But I couldn't fight the current. My foot felt pinned down. Something was weighing me down besides the rushing water. Panic threatened to force me to gulp in air.

It occurred to me in a soft warmth settling over my body that this may be how I died. How silly. Of all the adventurous things I'd done in my life, crossing a flooded bridge was what finally did me in. But I had always suspected it would be this way. Only the good die young, as they say. I'd had a good run.

At least I'd seen her face one last time.

* * *

Roxy

"SOME IDIOTS WENT DOWN the Little Creek Trail," the front desk clerk called out to me as I came into the lobby from my lunch break.

"Sh—" I started to say, then remembered myself. "Just now?" I asked instead.

"Little bit ago."

I blinked at him. He flinched.

Did it occur to him to stop them from going? Knowing the rain was pouring down? Apparently not. But I learned long ago not to expect other people to behave like I would in a situation. That way led to disappointment.

"I assume you're telling me because they haven't come back. Where's John?"

"Who's John?" The kid looked at me blankly.

"Our security guy."

"Oh. No idea. This Lodge has security?"

I blinked at him. He blinked back.

It never failed. Despite at least three different signs warning about the trail during rainstorms, almost monthly, someone would head down there.

I frowned down at my clothes and heels. "You seen Vincent? A manager?"

The kid shook his head, he was already over this conversation and moved on to help the waiting guest.

"Dammit. Dammit," I grumbled. "If I don't come back in twenty minutes, please send someone. And try and get ahold of Vincent. I'm taking the walkie."

"Will do."

This was definitely karma's doing for explicitly disregarding Vincent's instructions to work with Sanders. I was going to. Just on my own terms. That didn't mean I had control issues.

I headed to the back office and quickly traded my heels and blazer for the extra pair of galoshes and the massive poncho I kept on hand for this exact reason. Both had come in handy more than once. I left the side door and jogged to the trailhead. The grass squelched with every step and the rain was unrelenting. Little Creek had most likely become Rushing River already.

I could just make out the shape of two grown men heading back down the trail through the rain at a good clip. I let out a tense breath. At least we wouldn't have to call search and rescue. Good Lord, was Jethro still a ranger? Last thing I wanted was to see him. I made my way toward the men just so I could chew their asses out for not paying attention to their surroundings. And not reading signs. And for making me get soaking wet.

As I slowed, the first man sprinted across the bridge. He grazed across like a skipping stone on a smooth lake. Recognition set in. It was the co-owner of Outside the Box, Skip. It was so confusing to see him here in this setting, it took me a minute to register. What was Skip doing in Green Valley? Had I offended Sanders so much that he left? Had he turned tail and run as soon as he heard I wasn't going to …

No wait. Then that meant …

"Oh, you're clucking kidding me." I picked up my pace just in time to see the second man, definitely Sanders, start across the bridge. My feet slipped in the muddy bank as I halted abruptly on the deep slope.

His initial leap was as smooth as Skip's had been, but a fraction of a second later, once he was already in the air, time suspended. It was like a scene from *Final Destination*: a few otherwise harmless events lined up in just the right way to set him up for disaster.

The flap of his poncho that caught the railing. The log that popped out of the water, slamming into his ankle. There was nothing I could do but gasp and wait for the dominoes to fall. And fall he did. One second he was vertical. The next he was horizontal.

I gasped and lunged forward.

I was going to kill him. As soon as he came out of this alive, I would kill him. I could picture him, laughing it off, saying he'd felt like a swim. I half ran, half slid down the hill that led to the bridge about ten yards away.

But when he didn't immediately pop back up, it was clear something was wrong. I could just make out the shape of him—unmoving—under the dark, rushing water. Skip had already jumped back toward the bridge.

On the walkie-talkie I shouted for help. I didn't have time to hear their response. I tucked it away and ran to Skip's side.

Skip was gripping the railings, fighting the now knee-high current.

"His leg!" I shouted and pointed to the log that was now stuck between Sanders' leg and the bridge.

Skip's pale face shot to mine. If he was shocked to see me, there was no time to acknowledge it. He nodded and shouted back, "I'll get his head."

We moved into action. Skip somehow straddled the railings to get behind Sanders as I waded into the rushing water.

"Can you lift his torso out? I'll try and unpin him," I yelled.

Fear gripped my heart. In all my years at the Lodge, there had been a few emergencies and typically I slipped into action mode easily. Each time I was able to take the necessary actions with clarity, following established safety protocol without hesitation. This time hot fear sliced through me, filling my mind with panic. Why wasn't he out of the water? *Just sit up, Sanders.*

My fear went icy.

Sanders was unconscious. Pale as a sheet, his blond hair plastered to his forehead and his mouth slack. No time to think. I felt around his legs. Sure enough the current was pushing the log directly into his ankle, lodging it at an angle.

"Can you pull him back?" I yelled.

Skip hefted Sanders under his armpits. His face was taut with focus and fear. I gripped the log to keep the weight off as he worked. The freezing water made my fingers clumsy but pure adrenaline gave me determination. Distantly I was aware of the rough knobs and bark cutting into my fingers. The water was leaking into my ears, my whole lower body submerging in the frigid water as I dropped to leverage my weight. I shook with fear or cold. I couldn't be sure. None of it mattered. There was only getting his leg unpinned. My hands kept slipping. Getting a grip was near impossible. I had to angle my feet on the opposite railing and shove with all my upper-body strength.

As Skip shifted the weight, there was just enough wiggle room to push back the log from its stuck position. Instantly, the gushing stream shoved the log roughly past. It floated away like a crocodile down the river, none the wiser that it almost killed a man.

Without discussion, I grabbed Sanders' ankles, as Skip hefted the bulk of his friend's weight across the bridge. It was a struggle. Sanders' unconscious body was heavy. My galoshes slipped with every step. I fell to my knees. Skip yelled something at me but I couldn't hear him. There was only carrying Sanders up the hill and away from the water. Finally, we made it to a picnic table a few yards away. It was up a mound and under some thick pines protected from the worst of the rain, cocooning us in dry safety.

Skip and I hefted him onto the table. Every muscle in my body strained at the effort. As soon as his back was on the table, Skip checked his mouth for obstructions as I pressed my ear to his chest.

Why wasn't he responding?

I climbed on top of him, straddling his body so I could leverage my full weight. I hammered on his chest. His face was so pale.

"Wake up, dammit!"

Where was his ever-present smile? He looked so lifeless. I hit his chest with my fists. Why wouldn't he respond? His heartbeat was strong.

I had been about to start mouth-to-mouth when he finally coughed.

"Let's try getting him on his side," Skip said in obvious relief.

I lifted off of him and helped Skip turn him on his side. Sanders threw up water and coughed out such a ragged gasp for breath, my own throat felt raw from sympathy. He lay back up and looked up at the sky, getting his bearings. He blinked rapidly as a few raindrops leaked through the branches and hit his face. I leaned over him to block them from falling on him. The moment I did his entire face transformed. His eyes widened and a huge smile revealed his goofy teeth.

I'd never been so grateful for a smile in my whole damn life.

"Hi," I said.

"Hi," he said back.

I gently pressed my hand to his icy cheek. "I'm gonna kill you." My voice shook with emotion I hadn't expected.

"With kindness?" he asked.

A laugh-cough broke out of me. My own watery smile split my face at the sight of his. I couldn't help it.

His gaze moved to my mouth. He closed his eyes with a sigh and dropped his head back to the table. "Totally worth it."

Hands pulled me off him as two EMTs got to work checking on him.

As I moved back, it was like the rest of the world reappeared. It had been complete tunnel vision since the moment I saw Sanders fall. It felt like years of my life had passed but it could have only been a few minutes.

Skip came to stand at my side.

"He's gonna be fine." I said it to him as much as I did to myself.

Skip nodded. "He always is."

Tension lined his gaze. I realized this wasn't the first time Skip had experienced this level of fear for his best friend.

Skip and I followed the stretcher as the EMTs carried it back to the Lodge.

Sanders was fully conscious and already charming the pretty EMT with thin braids that stretched down to her lower back. "Just felt like going for a quick dip," he said.

Skip and I exchanged a look.

"Yeah, I think he's gonna be just fine," I said.

I'd been pushing him away since the movie night because of the fear of losing the life I'd built for myself. Within a few horrible minutes, I understood there was way more at stake than my career.

CHAPTER 12

ROXY

A few hours later, Skip and I sat under separate plaid blankets, sipping tea, and chatting by the great fire in the main lodge. Or what would be the great fireplace. Right now it was still a regular fireplace that matched the rest of the art deco vibe of the Lodge. If Diane Donner had her way, the whole place would soon resemble a modern-style cabin. The Lodge kept the fire going year-round because it added to the aesthetic. It made for a cozy setting, set off from the main lobby.

We were waiting for Sanders to come back down after he showered. He had a goose egg on his head and a nasty bruise forming on his ankle, but all things considered, he was fine. Surprisingly fine for how terrifying the whole experience had been. On my end, incident reports had been filed and the EMTs sent on their way. I'd cleaned off in the staff shower and changed into backup clothes I kept in my locker. My body felt warm and borderline high with a post-adrenaline buzz.

Skip was good company. Just like in Denver, we chatted like old friends catching up. He didn't drain me of energy like some people. His beardy ruggedness should make him so much more my type than Sanders. And yet any feelings I had for Skip weren't even comparable to the buzz I felt around Sanders. Skip was like slipping into your favorite sweatshirt. Sanders was like … Sanders was like nothing I'd ever felt. How I imagined it felt to have a couture silk gown slide off my body until I stood naked in nothing but Louboutin heels and a wicked grin.

"I'm good on excitement for a while," I said to Skip taking a sip of the steaming tea before setting it on the coffee table.

He chuckled from the other end of the brown leather couch and I glimpsed his bashful smile before he ducked his head. He was the definition of Colorado beautiful. He wore flannel authentically, his beard was full and brown, and he was built like someone who could actually chop wood and rescue five children under each arm. A grizzly bear with a marshmallow soul.

"You're probably used to this though with the corporate adventuring," I said. "Saving lives, no biggie."

"Not as much as you might think for what we do. Most people are pretty respectful of the rules. And because of the liability, Outside the Box has a lot of safety measures in place, more than if it were just a group of guys going camping with a few kegs and a shotgun," he explained.

"Is Sanders always this …" I trailed off wanting to say "stupid" but knew I was just cranky because he'd scared me so bad.

"Reckless?" he finished for me, then said, "Yes."

I remember the way he looked at his friend earlier. Concerned but also tired.

"He definitely strikes me as the leap-before-you-look type," I said.

This added to my overall anxiety regarding Sanders. He was just too big. He overflowed with too much life. He didn't fit in this life here. Not that it mattered. Not that I worried about how we would fit …

"He's always been like that. It's great in some ways. He's always so inherently sure of OTB's success that it's impossible not to feel some level of that confidence."

I chewed on my cheek. "But sometimes?"

"Well, then sometimes he jumps on a plane without telling me to go after ..." I didn't mean to react but I must have tensed slightly because he trailed off, finishing lamely with, "... a possible business venture."

I nodded feeling slightly disappointed. "You're so close."

"As close as two friends can be." Skip studied his mug of tea.

I had just been about to dig for more information when Sanders popped up. He was always popping up. He was like a little bubble rising to the surface, nothing could keep him down. Carbonation must have been contagious because it felt like I was filled with bubbles too as soon as I saw him.

"We're closer than that, hey?" Sanders said. "We're brothers." He sat directly between Skip and me, forcing us to scoot over to make room.

Skip carefully lifted his tea to the side table to avoid spilling it. "How are you feeling?" he asked.

"Great. That shower did me wonders." Sanders stretched out so his legs were propped up on the table and his arms stretched behind Skip and me respectively. The smell of fresh laundry and the hotel bar soap shook up the bubbles inside me, sending tiny bumps down my neck and arms.

How was this the same man that was unresponsive not that long ago? The tension I'd been holding on to started to relax seeing he was back to his old self. Or at least pretending to be.

"And your ankle?" I asked cautiously.

"It smarts a bit, but it'll be okay." Sanders' head twisted from me to Skip and back again. "So what're we talking about? Me? Go on. Pretend like I'm not here."

"We're talking about how you continue to put yourself in stupid situations with no concern for your own safety," Skip said in his normal even-keeled tone but there was just the slightest edge to his voice.

"What? I did no such thing. I had you with me. You're first aid trained," Sanders said to Skip. "And see, it all worked out."

"No thanks to me." Skip held up his hands quickly before tucking them back under his arms. "If it wasn't for Roxy, who knows where you'd be."

"Roxy, hey?" He raised a cocky eyebrow.

"We're lucky I got there in time to help carry you," I said ignoring Sanders' ridiculous smile. This one would be called "aglow."

"You two worry too much. The water was a bit of a shock. We've been trained to not react to freezing water." He glanced to me. "When you experience cold water—the body wants to gasp and flail and that can do more damage. When I got pulled under, I was just trying to stay calm until you guys got me out. I knew you would."

"You weren't responding," I said flatly. How could he be so calm about this? I was getting pissed off. His life wasn't a toy that could be easily replaced. Did he not understand that? Did he not see how bad he scared his best friend?

"I knew you'd save me," he said and squeezed my shoulder.

I stiffened and chewed the inside of my lip unable to look at him.

Skip said, "I'm Red Cross certified too. But I was referring to the CPR. Roxy all but knocked me down to get on top of you to start chest compressions."

I sat very still keeping my breaths even in hopes of stopping a blush from giving me away. "My training must have kicked in. We have to take a course to work in management."

Of course there was nothing in my CPR training that suggested straddling the victim. I hadn't been thinking clearly at the moment.

"And then it took two full-grown men to pry her away from you when the EMTs wanted to examine you," Skip finished oh so helpfully.

"I don't remember it happening that way," I mumbled.

But I had been experiencing a sort of tunnel vision in that moment. I had only been focused on making sure he was okay. He was the Lodge's guest and soon we'd be working together, of course I was concerned for his safety.

"You were yelling at him too," Skip said.

Had I? I remembered swearing him out in my head. Had I been saying that out loud? That would explain why my throat felt sore.

"Aww, my hero," Sanders said.

He clasped his hands, pretending to swoon. When he dropped his arms again, his left hand fell briefly onto my thigh. He immediately pulled it back but the damage had been done. All the bubbles dancing in my stomach fizzled through my body, tingling from my breasts to my toes. My mind flashed us back to the club when my body rocked against his and his hand ran up my thigh.

Just like that, the anger I'd been feeling at his complete lack of concern for his health melted into relief. As though the stress of the day was cotton candy left out in the rain, it dissolved around me into a sticky mess of confusing feelings. His thigh pressed up to mine was so warm when he'd been icy cold only a bit ago. All I wanted to do was wrap my arms around him and tell him I was so glad he was okay. And then punch him for scaring us.

I stared at his lap, without really seeing, as the memory replayed in my head.

When I realized where I had inadvertently focused, I shot my gaze up only to find him watching me closely. His face remained neutral, or rather his sort of neutral, which was a half-cocked grin. We were so off track we'd somehow missed Old Friend Town and landed at Awkward Moment Junction. Time to get this conversation back on a more professional track.

Skip cleared his throat and stood up. "I better call the office and see how they're doing without us. Glad you're okay, bud."

"Always," Sanders replied with a smile.

"Bye, Skip. I'll call you about dinner tomorrow," I said.

"Love you, Skippo," Sanders said.

"Love you too," Skip said and left.

It was refreshing to see such closeness in two men that didn't need to be wrapped in bravado. They loved each other and they told each other. There was something sweetly simplistic about it. I felt an ache of jealousy thinking about Gretchen. I still hadn't spoken to her in a couple days. Even though I thought about texting her a hundred times. But even when we were talking, I don't know that we ever shared that level of affection. I didn't really show affection, period. Just thinking the L word made me itchy.

I forced those thoughts away. The whole third of the couch to Sanders' right was now unoccupied but he didn't scoot over.

"Is he okay?" I asked after Skip was gone. I couldn't shake the fact that something was bothering him. "Besides seeing his best friend almost drown," I added.

"Skippo? He'll be fine."

"He mentioned you'd been hurt before?"

"Nothing major. Hazards of the profession." Somehow I thought it was more than that. "Are you worried about me?" He grinned at me and I glared.

"No." *Yes, you freaking fool.*

"You've saved me twice today," he said in a deep, rumbling whisper. "I'm feeling quite emasculated."

"Somehow I doubt that."

There was something intriguing about Sanders' cool confidence. I was used to men with big swagger and lots of talk. Tattoos and hairy beards to shout out their manliness. His confidence seemed to glow deep within him like an ember that never went out. Whereas one strong breeze could knock out the ego of most men.

Nothing about Sanders was like the usual masculine energy I was used to. And it was … attractive. Even now I saw the workers at the front desk eyeing him. I glared at them until they got back to work.

"Here I am, the Australian adventurer felled by a stream. I feel silly," he said.

I held his gaze, remembering how lifeless he looked earlier. The firelight jumped in his eyes. Emotion tightened my throat until I cleared it.

"That shouldn't make you feel silly," I said. My focus traveled to his feet. "Your slippers should do that."

He followed my focus where he tapped the toes of his horrendous shoes together. They were black rubber Crocs-style slip-ons lined with fur. They were horrendous. How could a man with those shoes cause me to have all these bubbly feelings? Roxy ten years ago wouldn't recognize this girl.

"Don't hate on these beauts. Like walking on clouds," he said.

I sighed and let my head fall back on the couch. Now the buzz was wearing off into exhaustion. I'd have to get up soon. Just five more minutes.

"This Lodge is gorgeous," he said.

"Mmm," I agreed sleepily. "Wait until you see the changes they're making."

But he wouldn't see them, would he? Eventually, he'd go back to Denver and a life I knew little about.

"And the forest, for what I've seen is just lovely. But that bridge is a bit dangerous. You guys might want to think about marking that."

I slowly turned my head toward him. "You're kidding me."

"What?" He too had his head leaned back, and his eyes were heavy. He must be exhausted too. With both of our heads back and legs up and me wrapped under a blanket, it was almost like we were sleeping together.

"Did y'all really not see the five different notices posted about flash flooding? And how it very specifically says not to take this trail if it's supposed to rain?"

Sanders looked up and around. His eyebrows furrowed. "I guess we missed those."

I sighed but was really fighting not to smile. He made it very difficult to stay mad at him. "You. You are the reason we have umbrella insurance."

"Would you believe that isn't the first time I heard that?"

That time I couldn't hold back the laugh. It was a cough that I quickly covered up. His eyes were lit with joy before they dropped to my mouth. My head fell back and I watched the fire. My heart was pounding with nerves.

"That knob took his blanket with him." Sanders rubbed his hands up and down his goose-bumped arms.

I fought the nervous shudder, doing something I'd probably regret. I sighed in frustration. At myself. I was an idiot. I untucked myself and stood up.

Sanders frowned. "Was it something I said?"

"Shut up," I said as I unwrapped the blanket from around me and shook it to spread it out. I covered us both as I sat back down, keeping a healthy, professional distance between us.

Under the blanket. Which we were sharing. Next to a fire.

I was a damn fool.

"Cozy," he said quietly.

I didn't respond. I just kept my focus firmly on the fire. My hands were loose by my sides, palms down. Sharing this blanket shifted the entire energy of the room.

At first, I wasn't sure that I really felt it. My right pinky was nudged slightly. Without moving my focus from the fire, I studied Sanders in my periphery. He, as always, seemed perfectly relaxed as he settled into the couch. His eyes shut with a contented sigh.

Did he notice that his finger grazed mine? My heart was pounding so loud that he must have felt the couch shaking. A slight brush of skin and my body was as enflamed as it was that night in Denver. I tried to calm my breathing. I would just twitch my finger and cough, alerting him to the fact that we were touching and he'd pull away. I supposed that I could pull away too. But no reason to make a mountain out of a molehill.

Too late.

I shifted my weight, under the guise of settling in. My hand definitely moved. It moved a lot more than I intended. Now the entire sides of our hands were flush. Why wasn't he pulling away? Was he feeling this too? Or was he so used to physical intimacy that this was no big deal. My chest was moving up and down in an embarrassing fashion. I needed to get myself under control. Normal people didn't act like this when they were casually touched.

Neither of us moved. We still faced the fire. What if someone saw us? Could they see the conflicted emotions on my face?

Just move, Roxy. Just pull your arm away. What would the SWS do?

I did move, but my damn traitorous body did not obey my screaming mind. Instead, my hand inched closer. His hand instantly reacted. As I slid mine closer, his flipped over. Our fingers intertwined. His was calloused but tender. Warm without suffocating. It fit mine perfectly. He squeezed it lightly.

I couldn't explain the moisture that burned my eyes then. The emotion that made my throat feel too tight. I swallowed it all deep down. I kept my face neutral. I'd been so scared earlier. More than I would ever admit. Having him next to me felt like a second chance. How many second chances could one gal get before her luck ran out?

None of this made sense. I knew pushing him away would keep my control in place. It would protect me from making any more mistakes with my life. But I couldn't move from that spot. When he held my hand, I felt more tethered to life, not less. He made me want more.

I swallowed and turned my head toward him. The second I did, he turned too, like he'd been waiting for it but didn't want to make the first move. His fair cheeks were splotchy with color. His chest, too, rose and fell quickly. His Adam's apple moved up and down on a swallow.

What does this mean? I thought.

It doesn't have to mean anything, he seemed to say in return.

His thumb moved gently on the back of my hand shooting electricity through my whole body.

I opened my mouth to speak when I heard my name.

"Roxanne," Vincent said.

I glanced up to find my manager glancing between Sanders and me and the blanket.

I'd never moved so fast. Pulled my hand away and stood up so fast.

Felt ashamed so damn fast.

* * *

Sanders

ONCE ON A CAMPING trip as a kid, Dad came across a rattlesnake hanging out near a ditch. My dad, who was never afraid of anything, jumped a foot in the air. I'd never seen someone run away so fast. At least, not until Vincent approached us and Roxy shot up like she'd been bitten. I fought to keep my face easygoing but her reaction stung.

It was probably a good thing.

I'd been struggling. When I learned the lengths that Roxy went to save me, my affection grew. How could it not? But I couldn't just forget everything she'd shared with me earlier in the day. She wanted to be friends. I could and would respect that. As we sat next to each other on the couch, every thought in my head consisted of "would I do this with Skip?" If I would do it with Skip, then it was all good. Skip and I were affectionate. Skip and I hugged. I could potentially hold hands with Skip ...

But then again, it never felt that way when I touched other friends. It never lit me up with a million tiny shocks of electricity when our skin grazed. Holding Roxy's hand for that minute had felt like a gift. I'd been about to do or say something very stupid when Vincent came up.

Roxy was up and standing next to him before I registered the coldness of her absence. She tossed the blanket onto my lap, thankfully, as she jumped up. They stood side by side, Vincent in his expensive suit, Roxy with her hands clasped, her demeanor as professional as his. His face remained neutral except for one small tic in his cheek that disappeared as fast as it came.

"Mr. Olsson, I heard about the accident. Glad you're okay. Can we get you anything to make you more comfortable?" Vincent wasn't a tall man but he seemed to tower now as he quickly glanced at his flashy watch.

I was painfully aware of the blanket and the heat flushing my body. I sat forward, elbows on my knees.

"Not at all. I'm totally fine," I said. If I were him, I'd be worrying about a lawsuit, so I quickly added, "I feel stupid for ignoring all the clearly marked warnings."

Vincent flared his nostrils to let out a slow breath. So maybe that had been worrying him too. "We're just happy it wasn't anything more serious."

"Thanks to Ms. Kincaid," I added.

He glanced to Roxy, his features softening ever so slightly. She was too busy glaring at the floor to notice. "She keeps surprising us with her talents."

There was something I didn't like about the way he looked at her. Well, he had eyes, so I couldn't blame him. The admiration worried me a little more. Did she feel it in return? Was he the type she'd go for? Suave, rich, more self-contained. I fought to still myself but my leg jumped up and down.

Vincent frowned to Roxy. "We'll have to add this to the ever-growing list of fixes to the Lodge to avoid this ever happening again."

She nodded tightly. "Of course."

"Please let us know if you need anything," he said to me, and then to Roxy, "Roxy, can I talk to you for a minute?"

They stepped around the corner together, into a staff hallway. I pulled out my phone and pretended to work. I couldn't hear much of their conversation, but based on her rigid stance and her frequent nodding, she was mostly listening anyway. Her short answers in soft tones came across even less than his smooth baritone.

Getting hurt really had been my fault. I'd been hoping to get away with my buddy and give her space, but once again I managed to muck up a situation. It had been reckless and stupid but I didn't want Skip and Roxy to see how ashamed I felt, so I played it off like I was fine. I was so sure the universe wanted me to come down here but nothing had gone right since I showed up. I was supposed to be making things better, not worse.

I frowned at my phone screen, feeling a creeping sense of anxiety. Somewhere a person stopped vacuuming or a motor shut off because suddenly their conversation was audible.

"I had a plan," Roxy said and her drawl a little more pronounced than normal. "I didn't—"

"But had you followed my instructions as I intended them, this whole situation would have been avoided."

She said something that I couldn't quite catch.

Vincent responded, "I've been reading through your old performance reviews. Every area is strong except one. You don't accept help. If you want to be in management, you have to learn how to delegate and work with other people."

"I understand," she said.

"I hope you do, because this can't happen again."

"It won't," she said firmly.

"Roxy, I fully expect you to succeed in any position you're in, but there is an inherent trust you're missing. People will sense that. They won't want to work with us. Neither of us wants that."

"No."

"It's imperative to me that you learn how to share the reins. I can't be everywhere at once and neither can you. The Lodge is changing fast and I need you to keep up." I glanced up to see him quickly squeeze her shoulder.

Roxy shot a look my way and I buried my face back in my phone hoping she hadn't noticed me eavesdropping.

If she responded after that, I didn't hear it. I fought the urge to stand up for her honor. I wanted to go to this Vincent and tell him that she was only trying to maintain a professional relationship. That I'd been distracted and put myself at risk. Skip could have been hurt too. My actions were self-absorbed. This was my fault, not hers. She didn't deserve to be scolded for wanting to do her job well. I vowed to be better.

They exchanged a few more words before Roxy came back. I continued to play on my phone. Nothing to see here. I definitely wasn't eavesdropping.

"I know you heard that," Roxy said.

She stood in front of me with arms crossed. All the heat between us while holding hands earlier iced over in an instant.

"No, I didn't," I said.

She raised an eyebrow.

"Not all of it," I said, standing up.

She crossed her arms and chewed her lip. Anybody else might think she was scowling but my gut told me she was ashamed.

"Do you want to talk about it?" I asked.

"No," she said instantly. Then deepening her frown, she added, "I just got reamed."

"That was a reaming? He didn't even seem mad."

"I'm pretty sure that's mad for him. He's hard to read," she said without anger.

I yearned to scoop her up in my arms. To be fair, if this was Skip, I'd definitely hug him if he was upset. But I was lying to myself again trying to justify getting what I want at the cost of her. No. I was trying to be better than that.

"He told me that I need to be better at accepting help. Apparently I don't play well with others."

"Well, that's true."

Her gaze went icy.

"What?" I asked. "You did send me away the second we were supposed to work together."

"And you didn't read the signs," she snapped. Confusion at her words must have registered on my face. "For the river. You didn't read the flash flood signs," she added.

Her frustration grew as a flush spread across her neck. This wasn't what I intended. I certainly hadn't meant to offend her. I thought it was obvious that she was the independent type. I didn't know that was an insult or up for debate.

"What can I do?" I asked.

She blinked at me. After a second, she shook her head and said, "This is my fault. He told me to work with you as a team and I didn't want to."

"I was at the meeting too. I could have insisted," I said. "You don't have to bear this burden yourself. Not everything is on these shoulders." I squeezed her shoulders, actively fighting the urge to pull her

118

in. She looked at my hands before looking around the room. I dropped them back to my sides. "There are benefits to working as a team."

"It's not that. I'm happy to utilize people who bring more experience than me."

"So long as it's completely on your terms." When she didn't respond, I added, "That's what I thought."

"You have all the answers for someone who can't read," she mumbled but the side of her mouth tugged slightly.

"Har har," I said. "I'm just saying, let's be a team."

She was chewing on her lip again. How the hell was I supposed to focus when she did that? I'd tasted those lips. I knew their fullness in my mouth as I sucked on them. You don't eat filet mignon and then crave a McRib.

"I'm planning on that. I just need to—"

"Ah, ah." I held up a finger. "No 'I' in team. We work together from here out. Even now."

"Fine. Okay, yeah. You're right." She rocked her head side to side, popping her neck like she was preparing for battle and not simple team building. "Where should we start?" she asked.

"I have an idea. Are you free tomorrow?"

"I'm free after lunch," she admitted. "Why?"

"It's a surprise."

Her nostrils flared. She really was like Skip. That's exactly how he'd feel about a surprise. Luckily, I garnered trust for a living.

"None of that, hey. It'll be great." I grinned.

She made a sound like Marge Simpson when she was disappointed with Homer. She fiddled with the end of her shirt.

I said, "You don't have to do anything. Just meet me here tomorrow around one. Wear hiking clothes."

"Fine."

"You won't regret it."

"Somehow I doubt that," she said.

CHAPTER 13

SANDERS

We'd been walking for ten minutes and I could feel Roxy's anxiety ratcheting with each step. My ankle was still a little sore but it was worth it to take a hike with her.

"What sort of trust exercise involves this much walking?" she finally asked.

I held back a triumphant smile. I had bet myself that she wouldn't last fifteen minutes until the anticipation got to her. I could only imagine the scenarios going through that head of hers.

"Oh, there you go again with the smiles," she said.

"I just like to smile, smiling's my favorite," I said, echoing Will Farrell's character in the movie *Elf.*

"Yes. I noticed this about you," she said dryly.

As the path inclined, our breaths grew more labored. I didn't actually have a fully formed plan as to where we were going. I just knew we needed to get her away from the Lodge. She needed to feel safe to be herself.

"You're not a big smiler, I noticed."

"Does it matter?" she asked sharply.

"Nope," I said truthfully. Her face appealed to me no matter what expression it held. Like a piece of fine art I could never hope to interpret, it only grew more fascinating to study.

"Is the exercise me trusting that you aren't a serial killer, luring me out to the middle of nowhere to kill me?"

"Ah, no. I could have killed you loads of times by now. I don't need to get sweaty to do that." I grinned at her.

She rolled her eyes. "I feel much better. Thank you."

We reached an outcropping of heavy granite slabs jutting out over the valley of lush green trees.

"Here we are," I said.

"How did you know about this place?"

"I didn't."

"This is not encouraging," she said.

"Roxy, Roxxo, just tru—"

"Trust you. Yes, I get it. Let's just do this. I have to prepare for a graduation party this weekend," she said, fussing with her fringe when the wind blew it around.

"At the Lodge?" I asked. "Do Americans have to make such a big deal about everything?"

"How else will everyone know we're the best?" She bit back a smile. "It's a well-paying customer. Their little princess only graduates high school once. It's a huge party. Like a hundred people. With a DJ. It's a whole thing."

My eyebrows shot up. That was the first time I heard her ever say anything like that. Like Vincent wasn't standing there watching her.

Instantly she frowned. "I shouldn't have said that. That was … unprofessional. I'm happy to give them an experience she will never forget."

I dropped my backpack and pulled out a bottle of water and handed it to her. Without the protection of the canopy, it was a lot warmer. At least there was no worry about rain. I checked.

"You don't have to do that," I said. "I know clients can be a huge pain in the ass. So did you have a big old graduation party too?"

"Not exactly. I didn't technically go to graduation."

"Prom?" I asked.

She raised her eyebrows at me. "Do I seem like the type to go to prom?"

I shrugged. "Yeah?"

She shook her head. "No. I didn't go to prom. There was a whole thing with Gretchen." She frowned at the mention of her friend. "It doesn't matter. Let's just get going with all this."

"That's not a very healthy attitude," I said.

"What do you mean?" she asked.

"The rushing to get back to work. Always waiting to be done and on to the next thing. There is only the journey."

She took a drink of water and handed it back to me. "How very zen of you."

I shrugged. "I've just thought about it a lot. There is no final point that I can reach and think 'ah, now I can be happy.' Life is just a series of ups and downs. Best to be in the moment instead of worrying about things that have already happened or, worse, haven't even happened yet. What an exhaustive waste of energy."

She sighed but grabbed the other end of the blanket I'd pulled out and helped me lay it flat. "Some people just aren't wired that way."

"Sure. If that's the story they tell themselves."

"It's that easy?" she asked. "Just stop worrying. Oh, okay. Thanks, I don't know why I haven't tried that."

"The sarcasm is strong with this one," I said trying to crack her prickly facade. "I'm not trying to preach. But yeah, it's that easy and it's the hardest mental exercising that you can do."

She gave me a doubtful look.

"I know. Skippo gives me the same face when I say that. We're hard-wired to want to suffer. We want to reaffirm all the negative thoughts we have, so when something bad happens, we can say 'see, I was right, everything is awful, this is why it's best not to try.' We have this idea that pain is a badge earned in adulthood. Americans especially, I've noticed. The long-suffering intellectual."

Roxy skidded on some stones as she bent to fix the blanket. I was around and helping her before I realized. I helped her slowly stand up. She smiled at me before fixing her fringe. "Thanks," she said. "You've thought about this a lot." Her tone softened in a way that felt encouraging.

"Yeah, I have." I dropped my hands back to my sides and walked to the other side of the blanket. I had read a lot about these things when Dad started to get sick. It felt too soon to talk about that. When I glanced up at her, she watched me carefully and I worried I'd thought about Dad out loud.

I cleared my throat and went on, "Maybe some think I'm just not smart enough to know how dark and horrible the world is? I'm perfectly aware. Maybe I'm naive? Also, no. I've just decided to try and live in the moment as much as possible. I can walk this earth with the weight of the past on my shoulders, or I can drop the load and walk easier. It doesn't mean the wounds aren't there. It doesn't mean I don't feel things. It just means I acknowledge them and move on. But it takes work. It takes constantly telling your mind not to go there. Move on. Let it go. Not now, dark thoughts."

We sat cross-legged on the blanket across from each other.

She picked up a few small rocks and rolled them around in her hands. "Aren't you just avoiding things? Pushing them off until one day they'll all come crashing on you? Not thinking about how your choices in the moment impact your future? Or those around you?"

As soon as she said the words, it was obvious she regretted them. I thought I'd been clear in the message I was conveying but it wasn't coming across how I meant. Did she think I was selfish? Was I selfish? My words had hit too deep. This was not the foot I wanted to start on. I wasn't avoiding things.

A dark cloud moved over my thoughts. The storm that was always right behind me.

I gently scooted the pebbles from her hands into mine and tossed them to the side. "Just be here now with me. That's all I'm saying."

Her swallow was audible. "Okay," she whispered. Her eyes shifted to the horizon and she seemed lost in thought.

"Phew," I said blowing out a long breath. "Didn't mean to get so heavy. Let's get started and save the new-age babble for later."

"Yes." She rolled her shoulders and rocked her head side to side.

"Are you about to start stretching?" I asked with a cocked eyebrow.

"Do I need to?" She had one arm stretched across her chest.

The image of her doing downward dog floated into my mind. Me pulling her hips back to deepen the stretch.

I cleared my throat. "No," I said but it came out as a squeak.

"I thought maybe we were going to do trust falls or something."

"That's a great exercise but not for two people. This is simpler. All we have to do is sit across from each other and make eye contact."

"What? That's it?" she asked.

"That's all we have to do. Sit still and hold each other's focus. At least thirty seconds, but a few minutes would be best. Time to sink into the connection."

"We can't blink or something?"

I threw my head back and laughed. "No, we definitely can blink. We just can't look away."

"Don't laugh at me," she said with a scowl.

"I'm not!" I sobered immediately. "You're just cute is all."

She tucked her hair back. "You can't say that sort of thing."

"I tell Skip he's cute all the time," I defended without thinking.

"I don't get it." She pulled the sleeves of her shirt over her fingers, hiding her hands in them.

"It's surprisingly difficult to do," I said seriously.

"Not surprising at all," she said. "Eye contact for that long is usually limited to babies and sociopaths."

Seriously, adorable.

"Stop laughing at me," she said.

I tried for serious. She frowned deeper. If smiling was my natural state, then frowning was hers. It was so damn sexy. That pout brought more focus to her already distracting mouth.

"Well, I'd say that's generalizing. But yes, to your point, that's why it makes it a good exercise. You're trusting me to see you uninterrupted. And I'm trusting you to do the same."

She put a hand to her chest. "Why is my heart racing? I almost wish we were doing trust falls," she admitted.

My heart was pounding too. In fact, I was beginning to regret this plan. Eye contact was a trust builder for sure. But it was also terribly intimate.

"It's just me," I said. "If you start to feel uncomfortable, remember when I biffed it and you had to save me."

"I don't like to think about that." Her brows knitted. "Let's just get started." I started to speak and she cut me off. "Calm down, calm down. I'm not rushing the moment. I just want to see if I can do it."

"Okay, good." I set the timer on my watch.

"Oh wow, you're really timing it."

"I don't mess around."

She took a deep inhale of breath and let it out slowly. "I suddenly can't remember what to do with my arms." She flopped them out.

"Ready?" I asked.

Turns out that when Roxy was uncomfortable, she was even more charming. This was a version of Roxy I doubted many people got to see. In that way it already felt like we were making progress. And damn if it didn't make me feel special.

She shook her hair back off her face. "Ready."

"Three …"

She looked up to the sky.

"Two …"

And then down to the rocks beneath us.

"One," I whispered.

Her gaze locked on to mine. It was as though the breath was sucked out of my chest. A physical reaction to her undivided attention punched me harder in the solar plexus than I thought possible. But I was the professional in this situation, so I had to make it look easy.

It couldn't have been three seconds and already the twitching began. Her fingers tapped on her knees. She breathed in and out. This was killing her.

"I keep feeling like I can't blink," she tried to joke.

"No talking," I whispered.

Interestingly, the more she fidgeted, the easier it was for me to pull strength and pretend that sustained eye contact wasn't almost as arousing as our handholding.

A few seconds later, she noticed how well I was doing and her competitive side kicked in. With her gaze still locked on mine, she blew her fringe off her face dramatically. She raised one eyebrow. She lowered it. Then she lifted the other.

I remained stoic.

Her gaze narrowed. She began to undulate her eyebrows. Lifting and dropping one eyebrow and then the other, like fans joining the wave at a football match.

I had been doing so well until she raised her lip in a curl that Elvis would've been proud of.

"You know, a lot of people use humor as a defense mechanism when they feel uncomfortable," I said coolly.

Her face leveled instantly.

I pushed, "If you can't do this, we can try something else …"

Her features sharpened. "No talking."

I should have challenged her from the get-go. If ever I needed Skip to do something, I simply appealed to his ego. Classic.

The air changed then. Her focus narrowed and her body stopped moving. We were having an entire conversation through our eye contact.

I told you, I could do this, she seemed to say.

I never doubted you for a second, I replied in my head. *I think you're wonderful.*

You shouldn't say that sort of thing.

There's nothing you can do about what I think.

Then the imagined conversation stopped and we simply existed in this moment. Her eyes had much more depth in this full light. Her pupils were so small that her full iris was visible. The darker brown was ringed with a lighter brown. The varying shades were textured like the glass marbles I played with as a kid.

A gentle breeze moved her hair. It carried the scent of pine and her to me. It was such a peaceful sense. This was two people seeing each other without masks or filters. This was pure. This was what screens, filters, and social media took away. This was human connection at a base level. I'd never done this with anybody before. I had made other people do it, of course, and saw its success, but living it with Roxy was like nothing I'd ever felt.

The stillness left no room to hide. I couldn't run or escape. Intrusive thoughts came poking at the edges of my mind. I tried to remain focused on Roxy, let her keep me from succumbing to them, but all of my feelings were on the brink of overflowing. The storm clouds of my mind blocked the sun and a chill ran over me. And for once I didn't feel happy at all. I felt a deep sadness overtake me. Any minute the clouds would break open and drown me. It would pull me under so fast there would be no hope of catching my breath. This was exactly why I always kept moving. The second I stopped …

"Sanders," Roxy said.

I blinked into the present. Brought my mind to the here and now. Roxy saved me a moment before it would have been too late.

"I think it's been thirty seconds," she said.

I glanced down at my watch. Three minutes had passed. "I forgot to set the alarm." My voice came out hoarse.

"Did I make it?" she asked hopefully.

"Of course." I forced a smile on my face.

"I knew I could do it," she said.

"I never doubted you for a second," I whispered.

CHAPTER 14

ROXY

*T*here were few things I loved more than blowing expectations out of the water. So when Sanders didn't think I could play his little staring game, I was set to prove him wrong. Of course, it was real weird at first. I'd been so worried that he'd be able to see the truth of me: my dark past and my growing feelings for him. I couldn't look directly at him at the best of times because I couldn't do it in glimpses. When I looked at him, I wanted to do it for hours.

At first, I couldn't sit still. I felt like I might crawl out of my skin. It made no sense. It was just eye contact and yet it felt like I was being forced to tell him my darkest secrets. But once I decided to just do it, I let go of the internal monologue. I simply focused on the way the cold stone felt damp through my hiking pants—incidentally, way more comfortable than my suit pants. The wind tickling my bangs across my forehead. My breath, moving in and out of my body in sync with my heartbeat.

I focused on Sanders. The bright, unclouded sky should blush in shame compared to the blue of his eyes. His face and mouth were relaxed so just the corner of one front tooth was visible. It was hard not to imagine leaning forward to close the distance between us and pressing a soft kiss on those lips. I couldn't forget the taste of him and I thought for sure all those thoughts were playing like a movie in my eyes. But then, something about seeing him so serious in the task pushed me to take it seriously.

Time stretched and I forgot all about being self-conscious. I wasn't sure what it proved but it definitely meant something.

I stood up and stretched, feeling more than a little pleased with myself. "What's next? Since I obviously nailed that."

He was slower to stand up. "You did great, Roxxo." His smile was in place but it seemed sad almost, which was an emotion foreign on his face.

My arms dropped. He looked anywhere but at me.

"Maybe we should head back? That was a lot for one day," he said. His voice was so casual. He would have fooled anyone else but I knew something was wrong.

"No." I crossed my arms.

"No?"

"You dragged me all the way out here. Forced me to look at your stupid pretty face. I'm not going back yet."

"Wait, wait." He shook his head. "Stupid pretty? Or stupid and pretty?"

"Sanders." I glared at him.

"I just don't have anything else planned." He scratched at the back of his head and looked at the trail leading back into the trees.

"You didn't even have this planned," I said.

"Fine. We can stay and try something else. But only because you're stupid pretty too."

"You can't say stuff like that." But there was no heat in my words. I was getting used to his bold flirting. He was like being around a plate of cookies when starving. How was I supposed to not sneak a little sugar where I could get it?

Sanders pulled out a battle-weary Nalgene water bottle covered in stickers from places like the Grand Teton National Park and the Great Wall of China. He took his time unscrewing the cap. After a few deep drinks, he smacked his lips with an "ah, better," then carefully spun the cap back on. Everything took an eternity.

"Are you stalling?" I asked.

"Not at all," he said giving me a look like I was crazy. Then he pulled out an apple and started polishing it on his pants. "Hungry?"

I blinked at him. "Nope."

He took a huge bite and chewed thoughtfully.

"Sanders." I shifted from foot to foot. "You *are* stalling."

"Not at all." He took another huge bite. The apple was already mostly gone.

"We've been gone a half hour." I glared.

"Can never be too careful. Low blood sugar is dangerous," he said through a cheekful of food.

Watching him eat was hypnotic. His jaw worked like a sleek machine. Like everything he did, his movements were so relaxed yet purposeful. His throat moved as he swallowed and it was impossible to not fantasize about biting him there and then, soothing it with a soft kiss.

I moved away and circled the small overlook. *That was weird. Don't be weird, Roxy.*

The apple core went whizzing through the air and into the valley below us.

"Okay," he said, wiping his hands on his pants. "This one is called, two truths and a lie."

I shot him a look. "I'm familiar."

"No holding back. Honesty."

In Denver we hadn't had a chance to really explore each other because we kept the details out. So what would happen this time if we pushed each other too far?

"You're going down, Colonel," I said.

He squinted at me.

"Colonel Sanders?" I clarified.

When my joke hit, he laughed. "It's not a competition," he said.

"Totally," I said instantly. "But if it were, I'd definitely wipe the floor with you."

"Adorable," he muttered. "Okay, you can go first. Sit down. Your pacing is making me twitchy."

"I'm making you twitchy?" I asked. "That's rich."

"Sit," he commanded.

With anybody else, being told to do something typically made me long to do the exact opposite. But when he told me what to do, a tiny shiver ran down my spine.

"Yes, sir," I said in a husky voice.

His pupils darkened and his nostrils flared. Those light blue eyes transformed into something more intense and I knew in that moment exactly what his eyes would look like when they looked up at me from between my thighs.

We sat back down in the same positions as a few minutes ago.

With no warning, I brought my hands up to cover the upper half of my face. I said, "I'm afraid to fly. My eyes are brown—"

"I'm going to stop you right there," he said.

"Cheater." I dropped my hand to point at him.

"You're the one who's cheating," he said. "It's two truths and a lie. And no covering your face, come on."

"You didn't let me finish."

"But you've already lied twice. You weren't worried at all about flying that night in Denver and your eyes are not brown," he said.

"Are you kidding me? You just stared into them." I threw out my arms. So much for him paying attention.

"Exactly. So I'm an expert. They aren't brown. Maybe in a poorly lit room a buffoon would classify them simply as brown. But in this light, they're a rich mahogany. Like a really expensive acoustic guitar that's been buffed to gleam. There's depth and texture. The edges have lighter flecks, more like an oak. But brown is weak. Brown is saying that the *Mona Lisa* is just a painting." He shook his head like he was disappointed in me.

"Oh," I said.

My eyes blinked rapidly, not sure where to look. I'd never been so aware of them. Was that true? Was it possible that he found that much depth there? My mouth closed when I realized it'd been hanging open. I swallowed, feeling completely flustered. How was I ever supposed to stay on track when he said things like that? He was so open and earnest. I told myself to clamp down the rush of adrenaline those words caused in me. Sanders talked like this to everyone. I was nothing special.

Eventually, I cleared my throat and said, "Stop trying to sidetrack me. You go, then."

With no preamble, he said, "I have two younger brothers. I'm lactose intolerant. Carrots give me the hiccups."

"You don't have any siblings," I said instantly. I wasn't sure how I knew, but I just knew. Maybe because he had only-child swagger.

"Dang. Yep." He frowned. Well, frowned for him, which meant he was still smiling but his eyebrows sort of turned down at the sides. It was confusing but made sense to me. "Your turn," he said.

"I can wiggle my left ear. I can also roll my tongue. My brother is three years younger." My face was completely blank. I'm sure I was the text-book example of RBF.

"Your brother is older," he said instantly.

I gaped at him. "Shit."

"Tried to throw me off, did you? Let me see your tongue roll."

I glared at him but then showed that not only could I roll my tongue, I could also sort of fold it in half and pinch it.

"Hot," he said.

I laughed. "You can't say that." I tossed a pebble at him. "Your turn. We're tied."

"Not a comp—"

"Yeah, yeah. Let's go." I rubbed my hands together.

He took a breath. "You're sick. I'm never playing Monopoly with you and Skip. It would destroy us."

"Stalling."

"I've only moved twice. I've broken three bones. I have a butterfly tattoo."

"No broken bones," I said.

This time his mouth dropped open. "How?" he asked seriously.

I threw my head back and laughed. "Oh my God. You have to show me that tattoo."

"What!" He stood up. "No way. There's no way you could have known about that."

"Show me this tattoo," I said threateningly.

I had no idea how I knew. Just like I had no idea how he knew so much about me. But I had to see that damn tattoo.

"No." He crossed his arms looking genuinely upset that he lost that round. I had spotted the hidden ace up his sleeve.

"Show. Me." I glared my most threateningly.

He reeled back with a grimace. "I'm going to regret this." He turned to put his back to me and started to unbutton his pants.

"No." I covered my mouth unable to contain my giddy excitement.

He lowered his pants just enough to show a tiny black tattoo at the base of his spine.

"It's a butterfly." I couldn't stop the laughter. I couldn't care less that I sounded like a crazed hyena. "You have a tramp stamp!" I had tears falling from my eyes I was laughing so hard.

He turned back to me and buttoned his pants. "I'll have you know that this was done by one of the best artists in Denver. This beaut set me back a few hundo."

In his defense, from what I was able to see, it was a beautiful tattoo. Black in a contemporary style with fine line work and clearly handled by a talented artist. I wanted more time to look at it but I couldn't exactly ask him to let me stare at his ass.

Or could I? No, be a professional.

"How? Why? I must know everything." I sat up and wiped the residual tears from my eyes.

"No," he said haughtily. "You haven't earned that story yet. Let's move on."

"Better than an ex's name, I guess," I said sobering.

"I would never do that. Everybody knows it's bad luck. Plus, I've never loved anybody near enough for that sort of commitment."

"Dark," I said. I wanted to ask more but wasn't about to delve into my past in exchange. Had that been a little skull hidden in the pattern of the wings?

"Your turn, Roxxo," he said, interrupting my thoughts. "That's it. No more Mr. Nice Guy. I'm out for blood now."

"I thought it wasn't a competition," I said. He growled and I chewed on my lip to think. "I was proposed to by the guy who married Sienna Diaz. My parents forgot me so many times after school the bus route added a special stop just for me. I had two dogs growing up, Rex One and Rex Two."

This time his answer wasn't immediate but his eyes wrinkled a bit at the side. Suddenly, I feared I gave too much away. I fussed with some gravel at my feet as he sat back down in front of me.

"No dogs?"

"No dogs." I shrugged. "Always wanted one though." He looked like he was about to ask another question, so I quickly added, "I'm still winning."

"Chris Hemsworth and I were born on the same day. I've never seen *Star Wars*. I'm an orphan."

"*Star Wars*," I said somberly.

"I may have a tramp stamp but I'm still a man."

I smiled softly at him. "I'm sorry about your parents."

He went very still. "Mom died when I was ten."

My heart absolutely ached for him. "I'm sorry."

"Thank you," he said and slid a smile in place. Always with the smile.

"Did your dad raise you?"

"Yeah. Dad's American from Colorado. After she died, he brought me back here to be closer to his family. Also, I think, to get away from all the memories."

I nodded. "I can understand that. Your dad?"

A shadow moved over his face. "Early-onset Alzheimer's."

"Was that hard? He must have been young, if you're only thirty-four," I asked. Suddenly I was desperate to understand more. I guess I'd assumed someone so happy must have lived a charmed life.

He scratched at his chin where there was a hint of a dark blond five-o'clock shadow. "So you were paying attention. Chris and I were twins separated at birth. I don't have any proof outside my stellar good looks."

"You certainly don't lack for confidence," I muttered.

He was avoiding the subject. I may have RBF but he hid with smiles and silly charm.

"Ah, don't make that face," he said. "I'm fine. I promise. I shouldn't have mentioned it. It's a downer."

"You don't have to …" I said but I wasn't sure how to finish. But really what I was thinking was that it was fucking tragic. I was about to ask if he was really okay but he stood again and brushed his pants off.

"Actually, we should probably head back," he said.

"Okay." This time I didn't argue. I felt … drained. And sad. I wanted to be alone too.

We packed up in silence but it didn't take long. I wished there was more to pack. I was ready to be alone but I also wanted him to talk more. It wasn't just his alluring accent either. This was a side of Sanders I hadn't seen and it intrigued me.

"Sienna Diaz, huh?" he said a few minutes later.

I rolled my eyes. "Yeah. It's a long story."

He nodded when I shut that line down. I was so not ready to talk about Jethro Winston.

"Why did your parents forget to pick you up?" he asked.

I froze. I had thought we'd skated past that accidental overshare.

"Geez, asking all the easy ones. They're just a little flighty," I quickly added. "Ya know what's weird?"

He held my focus for a beat before sighing. "What?"

"I've never lost that game before. I mean I still didn't *lose*. But I've never been so close," I said as we began to walk back.

"It is really weird." He studied the ground carefully as he stepped. More carefully than the trail required. "I've been playing this game with people for years and never seen this sort of success rate. I thought I had perfected lying."

"Not to sound like a psycho …" I said.

"Hmm," he said. His gaze was distant.

"I always win this game. No matter how many shots of tequila I drank, I always won against any Wraith."

"Wraith?"

"The Iron Wraiths. Just a club I used to hang around."

"What kind of club? Like that one with Gretchen? The book club."

"No. Not like that." I doubted most of the Wraiths could even read. "They're bad news. I don't think about them anymore."

"Okay," Sanders said casually. "If you ever want to talk about it …"

"And if you ever want to talk about your past," I snapped back.

I wasn't being fair but I wasn't about to pour my heart out because we played one game. Life wasn't that simple. People certainly weren't. We may be able to read each other easily—unnervingly so—but it didn't mean anything.

This closeness bridged felt like too much, too soon. But I'd felt like that since our first night together. A bird squawked loudly in the tree above us.

I backed up. "I better get to work."

He blinked a couple times and said, "Yeah, me too."

"In the morning, let's meet to discuss the plan," I said. "For MooreTek."

He smiled genuinely. "That'd be great."

Sanders and I might have a connection I couldn't quite explain, but he was leaving soon and I needed to focus on work. We could play nice together, but it wasn't any more than that. It couldn't be any more than that.

CHAPTER 15

SANDERS

*S*kip once told me about this thing called cry porn. It was when people purposely watched those videos of deaf babies hearing for the first time, or neglected dogs being rescued back to health. He said sometimes he watched them when the sadness got too close to the surface and he just needed to crack it open and let out some of his gooey softness.

I never understood that. Leaning fully into the pain of life. Better to keep moving, never settling. Let me be the river that washed around the boulder never moving it. I went on adventures, bungee jumped, skydived. Anything that spiked my adrenaline, reminding me I was alive. That's what I needed.

I needed to get away but I was already away in a new town. The intense session with Roxy inexplicably caused acid in my throat, sending me straight back to my room to pop more antacids. I was reaching for my phone when the air-conditioning unit clicked on in the room. Something about the Freon smell and the heavy hum of the unit in the tiny room sent my mind back in time to a month ago. Not even a month.

My dad, fifty pounds too light, sat in the stiff-backed chair at the care home. His pale flesh, papery and bruised. His eyes saw nothing at all. He wasn't speaking then. I couldn't stand looking at him like that. I physically couldn't stomach it. Sometimes he'd laugh. It was best when he laughed because then I thought at least wherever he was, he wasn't suffering.

I gasped for air as the acid churned in my gut.

"Shit," I said and ran to the bathroom.

I retched up the nuts and fruit I'd eaten that day. Guilt swirled with helpless anger. Roxy was still front and center in my thoughts which then only made me feel guiltier and angrier about everything back home. I needed to get it together. I couldn't let it own me. Hadn't I just said that to Roxy? Don't let things weigh you down, leave all the heavy shit behind. Just as I was rinsing out my mouth, there was a knock at my door.

"Sanders?" Skip's voice asked through the door.

I sniffed, rubbed at my eyes, and opened the door. "Skippo, what's up, mate?"

"Are you okay?" He looked behind me and I wondered if he'd heard all that.

"All good, yeah. Come on in. What's up?"

"Just wanted to see if you wanted to grab some dinner." His eyes shot to the roll of Tums on my bedside table. "Are you sick?"

I had to shut this down before concerned Skip took charge, so I quickly changed the subject. "I showed Roxy my tattoo today."

"Showed her?" He shook his head. "Actually, I don't want to know." Skip scratched at his beard. It was getting down right shaggy if you asked me. He liked it that way. He liked to push people away with his scary mountain-man look. Another thing he and Roxy had in common: trying to scare people off.

He moved to sit down on the edge of my bed. I hovered in the corner. He was winding up for a Skip lecture but I couldn't take it right now. I gnawed on the dry cuticle of my thumb and my leg jumped, shaking the floor.

Skip held my gaze before looking out the window for a minute. He surprised me when he finally spoke. "Remember that time your dad took us camping and we got lost?"

I hadn't fooled him. Somehow he always knew exactly where my head was at. Another thing he shared with Roxy. I laughed with effort. "Oh hell. That trip was brutal."

"How old were we, thirteen? Fourteen?"

"I can't remember but we definitely became men that trip," I said.

He chuckled softly. "Remember when I hit my head and he acted like it was totally normal?"

"The blood was everywhere." I shook my head. "I'd never seen anything like it. It was like a scary movie."

"He said, 'Ah, you're fine. Head wounds bleed.' But then I ended up needing six staples." His hand reached for the back of his head where his mangy hair covered a three-inch scar.

"And you turned out just fine," I said.

"Your dad saved my life," Skip said quietly, not quite meeting my gaze.

"Okay, now who's dramatic? You would have been—"

"I mean before that. Your dad took me in. He fed me and raised me as his own. He saved me. I have no idea where I'd be if not for him."

My Adam's apple sat so high in my throat I had trouble swallowing. "Yeah," I said.

"He was the greatest man I ever knew."

I nodded.

He went on, "But it's okay to not be okay yet—"

"I know, mate. Thanks." I held up my hand. If he even said another word, I wouldn't be able to hold it together. The last thing I ever wanted to do was break down in front of Skip. He'd known a real shit life and he never burdened others with it. He was a fucking hero. I wasn't about to make him feel worse.

He couldn't understand how angry I was and how that anger made me feel like the most selfish bastard on the planet. How the regret of how I handled those last months burned through my body all the time. Sometimes the overwhelming magnitude of it all hit me. I couldn't fathom how I was supposed to handle it. What was I even doing here? It was bad enough that I was away from home and the business. It was bad enough that I was hurting a decent person like Roxy. And I had dragged Skip into all this. I needed to focus on the business. That was why I was here. Forget everything else I felt. None of that mattered. The business mattered.

Skip asked, "Today went well? With Roxy?"

I was grateful for the subject change. "Yeah." I wanted to tell him about the staring and the sharing, but I knew it wouldn't come across like I meant. "We're meeting tomorrow to go over plans for MooreTek. I think she's finally keen to work with me."

"Good. Glad to hear it. And you're good too? Working with her?"

"Oh yeah. All that other stuff is behind me. We're just business associates."

He held my gaze a second too long and I didn't think he was buying it at all. "Want me to take over? Need to head back?"

My heart skipped. My palms instantly started to sweat. I should tell him yes. I should let him take over and so I could go home to take care of the shit I messed up. Wrap up Dad's estate and move on from Green

Valley and Roxy Kincaid. Skip was more than capable of conducting our business here.

"Thanks for the offer, mate," I said. "But I'm really just starting to make progress with her. I think it might be a dick move professionally if I pass her off now, you know?"

"I know the team would like to hear from you. They're really understanding of what happened. But you should maybe explain what happened at the conference. They'd understand."

This was as close to scolding me as Skip would get. I could see he was as uncomfortable with it as I was. He wouldn't quite hold my gaze as he rubbed his beard.

"I'll talk to them. As soon as I get back. I just don't want to return until I have awesome news. If I can do great with this client, I'm hoping the Lodge will want to do an exclusivity contract with us for all their corporate groups. Or any groups really. We could do wedding parties. Girls' trips. Those are big too. Communication and vulnerability are good for everyone."

He looked me dead in the eyes. "I agree."

I shot to the mini fridge and searched it. There was nothing inside except a couple bottles of five-dollar water but I couldn't look at him just then.

I heard him let out a long sigh. "Okay. As soon as you wrap up this thing with MooreTek, you'll head back? Right?"

He asked me directly. I couldn't put it off any longer. That was over a week away. By then I'd have good news. I'd have figured things out. I spun back around with an easy smile. "Sure. Yeah, of course, Skippo. That's perfect."

He nodded but I could tell there was something he wasn't saying. "And you're sure you're okay?"

"I'm fine. Just a little tired."

He stood up. "Okay. I'll let you get some rest."

"How was your day?" I asked, finally remembering not to be such a self-centered twat.

"Good actually. I met with Clifford Rutledge. He said you talked," Skip said.

"Oh Ford, yeah, he's a great bloke." I was happy to hear this. I really did want to get enmeshed in the local community and his Ford's Fosters seemed like a great program.

"He wants to do a camping trip with his students," Skip explained. "Wants to hire us to help."

"Excellent."

"I think so too," Skip said.

He headed for the door. "We'll talk more tomorrow. Just be careful with Roxy."

"Trust me. I won't do anything unprofessional. We're just friends."

"I trust you. But sometimes being just friends is easier said than done," he said and left the room. I frowned at the door and realized I wasn't the only one keeping things from my best friend.

CHAPTER 16

SANDERS

*A*fter a good night's sleep, I felt slightly better but not back to my normal self. When I passed my reflection in the hall mirror, I was frowning. As I waited for the elevator, I practiced my smiling in the reflection of the closed door. It fell off almost immediately. It didn't normally require so much energy.

I needed to rally before I saw Roxy. I had over a week to figure out how to get Outside the Box rocking again. I wanted to let things happen with Roxy at her own pace. Or not at all. Either way it would be fine. Okay, that was bullshit, but she didn't need to know.

Roxy and I met early in the morning in an empty office that had obviously turned into an overflow construction work space. Next to the small desk was a circular saw covered in a sheet of plastic and some stacks of two-by-fours. Boxes were stacked in the corner. We were forced to sit, knees almost touching, on the only free side of the desk.

"Nice place," I said gesturing to the ladder and paint buckets in the opposite corner.

"Yeah, the construction is a little bit of an eyesore." She took a sip of coffee.

She was back to her most buttoned-up self and my already shit mood darkened. As much as I wanted to be patient, it was always two steps forward, three steps back with her. This dance was much less fun than what we did in Denver.

"But if everything goes to plan, this will be my office one day," she said flicking a glance to me to gauge my reaction.

"And that's what you want? To be the events coordinator here?"

She sat ramrod straight and tugged the hem of her skirt down and crossed her legs. She didn't even look comfortable. Could that really be what she wanted?

Her brows knit. "Yeah, of course. I've been working my way up the ladder for years," she said.

I don't know why this bothered me. I didn't have any right to have an opinion on her goals but imagining her in this office all day and night, scrunched behind the desk of this windowless box ... She was like a beautiful wildflower trying to pass as a dull house plant.

"It just doesn't seem to fit your personality. The suits and the office and the bougie corporate title."

Her eyes widened and her nostrils flared. She frowned fiddling with her fringe, making it perfect. "Right. I could never be so corporate."

I frowned. "That's not what I mean. I just ..." I scrubbed a hand through my hair. What was my deal? I was being a bastard and taking it out on her. This wasn't fair. "I'm sorry. You could absolutely run this hotel if you wanted."

"I wouldn't want to run the Lodge. I just want ..."

"What?" I asked nudging her foot with mine.

"Stability. The assurance that if I do my job well, I will never have to worry about going back." She shook her head. "I just need to prove I'm worth the chance they took on me."

I looked closely at her. She was fighting hard not to fidget, her thumb-nail piercing into the paper coffee cup in her hand. I wanted to dig more, I wanted to understand what she was so afraid of.

I settled on, "You're brilliant. You could never disappoint people." I believed the words but they still came out flat.

"Thanks," she said but wouldn't lift her gaze.

There was an awkward silence. I needed to get my shit together but I was cranky and stubborn.

She cleared her throat. "I brought doughnuts. From Daisy's Nut House. You'll never have anything better," she said.

"We have doughnuts in Denver. Crazy. I know."

"Lord, you *are* a salty bastard this morning." She covered her mouth as soon as she said it. "Sorry. That was not professional—"

It was like all at once my tension melted away. I loved when she just said what she thought without filtering it. It was like the first night we met. God, all the times I wished to go back to that first night. The more time I spent with professional Roxy, the further I felt from her.

I nudged her again, and her smile grew. "I am a cranky shit today." I pushed her chair until she looked at me. "I'm sorry. Give me some coffee?" I pointed to the cup she'd brought me with my best puppy dog eyes.

She handed it to me, her lips trying to hide her smile as she rolled her eyes at me. "And one of these." She slid a chocolate masterpiece over on a napkin. "You're wrong, by the way. You've never had a doughnut like this. Just try a bite."

I was tempted to force her to feed it to me, but quickly shut that down. I definitely would not ask Skip to do that. I took a bite and moaned. Three bites later it was gone.

"Fuck me, that was good." I licked the remaining frosting from my fingers.

When I glanced back to her, she looked away, her cheeks blushing. Maybe because she seemed to work extra hard to get me to come out of my cranky shell or maybe because watching her blush was the sexiest thing I'd ever seen, it wasn't long before I was back to my normal cherry spirits.

"I do love hole foods," I said.

She blinked at me and I pointed to the center of the doughnut. *"Hole* foods, get it."

She rolled her eyes but laughed. "See, these are magic."

"I think it's the company," I said.

"You shouldn't say stuff like that." But this time when she said it there was no fight to her words.

I shrugged. If that's what it took to get a smile. I would break all the rules.

We spent the rest of the morning working through the itinerary for MooreTek. The team-building activities Outside the Box specialized in fit easily into what she had already arranged. Seeing her so focused and in her element of control shouldn't add fuel to my inappropriate-thoughts fire, but since I'm a selfish bastard, I might as well own it.

As the minutes passed, she slipped out of her heels and tucked her feet under her. The black pantyhose became sheer when she folded her legs, and her skirt rode up. I loved the glimpse of thigh her new position afforded me. Soon after, she shrugged out of her blazer. When she took out her hair to redo the twisty thing, I almost lost my mind.

Unaware of the direction my thoughts had taken, she fluffed her hair, the sweet scent of her shampoo wafting over me. "Yeah, that's a great idea. You could take them to do the rope thing, and then that night I'll coordinate a special dinner."

I only half listened as she spoke. Her arms lifted above her head as she expertly re-twisted her hair, recreating her earlier updo.

"Good, hey?" I said.

How did she learn to do that? How could she make it look so perfect without a mirror? With arms lifted, her shirt rose and a glimpse of a tattoo revealed itself on her waist. I swallowed and wished my gaze alone could move her shirt aside.

"Sanders?" she said my name like this wasn't the first time she'd tried to get me to answer. "Yo, Colonel!" She shoved my chair with her pantyhose foot.

"Yup?"

"Are you listening?"

"Of course," I said, forcing my focus back to her face. Roxy glared at me adorably.

"It has to be next week or nothing. This is a big deal."

"Okay." I smiled at her.

She sat back in the conference chair and stretched her arms over her head. "Don't you want to write anything down? We made a lot of plans."

"Roxy. Trust me. Remember?"

She sighed. Her thumbnail picked at the grain of the conference table.

"Vincent emailed me." She kept her features straight but she messed with her fringe. "He said MooreTek's CEO is bringing her think-tank. They're counting on us to inspire some brilliant breakthrough."

"Eesh. No pressure."

"This is what I'm saying. I trust you, Sanders. But I really want to make sure you understand how huge this is for the Lodge."

People sometimes underestimated me because of my easygoing personality. I was used to that. I repeated back the itinerary of the next week hour by hour. Her eyebrows inched up as I spoke, and by the time I was done, she was almost smiling.

"I'll also write it down, if that would make you feel better," I added softly. "I'm taking this as serious as you, okay?"

She let out a breath that puffed out her lips. "Okay," she said.

"Don't worry, Roxxo. I know you may not buy into all this new-age stuff, but I've worked with some of the biggest companies in the country. There's truly something to be said for learning to pull back your mask and show some vulnerability with your work mates. I've seen billionaires in tears who come up with their most innovative ideas from that rawness. I wouldn't be here if I didn't really believe in it."

"I trust you," she said.

We held each other's gaze and I could almost feel her opening up to me. Like a tight new bud of spring just barely starting to bloom. I would be gentle and patient. I would not crush her. I could be the sunshine that coaxes her to reveal herself.

Around noon my stomach growled loudly enough for her to hear.

I put a hand on my middle. "Shush, you."

She looked up from her notebook. "I think we're good for the day. Why don't you go get lunch. I just have a few more notes to take."

I stood and stretched, arms high until my back popped. When I looked back at her, she was chewing on her lip and looking at the little bit of skin revealed. She looked away, quickly pretending to take a note on a yellow-lined notebook. I took a steadying breath and straightened my shirt.

"Good idea. Need anything?" I asked.

She stayed focused on her paper, chewing the end of her pen. Did she understand that everything she did was so sexy? From this angle her cleavage was fully on display. A little flick of color flashed beneath her bra strap, stretching almost to her collarbone. What I wouldn't give to discover where that tattoo went. I needed hours to explore.

I must have gone noticeably still and quiet because she looked up. She pulled her shirt closed and I felt like a real prick.

"I think this went really well," she said.

"Agreed." I cleared my throat because my voice had gone a bit funny. "I look forward to working with you."

Her pen tapped rapidly on her notebook. "Let's go to dinner," she said without looking up.

I froze. My heart pounded like she'd just proposed marriage. "Wh-what?"

"Tonight. Let's go get some dinner and celebrate. There's this fun bar in town, I can show you."

"As a date?" I asked. That at least, caused her to look up.

"As two people who have had a great day and breakthrough," she said carefully.

"Okay," I said even as my brain screamed that this was a bad idea. I was just finally proving my professional self and showing her I was more than a good time. "That sounds good."

I was gonna regret this.

My eyes went to her wrist where a little glimpse of tattoo showed again. Were they trying to entice me now? They seemed to be jumping out more and more. She pulled the sleeves down to cover the area.

"Are you ever going to show me those?" I asked.

Her cheeks flushed. "No."

"I showed you mine. You show me yours." As soon as the flirtatious words were out, I could have smacked myself. I was nervous about dinner and it had just happened. I'd done so good—well, mostly good—all day keeping my feelings locked down and my professional demeanor in place. But those flashes of her tattoos were incendiary. I needed to see more.

"Not today, Colonel," she said.

I'd almost forgotten what we were talking about I was so lost in dirty thoughts.

"So you're saying someday?" I teased.

"Go. Eat." She playfully pushed me toward the door with her foot.

I grabbed her leg without thinking. My fingertips circled her dainty ankle. If I followed my gaze up her leg, I'd reach her skirt. And past that … I forced my focus to stay where I held her. I was hard in an instant. A glimpse of ankle and I reacted like it was the Regency era.

We both stared at my hand on her ankle. My thumb moved in a circle along the silky material and delicate bone. I shook with desire. What if I sank before her on my knees? What if I just pushed her leg up on to my shoulder? What if I kissed along her long, beautiful legs until she moaned my name, lost in pleasure?

"Sanders," she said. Her chest was flushed as my gaze finally tore away from her ankle. "I'll see you tonight? Okay?"

I gently lowered her leg to the ground. Time to get the fuck out of there. "Sounds good."

I left without another look back. Tonight was going to require a strong game plan.

CHAPTER 17

ROXY

*I*t wasn't a date. It definitely wasn't. I just wanted to look good for myself. It was just dinner with Sanders. It wasn't helping that I owned absolutely no clothes. A closet full of clothes and nothing to wear, a biography. I settled on jean shorts that would have been way too short if not for the black fishnets I wore under them and laced-up combat boots. I topped it with a black tank top that hid none of my tattoos. Sanders wanted to see them, well, now he would. I left my hair down, lined my eyes with heavy eyeliner, and slicked on lip gloss that stung my lips into a ridiculous pout.

Genie's was packed. Always. The country bar was the place to be when you wanted a drink and to hear some music without any trouble. I glanced at the table I'd sat at with the SWS not that long ago when Erik Fricking Jones played Elton John on the piano. That was crazy. I wondered if Kim was going to get me that autograph. Not that I would admit it but, Lord, that would be amazing.

I wished I could send a message to the SWS group text, just to tell them I missed them. But they'd definitely think I was dying if I sent a text like that. I wished I could explain that my distance was to preserve my way of life and that included our friendship. I just had to get through another week with Sanders and things would be back to normal. I held my phone in my hand, looked at the last text from a week ago: a less peppy Kim checking in and all of our half-hearted replies. I put my phone away.

I waved to Patty, as I made my way to the small table in the back. I felt a few sets of eyes on me but kept my face relaxed which was enough of a red flag for most people. Green Valley was filled with a bunch of nosey nellies. Nothing about me screamed "approachable."

She took my order of a vodka soda and I waited. Sanders should be here any minute. My hand lifted to fix my bangs but I dropped it back to my lap. I'd felt really good after our meeting this morning. I was ready to fully admit that I'd misjudged Sanders on a lot of levels but it was clear now that he took Outside the Box very seriously and had a mind for details. I wasn't ready for him to completely take the lead on this corporate retreat but it was so easy to trust him. Freakily so. I didn't like it.

After my drink was dropped off, the bar grew even more crowded. I fought very hard to not check the door every five seconds. I had to trust that he'd come. Tonight wasn't a big deal, just two people hanging out.

At the bar, a man I recognized from my old days at the Dragon Bar kept eyeing me. He wasn't a Wraith, they didn't hang out here, but there was something familiar about him. He was tattooed, bearded, sort of hot in that typical angry biker way. If you were to look up "Roxy's ideal man" ten years ago, this guy would be the top result. We made accidental eye contact. One more time and I would bet twenty bucks he'd head over here. Unfortunately, his seat at the bar was directly in line with my view of the door. Which meant if I checked the door for Sanders again, it would look like I was looking at him. My drink rippled. I'd been shaking my leg so hard, the table was wobbling. I crossed my legs and took another deep drink. What was my deal? I was sweaty and twitchy and excited …

Oh *shit*.

Everything I felt could be described as anticipation. I was looking forward to seeing Sanders again. Not even six hours had gone by and I couldn't wait to see that goofy grin. Most people seemed to suck energy from me but here I was looking forward to time with Sanders like a plant leaning toward a window for sunlight.

I swallowed the rest of my drink in one gulp. *What would the SWS do? Get it together, Roxy.* Gretchen would never sweat a guy, that's for damn sure. She preferred them eating out of her hand and far away from her heart.

Then Sanders walked in. I knew before I even looked up. I *felt* it. I was so screwed. My insides lit up. My skin tingled. I clenched my fists to keep from running up and wrapping my arms around him. He was here. He smiled at me and I smiled back. A full smile. If it were a movie, the needle would scratch on a record and everything would go silent. The whole place would be looking at me and my ridiculous grin.

Sanders' smile grew, and if my knees weren't tingling, I'd have stood up to greet him. His eyes moved over me before returning to my face, tripping up on my mouth. That same heat from earlier today was there. When he held my ankle.

And then.

Skip waved from just behind him. Skip was here. He brought Skip. The smile almost fell off my face but I knew how that would look. It would look like how I felt: crushing disappointment. I liked Skip. I enjoyed spending time with him but I hadn't been expecting him. I hadn't explicitly said it would be just the two of us but I thought ...

"Hiya," Sanders said when he reached the table. The two-person table. He sort of looked like he wasn't sure if we should hug or shake hands, but when I didn't move, he settled on a wave.

"Hey." I finally let my smile drop because it was beginning to hurt and experience told me that it was getting that strained look that caused the elderly to scurry away.

"Hi, Roxy," Skip said, his eyes darting from me to Sanders to the table.

"Hi, Skip. Sorry, this was the only table open when I got here. Let's move over there," I said. "Am I intruding?" I heard Skip whisper to Sanders as I picked up my bag and drink and headed to the new table.

"No way. You guys both wanted to get dinner and I wanted to get out. I figured we could all hang out."

"Sanders, if you—"

"Can I get you guys a round?" he asked brightly when we got settled at the new table.

I'd forgotten how to speak. Sanders dashed over to the bar before I could tell him the server would be over.

"Are you okay?" Skip asked me.

I found my voice again. "Of course."

"If I'm intruding …"

"Not at all." I waved him away. "I'm glad to see you," I said honestly.

"Me too," he said. Then he shot a look to the bar and leaned in to whisper. "Listen. Sanders brought me because he made it sound like a group thing."

"News to me," I said.

Skip frowned. "I think he's just afraid to be alone with you. He knows you want to set boundaries and he's still so raw from his dad's death, I think he's just trying to do the right thing," Skip explained.

My gaze searched his face. "His dad's death?"

"I thought you knew." Skip's face paled.

"I did but I thought it was years ago."

Skip ran a hand over his beard and swore. "No. It was about three weeks ago."

"What?" I gasped.

"He's still—" Skip stopped talking abruptly and sat back as Sanders walked up.

"They'll come by to get our order." Sanders looked around the bar. "Oh, a stage."

"They have live music sometimes," I said numbly.

I could share my Erik Jones story then, but I didn't feel much like talking just then. My throat was too tight. Sanders just lost his dad … My stomach was too bubbly but not in a good way. This news felt like an important revelation. Why hadn't he mentioned his recent loss to me? I felt like we were making progress and now it was like the Sanders I grew closer to was a facade. Maybe we weren't growing as close as I thought. Maybe he didn't think it was any of my business.

When Patty came around again, I ordered another vodka soda. "Make it a double," I said.

Sanders and Skip both ordered a beer.

I listened as the two men chatted. Sanders kept trying to get me to talk but my whirling thoughts held my tongue.

"Hey, Roxy," a voice said.

I looked up from slurping my drink to see Suzie and Ford. It took me a second to react. I couldn't compute seeing Suzie and Ford here while I was with Sanders and Skip. I was already off-balance and this only spun me out more.

"Hi, Suzie. Hey, Ford," I finally said.

Ford nodded a hello. Behind him I saw Jack and I greeted him too.

"Hey, Roxy," Jack said as he leaned in for a hug. I'd only hung out with Jack a few times but I liked him. To be real, he seemed way too cool for Ford.

"Have y'all met?" I asked, gesturing between all the people who now surrounded me. I sat back down without introducing anybody. They could figure it out.

My palms were sweating and my feet didn't seem to be working. My friends went about making introductions and I sat watching, as though I was an outsider. I couldn't remember who had met who the night of the drive-in movie. They could figure it out.

Sanders stood up and shook everyone's hands with a big cheesy smile.

"We actually met," he said motioning to Ford. "Good to see you again, mate."

Sanders and Ford did the bro-hug fist-bump back-tap thing. It all seemed very complicated.

Jack and Skip were introduced. A look passed between them my fuzzy brain couldn't process. Skip seemed a little distant and I couldn't figure out why. Maybe because Sanders was pumping out the charm and making it a party.

"You guys should join us," Sanders said.

"Are we interrupting y'all?" Suzie asked looking to me.

"Not at all. Just a bunch of friends having some drinks," I said with just a pinch of salt. She hesitated. I softened my words with a smile.

I felt Sanders glance at me. The guys gathered a couple more chairs and pulled them up. It was just such a culture clash to see Sanders and Skip chatting with Suzie, Ford, and Jack. I wasn't good at group things to begin with. This had the added confusion of mixing my work life with my personal. How was I supposed to act? In these types of situations, I typically shrank down and shut up because I could never quite figure out how to insert myself.

I downed the rest of my drink, capturing an ice cube to suck on. Jack sat down next to Skip who glared when the chair bumped his to make room.

"Just so you know," Suzie whispered at my side. "Gretchen is meeting us here. We can switch tables if you want."

I shook my head despite the ice in my gut. "No. It's fine."

Of course she was. Hey, while we're at it let's call up my parents and Vincent. Let's invite Jethro and the whole Winston clan and maybe some Wraiths because this couldn't get any more fucking awkward.

"Maybe you two could talk. Things have been so weird since the drive-in," Suzie said.

"She hasn't texted me either," I mumbled.

Suzie let out a breath. Her startlingly emerald eyes were sad. "I think her heart was in the right place," she said tentatively.

"It always is," I said.

"Just talk?"

"I just need to focus on work right now. Let's not talk about it right now." I tilted my head subtly to Sanders at my side.

Suzie sat up and looked to Ford and made a face. Fucking couples.

A hand squeezed my knee. My head shot to Sanders. He was looking straight ahead. Nobody would know he was even doing it. But it gave me strength I didn't know I needed.

Then Gretchen walked in. No, not walked. Gretchen arrived. It was as though the whole room turned to her. She wore denim short overalls that hugged her curves perfectly over a plain white crop top. Her red curls bounced happily as she spotted the group and came over.

Between her and Sanders, how could anybody compete? In some ways they were a perfect match. The thought caused a sharp pain.

"Howdy, y'all. Oh a party! I'll order shots," she said.

"Gretchen, no. It's a weekday," Suzie said.

"So what? Come on. We aren't leaving here until we've all had the best time."

"Why did that feel like a threat?" Sanders whispered in my ear.

Goose bumps tickled down my neck. "Because it was. I need another drink."

He pulled back to look at me with concern. "Are you okay?"

I said, "Of course. It's a party with half of Green Valley. Let's have a great time."

Gretchen and I exchanged a look. My heart ached. The irony, I realized, was that we were fighting because she pushed me toward a man I was avoiding to help preserve our friendships. *No ex left behind.* That was the promise we made to each other.

I lost track of time a bit after that. Bits and pieces came through my fog. Gretchen was chatting to Jack and Skip, flirting loudly. Jack smiled easily back and Skip frowned, looking a little uncomfortable. This only made her try harder to bring him out of his shell.

"Careful there, boys," I said. "Those're her scheming eyes." My voice slurred more than I wanted.

Gretchen crossed her arms. She was about to say something when Ford loudly asked Suzie to dance, to my great surprise. He didn't strike me as the type but the two of them on the floor? Well, shit, of course they looked good. They loved each other so deeply, when I watched them sway, my chest ached with something I couldn't identify. Sanders nudged me, asked me if I wanted to dance. My head dropped to the table. The world spun and it felt like that was the only way to keep me from flying away.

"Hell no," I said and turned my head to look at him. "Walkin' might even be a lot to ask."

He rubbed a circle on my back and slid some water toward me. "Need to go talk?"

I groaned.

My carefully controlled worlds were clashing together. This night hadn't gone to plan at all. I felt pulled in different directions and I couldn't handle any of it. I was embarrassed for misinterpreting closeness with Sanders. I wasn't sure how to act with both my friends and coworkers around. And seeing Gretchen reminded me of how much still needed to be said. It was all too much. For all of my attempts to tightly control my life, it was spinning out around me.

"I'll be right back," I said. When I stood, the floor slid sideways and I had to grip the table.

I felt Gretchen eye me as I made my way to the bathroom. I was tired of holding on so tight.

I needed some air.

* * *

Sanders

WELL, I screwed up.

Roxy's smile when I walked into Genie's made me soar. She was beautiful with her hair flowing around her, the artistic flowers and designs on her arms fully on display. Her long legs went for days in short shorts. She looked more relaxed that I'd seen her since Denver. She looked … happy to see me. Until she saw Skip. Her gaze shuttered and her smile became the fake one she used at the Lodge. I had completely misread the invitation. I wished I could go back in time and understand that this was Roxy's attempt to connect.

No, that was a lie. I knew. I was just scared. I didn't want to show up alone and cross a line.

I kept an eye on her as her friends chatted. Roxy kept tossing back drinks at a rate that surprised me. She had always tried to appear put together and professional around me and here she was getting hammered. Her lithe build didn't seem equipped to handle the vodka at the rate she was drinking it. I wouldn't be able to handle that much.

"Roxy, here." Suzie slid her a glass of water and a basket of fried pickles.

Roxy didn't say anything to her friend but did take a pickle and sipped the water. There was an aggression to her drinking that worried me. Like she was trying to prove a point. I wasn't sure if it was aimed at Gretchen sitting at the other end of the table. They carefully avoided talking to each other in a nonverbal ballet that was almost impressive.

They were a good group and under normal circumstances I felt like we would have all hit it off, but there was a weird tension in the air that made my skin itch. Even Jack and Skip kept arguing over every little thing. I'd never seen Skip like that. Skip was quiet not argumentative. Jack would say the sky was blue and Skip counter with, only during the day. Ford and Suzie were too lost in each other to notice. It was up to me to keep the jokes coming if only to get a single smile from Roxy.

"I chucked a boomerang once. Not sure where it went but it'll come back to me," I said.

Skip groaned and shook his head. Probably not the first time he'd heard that one. Despite my best attempts, Roxy seemed to slip further into a dark mood.

To add to my mounting frustration, this biker at the bar kept looking at Roxy. He had a thick beard and a shaved head with a tattoo on his neck. He'd blatantly check out her legs, not even trying to hide it. I scooted closer to her and put my arm around the back of the chair. If he looked over here again, I would have to do something about it.

I caught Skip watching the exchange. He shook his head and mouthed, "Calm down." I shrugged, and brushed my thumb across the exposed skin of her shoulder.

Roxy stood abruptly. "I'll be right back." Her words slurred.

As she walked away, I caught the guy at the bar watching her. He was eating up her body like she owed him and it pissed me off.

"I'll just keep an eye on her," Suzie said.

The scumbag at the bar leaned back and looked as though he was going to follow her when Suzie quickly caught up. It occurred to me in that this was one of the reasons why women go in pairs to the bathroom. I always thought it was just so they could discuss the deepest secrets of their mysterious sex. But they obviously had a more practical application for avoiding men who were waiting for drunk "easy targets" to break off from their friends.

I was going to kill him.

Skip nudged me. "You're glaring."

"He's just staring at her. He needs to mind his own business."

Skip followed my gaze to the bar. He frowned. The brute at the bar couldn't care less or didn't notice us.

"We'll keep an eye on her," Skip said.

I nodded. But I couldn't stop the growing irritation. Who was this guy? What right did he have to look at her like that? Then a sinking realization set in. Was I any better? I stared at her like she was the most amazing thing in the world because she was. But that didn't mean he could. Roxy mine. Fire good. Sometimes it was hard to beat back the caveman.

But no, it wasn't the same. I wanted to see her flourish. I wanted her to be who she was. I wanted to be the person that brought her unending happiness. It wasn't about conquering her for a night. Even that first night in Denver our interactions had never felt that small to me. It felt cosmic. Stars aligned. I would never treat her as something to be used and disposed of. She was everything.

I gulped and looked down at my beer.

"These girls can take care of themselves, trust me," Jack said amicably. "Gretchen probably has a weapon hidden under the table even as we speak."

"I wasn't saying that they couldn't," Skip said with quiet rage in his voice.

Jack blinked at him. "I know that. I was just saying—"

Suzie came back, her eyes were wide as they shot around the table. "She slipped out while I was "—her gaze flicked to me and Skip— "using the facilities," she finished.

Not sure why she needed to sugarcoat it for us but then her words hit. I glanced to the bar. The guy was gone. My heart took off at an alarming rate.

"That's sort of her thing, isn't it?" Gretchen said with sass but her gaze moved around the bar looking for Roxy, the corners of her eyes tight with tension.

"I'm going after her," I said as I stood. "Skippo, give me the rental, hey?" I reached for the keys.

He nodded and handed them to me. "I'll come with. Just let me close the tab—"

"There's no time." I was already wasting too much time standing here as they discussed what they could do. "I got this," I added looking at them all.

Gretchen nodded and Suzie grabbed Ford's hand, looking pale.

"I can take him back to the Lodge," Jack offered.

Skip frowned but didn't speak.

"I don't bite," he added with a smile, not looking at my sulking best friend. I didn't have time to figure out what that was all about.

"Thanks, mate. Nice seeing you all again."

I ran out of the bar.

In the gravel parking lot, the biker was just starting his bike. It rumbled through the air and shook my insides. A passenger with long brown hair sat on the back. I ran toward them with no plan. I was going to probably get killed but I didn't care. There was no fucking way this guy was ...

Roxy wasn't wearing jeans. Or a leather jacket. In fact, that hair wasn't even the same shade of brown. They both turned toward me. Not Roxy.

I stopped about five feet away and let go of a breath I didn't know I had been holding.

They both gave me an annoyed look before he spun out of the parking lot, kicking up gravel.

"Did you think that was me?" Roxy's voice caused me to turn around.

She stepped out of the shadows from the side of the building, arms wrapped tight around her middle. Her lips were more pouty than usual.

"I—I thought maybe that guy ..."

"I wouldn't just go home with some stranger," she said through ground teeth.

"I didn't think ... I don't know what I thought." I shook my head and stepped closer to her. "I was just worried about you. I didn't like how he looked at you."

Her arms dropped to her side and she took another step closer. In the light of the lamppost her eyes had little black smudges from her makeup underneath them. She looked tired and mournful, and swayed a little as she stood there. "Take me home?"

I swallowed. "Of course." I went to her side and slipped my arm around her middle. At first she stiffened, then she relaxed and put her head on my shoulder to let me guide her slowly to the rental.

Once in the car, I bent forward to buckle her in. As I clicked the buckle into place, the heat from her body wrapped around me. She inhaled deeply. I pulled back slightly to study her face. She blinked up at me slowly. Her gaze moved to my mouth.

"Are you okay?" I asked.

She shrugged and her bottom lip trembled. Then she shook her head, sucking in her lips.

"Let me get you home, hey?"

She nodded before I gently shook her fringe back in place. Her mouth pulled to the side in a sad half smile.

We drove in silence as I followed the map on the car's GPS through winding backroads to a small cluster of apartments just on the edge of town. Silence encased us as I put the car in park. Neither of us moved. The silence rang loud in my ears. I thought she might have fallen asleep, but when I looked to her, she was blinking out the window.

"Why did you leave the bar?" I asked. "It's like all I do is chase after you," I admitted softly. I hadn't meant to say that but I wanted an answer. I was confused and tired.

She turned to face me. "Why did you bring Skip tonight?"

"I-I wasn't sure about … I was trying to respect the friend boundaries."

She nodded with a small smile. "I did think about going home with that guy. He would have been my type. Old Roxy would have."

I frowned. I hated the jealousy that burned me. A man like that wouldn't know the gift they had in her.

"There's a lot you don't know about me, Sanders."

I waited a moment. "I'm trying to change that," I said.

She let out a small sigh. "Why didn't you tell me your dad died?"

I snapped to look at her. "I did," I said slowly. Technically.

169

"Skip told me it wasn't even a month ago. Have you even had a funeral for him?"

"It's not exactly something I like to talk about." I felt my temper changing. "He shouldn't have told you."

"He didn't mean to. It slipped out. Why didn't you tell me?"

"When would I have told you? That night we first met? 'Hi, my dad just died and I'm a complete fuckup.' Not when we weren't sharing details. Not when you looked at me like …"

"Like what?" she asked softly.

"Like I was something special," I answered honestly.

"You are special."

"Yeah, well, so are you." I wasn't sure why it came out so accusatory. "You're a fucking miracle and yet you refuse to let anybody in."

"What?" She glared at me.

"Tonight. This freak-out. What was it about? This drinking to oblivion. The attitude?"

"You can't talk to me like this. We don't know each other well enough."

"Lie," I said staring into her dark eyes. "And you know it. You see me more clearly than anybody ever has."

She swallowed and her gaze moved around the car. It was dark outside but she was illuminated by the streetlights around her apartment building.

"I have been trying to let you in." Her accent grew stronger. "I just hadn't expected everybody I know to be there. I didn't expect you to invite half of Green Valley to our date."

"I didn't know it was a date."

"Lie," she spat back at me.

I turned fully toward her, letting out a sigh. Secretly happy on some level to be called out. To hear her talking to me like she does when it's just us, without any masks. "I didn't know everybody else would show up. But I am sorry. You're right. I was worried it was a date."

She crossed her arms and looked out the window. "Worried," she mumbled.

"Not because I didn't want to go out with you. God, Roxy, you know how badly I … that's exactly why I was worried. I didn't know what to do. I can't seem to control myself around you." I poked her shoulder gently, to get her to look at me. "I didn't want to be alone with you and have you regret it."

Her shoulders sagged with a deep exhale. "I don't want either of us to regret our time together. You want to get to know me so bad, then here you go. This is where I'm from." She gestured to the apartments and back toward the bar. "Those are my people. Is that what you want to know? That I was a biker chick for a motorcycle club … If you met me back then, you wouldn't even look at me like that …"

"Like what?" I leaned closer.

"Like I was something special," she repeated back my same phrase.

"You're wonderful, Roxxo. All I ever want is for you to be yourself around me."

She fisted her hands, rubbing them along her arms. "That's the thing though, isn't it? I don't know who I am. I'm not Biker Roxy anymore. I'm clearly not pulling off this corporate shit. I don't know where I fit. Everybody seems to know themselves so well. Tonight, it was like all my worlds came clashing together. I shut down. I was embarrassed. I don't know who the hell I'm supposed to be." Her words shook with emotion as she finished.

She let out a long slow breath, her brows twisted with confusion. "I don't think I knew I felt this way until just now," she said with a huff.

"Who were you the night in Denver?" I asked.

Her gaze shot to me.

"Were you pretending that night?" I swallowed, afraid of the answer.

That night had meant so much to me. I had felt a connection to her on a level I never had experienced with anybody else. If she was faking it … I didn't know if I could handle it.

"That night I wasn't pretending to be anybody." I looked up at her words. "I think that's what scared me so bad."

I couldn't speak for the emotion that tightened my throat. I wanted to pull her into my lap and kiss her into oblivion. I wanted to tell her she fixed me that night. She took one of the worst days of my life and put me back together without even trying. How could I possibly even convey the depth of my feelings for her? I didn't want to scare her. She already ran away at every turn.

I grabbed her hands. She looked down at them, her chest rising and falling.

"I don't want you to be scared of whatever this is," I said. "I don't want you running away. I want you leaping toward me. There's no rush for me." I ran my thumbs along the soft skin of the back of her hands. "I don't want you to regret a moment with me. Life can be too heavy to handle sometimes. Let people share the load, Roxy. If you can't leave it behind, then let people help."

"Thank you. I'm working on that," she said with a grin.

I said, "There's seven billion people on this planet. You aren't alone."

"Neither are you, Colonel." Her bottom lip pulled into her mouth as she worried it. "If you want to talk about your dad …"

It was tempting to tell her everything but I just couldn't talk to her after a night like tonight. After she'd been drinking. I suddenly felt so tired. "Thank you." I squeezed her hand. "It's getting late. Let me walk you up."

Her mouth parted and then she said, "Sure."

CHAPTER 18

ROXY

*J*t was Saturday night in the Barn, the main event space for the Lodge, and the graduation party was in full swing. Or it should have been? I couldn't tell if the party was fun. The DJ spun a bunch of songs I didn't recognize and the teens took a lot of videos on their phones. They weren't dancing exactly. Or if they did it was only for like twenty seconds and then they'd clump together looking at the video they made. I do not understand teenagers. I didn't even fit in with them when I was one. When I was eighteen, I was partying with the Wraiths in ways that made this party seem like a toddler's birthday.

I stood on the edge of the room, watching and debating if it was time to leave. My responsibilities for the night were complete. I could use a cocktail and a break from these shoes.

"Someone needs to show these people how to party," a voice whispered in my ear.

The vibration trailed down my spine, kissing each vertebra before settling in my lower body. Just a whisper in my ear … just a scent of him and a cascade of horny rippled through me.

Get a grip, woman.

"Sanders," I said. "Hey." I fixed my bangs.

My relief at seeing him was instant. Things ended weird the other night. I had been drunk and knew I was acting like an asshole. I had been so overwhelmed I slipped into Old Roxy habits.

"You look beautiful," he said.

I wore a little black dress, my go-to for nighttime events. It was a simple shift dress made of a heavy jersey-type material but was slightly shiny, so it looked professional with my black heels and matching silk stockings.

He grabbed my hand and spun me around to get the full view. I rolled my eyes but liked the way he ate up my body like a sugary treat from the Donner Bakery dessert case. Maybe we could forget that the events at Genie's ever happened. My overshare. His refusal to share. Tonight, he seemed set on flirtation.

"You don't look so bad yourself," I said.

His black button-up shirt looked crafted to his body. The strength earned from all his time outside, pulled the material tight around his strong shoulders and biceps. He wore matching black pants and a thin belt, nothing outrageously fancy but he looked amazing. It was nice to see him in something other than khaki hiking pants. Not that I minded those either. I liked how he looked all the time.

"I clean up okay." He shrugged, backing away to look up at me with a pouty smolder. The dirty, little flirt.

"I remembered you said you had to work this party," he explained. "I thought …" He looked to the side and then turned back to me. His focus snagged on my legs before returning to my face where it moved from my mouth to my eyes and all around. "Well, you mentioned never having prom or graduation, this is the next best thing."

He looked so earnest as he spoke, so hot with his slicked-back hair and freshly shaved face. He was so sexy I couldn't stand still. I wanted to rub my thighs together just to feel the silk material. I wanted to feel him roll the stockings off my body slowly, one at a time.

"Such a romantic," I said having no clue how to even handle such a thoughtful gesture. "Thank you," I added.

I reached out and squeezed his biceps without meaning too. The action surprised us both. I didn't even know what happened. One moment I was standing there and the next my hands had a mind of their own.

He raised an eyebrow and cracked a smile.

Something shifted in me then. Like the final remnants of an ice cube dissolving, I gave in. I'd been trying so hard to maintain control when all I did was make everything worse. He came here to comfort me, to give me the dance I never had, even after my freak-out at Genie's. It was time to just let our bodies take the lead for once.

"I was actually just about to leave," I said, hoping he'd take the hint. Maybe we could go have a drink at the bar ... maybe I could share with him the very expensive La Perla garter belt—purchased at sale seventy-five percent off—that held these stockings up.

His smile dropped. I realized too late how he would take that.

"Not sneaking out," I said quickly, trying to poke fun at myself. "Maybe you and I ..."

"This party is a stinker," he said glancing around.

"Wait. What? What do you mean?" We looked around the room. More kids had moved to play with their phones at the tables.

He nodded looking concerned, hands deep in his pockets. "We have to do something."

"I've done everything." I started mentally going over the checklist for the party, the food, the decor, the music, everything had gone off without a hitch. But something was missing, I admitted to myself. It was ... a bit of a snoozer.

"Let's dance. Show them how it's done," he said.

"Right." I laughed.

"I'm serious. Somebody needs to show these whippersnappers how to dance."

"Whippersnappers? You're so cool," I said dryly.

He grabbed my hand and started tugging me to the floor. I froze. "What are you doing?"

"Come on. We have to pass on our traditions to the next generations. This is crucial." He tugged me.

"Sanders. No. I'm serious. I do not dance."

"Are you kidding me?" he asked and I realized my mistake.

"Okay, I dance. But I already told you I wasn't myself that night."

"Lie." He threw out his arms frustrated. "Come on, Roxxo. Who cares what they think? You're never going to see these people again."

"Are you kidding me? It's Green Valley, I'll probably see half this room tomorrow."

"True. Still, who cares? Aren't you tired of holding on so tight all the time?" He came closer. He brought his hands around my head. For a moment, I thought he was going to pull me in for a kiss. I didn't want that. Or did I want that? "Aren't you tired of thinking all the time?" He pressed his forehead to mine in a frustrated growl. "Don't you just want to dance like we did that night?"

I widened my eyes.

"Okay," he amended. "Maybe not exactly like that night. There are impressionable young minds around us."

His hands reached around for the clip that held my hair back. He pulled it out and ran his fingers through it. He was right. I just told myself to let go. Now I had to follow it with action.

"You're broken in the brain," I said but it came out a husky whisper.

"Likely. But you have no idea how long I've been wanting to do that." He scratched his nails against my scalp and ran his fingers through the length, until it flowed around me. I smelled my shampoo from my slightly damp hair and he leaned in to inhale it deeper. Little freak. I bit back a smile.

I was tired of overthinking. I was tired of being so afraid that a little fun would cause an entire backslide. Just then the peppy beat of the Electric Slide blasted from the speakers. My shoulders started to rock back and forth like some base Pavlovian reaction to the music.

"Come on, you know you want to," he said with no shortage of flirtation in his voice.

I rolled my eyes. "This is insanity."

I grabbed his hand and we went to the floor. "That's my girl!" he shouted and I couldn't help but feel delirious from his words.

"So is this like the Nutbush?" he asked.

He watched my steps and caught on quickly.

"I have no idea what that is," I shouted over the music.

He stilled. "I have so much to teach you." After a disappointed shake of his head, he started to move again.

A few girls hovering on the edge of the dance floor giggled and pulled each other to the center. I moved to the front to show them. It's a superpower women sometimes have, the ability to learn line dances instantly and follow with ease.

"There you go," I said to them. They laughed and shimmied without shame. I could tell they felt cute too and that made me feel good.

Who was I? Maybe this was the joy Suzie felt teaching a class at Stripped. I let the music take over. It was fun to line dance. I didn't look cool but I didn't care. This was *fun*. I could have fun, I was allowed.

More people moved to the floor. Soon at least thirty of us were dancing. Step forward, rock back. Shimmy.

"Alright, now. Come on, y'all!" the DJ yelled.

Sanders grabbed me and twirled me out. I let my head fall back, as the flashing colorful lights and the music made me feel a little drunk.

He pulled me back in, and we ground our hips in tandem, back and forth to the tempo.

"It's electric," he whispered in my ear. Sending chills down my arms despite the very cheesy retro song. I threw my head back and laughed. His eyes lit up. "There she is," he yelled.

I covered my face, embarrassed for him. And yet … I was having fun. Even the parents joined in, most were closer to my age than the kids dancing. They knew this jam and the second the music started they recovered a piece of their past.

The energy pulsing through the Barn reminded me of that night the SWS had joined in with the rest of the crowd at the bar, dancing to Erik Jones' singing. That very specific type of connection that comes with this sort of group bonding. *God, who was I?* I was a woman having fun.

I did a fancy shuffle and twirl just to show off.

Sanders fell to his knees and bowed in front of me. "I'm not worthy," he yelled.

"You're insane," I called out, trying to tug him up. But he crawled on his knees as I dragged him along. I hid my face and laughed.

A few teens giggled at his antics. Some of the girls were doing their best to get Sanders to see their flirty smiles.

"Alright, let's slow it down now," the DJ crooned as the music melted into a slow country song.

Without discussing it, Sanders pulled me into his arms and we switched to a slow two-step.

He was a little sweaty as I dug my nails into his back to hold on. I had to admit, my lady bits quite liked the sight of that. I was taken back to our first dance together.

"Admit it, you had fun," he growled in my ear.

"I admit you are crazy."

"And you like it." He pulled me so there was no space left between our bodies.

I did like it. I liked him so damn much. He didn't even have a clue. I would have never done this for anybody else. He made me feel like nobody else ever had. He pushed me to my limit and then nudged me over the edge with one look. My body felt like it was tumbling head over feet into an abyss that I would never escape. He made me want to have him around all the time. He made me want things I couldn't have.

"Let's go outside," I whispered.

His eyebrows rose slightly and he followed as I led him outside.

* * *

OUTSIDE, A few teens vaped under a flood light.

"That'll kill you," Sanders said to them.

They rolled their eyes. "Thanks, grandpa," one said. But one look at my glare and they made their way back inside.

"I'm wounded," he said dryly. Turning back to me, he said, "What's going on, Roxxo?" His eyes pleaded with me. The deep blue of those depths drowned me.

I wanted to just give in to what felt good and right. Him.

"Remember how I mentioned that crew, the Iron Wraiths, that I used to party with?" I asked.

We stood near the wall, leaning against the brick. He said, "Yeah, and you didn't want to talk about it."

"Well. I'm ready to now. I'm not going to go into all the details but I need you to understand something. Because I know I'm frustrating to be around. I wish I were as easy as my friend Kim. I'm not the most likable."

"I disagree, but go on," he said.

"I had a rough childhood. Not terrible but my parents forgot about me a lot. My brother was never around and skipped town the second he was old enough. When Gretch and I met, we were inseparable. We were everything to each other."

He reached for my hand and tangled our fingers. I studied our inter-twined fingers, finding the strength to share more.

"Well, little girls grow up and meet boys. Gretchen started hanging with this guy that was in a motorcycle club here in Green Valley called the Iron Wraiths."

Surprise crossed his face.

"Yeah. It was bad. We got mixed up in their crowd. Then I started seeing this guy Jethro."

"Ah, Sienna's Jethro," he said.

"That's the one. And incidentally the reason the SWS exists—it stands for Scorned Women's Society." I cleared my throat. "We are all, uh, Jet's exes."

"That's not weird?" he asked.

"It's really not. It's hard to explain. Plus, if I wasn't friends with any of his exes, there wouldn't be anybody left to be friends with," I teased. My fingers itched for a smoke though I hadn't since I left the Wraiths, just talking about that time brought up muscle memory.

"So, Jet and I dated. I worked at the Dragon Bar, this place where bikers hang out, to be closer to him and the MC. To a kid who had basically been abandoned, hanging out with the Wraiths felt more like family than anything I'd ever had. Gretch too. But she was gone with her guy more and more. Then they got engaged and she stopped coming around completely. She was trying to get him to leave. Anyway, that's a whole other story. But the point was, I was Jet's old lady. I had a place ... even if it was a pretty shitty one in hindsight."

I blew out a long breath.

"Then one day Jet stopped coming around the bar. Stopped coming around at all. He got out of the MC. I still don't really understand how, to be honest. But he was gone. He left without a single look back. I was pissed. And I found myself abandoned to a group I wouldn't have even been with if it hadn't been for Jet and Gretch in the first place."

"I'm so sorry," he said.

"This is turning out to be a longer story than I thought." I fixed my bangs unable to meet Sanders' gaze. "Anyway, I was pissed. One day Gretch comes and says she was taking me away and Jet wanted to marry me to make things right. I just had to go with her." I shifted on my feet.

"But I was pissed off and stubborn and let myself think I had found people who really cared. I told her to leave without me. After that, things got pretty bad. When you aren't a single person's old lady, you sort of become shared property." I shook my head. "I won't go into it. I convinced myself I was okay with things that I wasn't. I did drugs and drank a lot just to cope. It was bad."

"But you're here now?" he prompted.

"Yeah. I got a second chance," I said. "A few months later, Gretchen came back again. She was on a rampage. Her lover was dead. And I had been completely oblivious. Nobody told me anything. It broke through my fog to see someone I loved so fucked up. Her pain cracked right through the shell of hurt I'd built around myself. She was screaming over and over that they murdered him. That she was going to kill each and every one of them. She was drunk and sloppy, her clothes were a mess, her makeup was running. She looked skinnier than I'd ever seen her. Nobody was scared, a few of the guys laughed at her. But the gun she was waving around was real. That look in her eyes was real. I knew that girl well enough to know that she wasn't messing around.

"I was pretty coked out of my mind and wasted, but I knew I had to distract Gretch. I had to make her see me. I went stumbling up to her. I can't imagine how terrible I must have looked after so many months apart. It took her a moment to even register me. She was so far gone and lost in her own head. But when she did, the arm holding the gun dropped and she looked at me with sadness. Even in that situation I was the pitiable one.

"It was like a lightbulb suddenly turned on and I could see that I was in a room with cockroaches and filth all the while thinking I was in a palace. When she saw me, it seemed to break her too. In that minute, I made a choice. I never wanted to end up like this. I didn't want either one of us to be broken by the Wraiths. I knew in that moment that if either of us wanted to be saved from that life, we'd need each other."

I took a deep, shaky breath in. I had never shared this with anybody. But seeing Sanders' patient, open expression, feeling his concern for us without judgment gave me strength to finish.

"I told her to take me away. She looked me up and down and she saw it too. The nights ahead of us. Prison maybe for her. Me being passed around like an object. Slowly morphing into my parents at best, a whore for the Wraiths at worst. It was this moment of extreme clarity. I knew we couldn't go on like this. Even though no one had ever told us, we both understood that we were made for more than this. We believed in each other."

"I'm so glad you did," Sanders said in a low, steady voice.

I squeezed his hands. "She wiped away the tears from her face, then nodded once. I took her hand and grabbed my bag from the bar, shoving the gun inside it. We turned to the door, holding hands like a lifeline. Some random biker tried to stop us but Gretchen looked him straight in the eyes and said, 'I'm taking my best friend and we're getting the fuck out of here. If you try to stop me, I will kill you.' Completely sober. He stepped right out of the way. Out front she turned to me and said, 'No ex left behind.' She saved me that night."

When I finally stopped talking, tears hovered in my eyes. I blinked them away.

"You saved each other," Sanders said as he pulled me in for a hug. "And I'm so glad."

I squeezed my eyes tight and the tears leaked out. When we finally pulled away from each other, I sniffed and said, "So now you see."

"See?"

"Why this job is important to me. Why maintaining my focus is so important. Gretchen gave me a second chance at life."

"And you're worried that I'll mess things up?" he asked with a small crinkle in his forehead.

"I'm worried that *I'll* mess it up."

I frowned. For so long that's what I had thought. I thought if I gave in even a little to deeper desires, then I'd totally backslide. That I would ruin the second change Gretchen had given me.

"I don't want her to feel like I'm wasting my chance," I said honestly.

"People who love you, love you for the person you are, not your job or your clothes," he said, our hands clasped together.

184

"I know she loves me, but I don't have anything else I can offer."

"She doesn't need you to offer anything." His gaze was piercing with intensity as he spoke. "I guarantee she just wants you to be happy. For you to feel like enough. Roxy, you as you are, is enough. You are more than enough. You are everything."

His words soothed my loudest anxieties the way falling snow quiets the earth. I was enough. Could it be that simple? Sharing my past out loud, my fears felt so silly. But that was what I thought. That was how I'd been living my life. Of course Gretchen wanted me to be happy. Of course I could have some fun without losing everything I've worked for. But I needed to test this new revelation. I dropped his hands to pull him close to me.

"You shouldn't say stuff like that," I whispered as my heart pounded.

"Why?" His arms brought me closer so no space was left between our bodies.

But there was no more time for talking. There was only one thing left to do: to kiss the hell out of that man.

* * *

Sanders

THERE WAS no doubt in Roxy's kiss. No hesitation. I kissed her back, her tongue flirting with mine, as I walked her back to the wall.

I'd missed these lips. I'd wanted this woman for forever. Before I even knew her, I needed her. The thought struck me so hard it would have taken my breath away if she wasn't currently breathing new life into me. Her lips. Her touch. It all gave me life. A desire to be here. Be more. I understood now what she thought was at risk, that's what made this moment all the more valuable.

My thoughts were a tangle of warring desires. I couldn't rush this. I couldn't slow down. I wanted to respect her and take things slow. I wanted to make her scream my name as I licked and tasted her. My hands were on her hips, stuck in place with indecision. My fingers restlessly worked the soft material of her dress.

I pulled away to take a breath, to check and see where her head was at. When I found her gaze, it burned with the same heat that ignited me from the inside out.

Okay, man, breathe.

My forehead dropped to hers. My whole body shook. I realized my hands were still at her hips, tugging her dress until I could palm handfuls of the material without meaning to. It stretched tight across her ass, revealing the tops of her stockings high on her thighs. I leaned back to confirm that they were indeed edged in black lace and bit my lip to keep from groaning at the sight. Panting, lips even more swollen than normal, Roxy blinked up at me through her lashes. If she noticed her fringe was a mess, she didn't worry about fixing it this time.

"I like those." I let go of her dress to drag a finger up the silky stockings clinging to her legs.

I was rock hard and had to shift to ease the pressure against my belt. Her gaze followed the action.

"Oh yeah?" A small smile crept up her lips up as she grabbed the hem of her skirt. Instead of fixing it lower like I expected, she slowly lifted both sides to reveal delicate black clasps and a garter belt. She stopped lifting just short of what I wanted to see the most.

"Holy shit." I bit my fist.

She moaned as I came back to kiss her more. More like attacked her. She had just enough time to drop the skirt and grab my hands before our mouths met again. Our clasped hands lifted above her head, the backs of mine pressing into the rough rocks of the building. It had the added bonus of causing her body to arch into mine.

I ground my body against hers and she hooked a leg behind me to push my hardness against her with a moan. Only our gasping breaths filled the night. The soft shuffle of our clothes rubbing restlessly against each other.

She smelled and tasted amazing. I never wanted this to end. Never. I would figure out how to work with my face on hers.

The heavy metal door to our left squeaked loudly against the quiet night.

Vincent walked out and I stepped back instantly. She straightened and shifted her dress back down, discreetly wiping her mouth. I glared up at the sky. *Come on.*

"Roxy?" he called out.

We were a few feet apart by the time he spotted us. I braced the wall with one arm, slightly turned away, pretending to observe the trees surrounding us, but mostly trying to hide the evidence of what we'd been doing. He would definitely see.

I glanced over my shoulder to find Vincent looking between us with a raised eyebrow. Roxy strode toward him smoothly, twisting her hair up into a bun as she went.

"What's up?" she asked coolly.

I turned back to the forest and wiped my face. Her taste still filled my mouth. My body was rock hard and wound up, humming like a running motor.

"The DJ needs another mic, is there a backup somewhere?" Vincent asked.

"Sure. In the back room, I'll show you."

I let out a breath. I had hoped after our talk that she had finally begun to trust me but it was obvious we were back to the same old story. We'd get close. She'd pull away. She'd say sorry later. I wished we could just go back to that first night and start all over. Just let me go back to the beginning to do it right the first time. I should have never let her go. Instead, it felt like the closer we grew, the further she pulled away.

I still looked out into the trees, a darkness threatening to take over. The first hint of acid churned in my throat when her hand rested on my shoulder.

"Hey, Colonel?"

When I turned to meet her, I found her smiling shyly at me.

"Busy tomorrow?" she asked.

"Tomorrow?" My thoughts scrambled to catch up. "Sunday? No. Wide open. Free as a bird."

"Good," she said. "Let's hang out."

"Hang out. Yup. Sounds good."

She bit back a grin and walked away.

I looked to the sky again. This time I grinned.

CHAPTER 19

ROXY

*T*he forest floor was easily thirty feet down. The only thing that stood between me and certain bone breaks was the flimsy harness wrapped around my hips like an oversized diaper.

"I don't think this is what Vincent had in mind when he told me to trust people," I said.

"Sure it is." Sanders smiled at me.

It was Sunday afternoon and the sun sparkled through the canopy of the tall pines. Though I preferred to enjoy trees much closer to the ground. Man wasn't meant to be this close to heaven.

In preparation for MooreTek's arrival tomorrow, Sanders suggested we go explore a local zip-lining company and discuss the logistics of liability. Sanders also insisted that experiencing the adventure firsthand would help me understand the process and a little trust never hurt anyone. Sanders was an idiot. And I was just as bad for going along with it.

Now that there was thirty feet between me and the earth, I decided that somebody could most definitely get hurt. Somebody being me. I double-checked the clips—he called them carabiners—that attached me to the rope in two spots.

"Thought it might be best to show you the ropes." He raised an expectant eyebrow at me. "Little zip-lining pun? Never fails to get a chuckle."

"Har. Har."

My palms wouldn't stop sweating. How was I supposed to hold on for dear life when my palms couldn't grip anything? This seemed like a major design flaw in humans. Like putting our only air pipe next to the place where we swallow food.

"Are you okay? You've gone quiet." He nudged my arm lightly until I looked at him.

"This is safe, right? Board certified? The government approved this? What sort of safety requirements did this pass? Where can I read up on the regulations? I should have checked all this before we left."

He studied me closely enough that I started to wonder if there was something on my face. A smile tugged at the side of his mouth.

"It's totally safe. No accidents to date," he said, then added, "The worst thing that has ever happened was the guy who drank too much the night before and lost his lunch."

"You deal with a lot of vomit in your job?"

He shrugged. "I weirdly do. Preparing me for fatherhood I guess."

My brain instantly imagined him gently bouncing a baby on his shoulder with one of his giant grins on his face. It did weird things to me. I shoved those thoughts way down. I'm on to you, Mother Nature. Calm yourselves, ovaries, we ain't the breeding type.

Sanders gestured to the zip line that stretched from the platform we stood on to one about twenty meters away. "This is just a small example of what Outside the Box has in Denver," he explained. "We have basic zip lines like this, longer and shorter distances and different heights off the ground. But we also have obstacle course-type experiences, like rope bridges and free falls."

"Good Lord," I muttered. I smoothed my ponytail, my damp palms pulling on the loose strands. I took a quiet deep breath in.

"Hey, trust me. I won't let anything happen to you." He held my gaze and I found there complete and open honesty. I believed him. He'd already explained how everything worked, how to hold on and place my hands. I knew, in theory, what to do, but that was very different than in practice.

"Okay." I nodded.

Unfortunately, even though I believed him, my body didn't move. I gripped the rope as though my life depended on it. Oh, that's right, because my life did depend on it. My feet remained planted, turned toward the inside of the platform, away from the taunting distance below.

"Are you afraid of heights?" he asked.

"No," I said instantly. "No sane person puts themselves in this position willingly."

He looked at me again. Too closely. Why did he keep doing that? He hadn't talked about our kiss and so I hadn't either. It was pretty clear that both of us enjoyed it but that didn't make the aftermath any less awkward. I thought maybe we would continue what we started last night when he picked me up today. So when he suggested this suicide mission, I was a little thrown off.

Also how did one bring that sort of thing up? *"Hi, how are you? Nice to see you again. Can I suck your face now that we've gotten the pleasantries out of the way?"*

"You don't let go of control easily. Neither does Skip."

"Really?" I asked momentarily distracted.

"Yeah. He only started OTB with me because I needed a partner." He frowned a little as he focused on the horizon. "He's much better at the business side of things. I just like taking people out of their comfort zone."

"Clearly," I said. Then added, "So he doesn't like—"

"You're stalling."

This time it was my turn to snap. "No. I'm not. I'm up here, literally so outside of my comfort zone I don't remember what it looks like. You push and push me." I couldn't believe I was able to articulate precisely what I was feeling at exactly the moment it needed to be said. Sanders made me braver, but he needed to return the favor. "You want me to trust you. I'm asking you to do the same for me."

I held his stare looking as pissed off as I possibly could, wearing this goofy-ass helmet.

He swallowed, the tendons of his cheeks flexing as he clenched his jaw.

"I don't like to talk about this stuff. It makes me sound shitty."

I wanted to reach for his hand but I wasn't about to let go of this rope. Instead, I shuffled my foot slowly to nudge his. "I shared my dark past with you last night. You can trust me."

He scratched at his chin. "I don't think Skip in particular likes this business, no. I think he became my partner to help me. And then it took off and I'm not really good at managing the details all the time. And now it's too hard to imagine doing this without him."

I nodded like I understood. But I didn't really. I couldn't imagine counting on people in such a big way. It was just asking for failure.

"He typically has to handle the stuff I just plain don't want to. That's the reason I missed the conference in Denver. Recently a lot of companies like ours have crept up. We were losing business because I kept making these stupid mistakes. I was really distracted toward the end of my time with my dad. And when he passed, I well, I couldn't function for a few days."

"I'm sorry," I said and quickly managed to squeeze his shoulder.

He sucked in air through his teeth and rubbed at his collarbone, shoulders stretching beneath his shirt as though to get some air. "The day of the conference, a big group came to town. They went to the hotel where they were supposed to be staying." He winced. "I forgot to book their rooms. They showed up, about twenty of them, and there was nothing available. I rushed to go meet with them and find a place but everything was booked for the conference. I had to smooth feathers. But I fucked up. Big-time. Skip stood in for me at the trade show as I groveled to the customer and got them a place to stay at some Airbnbs. It was awful."

He closed his eyes.

"I'm so sorry," I said. Admittedly, that made my skin itchy. That type of mistake was my biggest fear.

"Skip is always there to clean up my messes. Following behind me with his sweeper to pick up my pieces."

"Is that why he came to Green Valley?" I asked cautiously.

He glanced to me. "Yeah. Between my dad and the business"—his eyes flicked to mine and away—"I think he thinks that I'm struggling a bit."

This made me frown. Sanders always seemed so put together. So confident. It was hard to imagine him needing help at all.

"One day …"

"What?" I asked.

"One day, he's going to stop coming to my rescue." He chewed his lip thoughtfully.

"And you will be fine," I said. Reluctantly I released the rope to grab his hand. "You'll figure it out and he'll still be your friend. You're more than capable of handling the business. I've seen it. You're fantastic with customers. Skip is a great friend, but you could handle the business yourself if you wanted to let him go. You handled the mistake you made with the conference. You can handle more than you think, I bet. You're whip smart. You're just dealing with something terrible."

"Thanks." He glanced away and back, scratching at the back of his neck. "That's why I'm out here. To help fix the damage I've done."

"You will. This week will be great and you'll get a ton of business. Maybe you could even open another branch out here?" I said hesitantly.

His gaze held me in place. "That would be great."

We smiled at each other and I felt myself blush. *God, I'm such a sucker*. But I was honored that he shared with me. I knew what it cost him.

"See? Look at us. Sharing. You can see why this is good for people. Nothing enables trust more than putting your life in a stranger's hands," he said.

"Gee, when you put it that way." My head shook. I didn't put my life in others' hands. I didn't even put my laundry in other people's hands. If I wanted something done right, I did it myself.

"You're going to need to move eventually," he said.

"I know." I nodded a few times rapidly but still didn't move. Now my eyes wouldn't open.

Two large hands squeezed my shoulders. The sudden contact was so jolting my eyes shot open.

He gently squeezed. "Why don't we try something else?"

"I'm not camping," I said.

"No." He chuckled. "I didn't realize you were so scared."

"I'm not scared. I'm sane. This isn't healthy. Millions of years of evolutionary instinct yelling that this is a bad idea."

"I understand." He seemed genuine. "Let's climb back down." He started to reclip his carabiners.

"I'm not falling for your reverse psychology."

"Roxy, I promise that's not what this is. I wanted to show you what Outside the Box does. I'm not trying to force you into something you aren't comfortable with. I have other activities we could try. Or we can hang out and watch the next group."

I crossed my arms. "Screw that. I'm doing this." I double-checked the chin strap of my helmet.

He was being honest with me. I could do this. Take a leap of faith for once. Even if it was just a tiny one. I crouched and pushed myself off without another word. My body zipped through the air. The forest blurred around me. Okay, I was only going like five miles an hour but it felt much faster.

I screamed, clamping my eyes shut. I was definitely making a fool of myself and knew that Sanders was laughing at me. It was all over fast. The next platform was waiting only a few yards away. I did as we practiced and landed with a gentle thump on the mat.

My whole body shook as I clipped myself to the next rung and the next until I was secured to the platform.

"That was awful!" I screamed across to him.

"You were great," he yelled back with a big stupid goofy grin that made me want to kiss it right off.

He was across and on the platform with me not ten seconds later. I was beginning to sense this was the bunny hill of zip-lining.

"Okay, I admit it, Colonel, that wasn't as terrible as I thought it was going to be."

"Just wait until you do the ones that are three hundred feet in the air. Or half a mile long." He grinned and it was infectious.

"That's never going to happen. I'm good for the rest of time," I said, dead serious. I was proud of myself but saw no reason to tempt fate ever again. "Can we get down now?"

He laughed. "I'll go first. Just remember lead with red, unclip, clip, then green, unclip, clip."

"Got it," I said.

The platform was only about twenty steps but it took a few minutes to do the clip and unclip thing, so that by the time I almost reached the bottom, my already shaking arms were fatigued. Okay, I needed to work my upper body more. More classes at Stripped and maybe I'd be able to hang, literally, like Suzie.

"There you are. I went and made some tea and came back," Sanders said a few feet below me.

"Aren't you hilarious," I said.

But I wasn't paying attention. I'd let myself get comfortable in the rhythm of the work and realized I grabbed the green clip first.

"Shit," I said, my brain short-circuiting.

"Okay, Roxxo?" he asked.

I clung to the rung. This was ridiculous. I could literally fall from here and I would be fine. Worse case it'd knock the wind out of me but it was as though my fear was on a delay and I physically couldn't move. I looped my arms through the rung and closed my eyes.

"I'm fine. I live here now," I called. I was humiliated. I tried so hard to keep my shit together around Sanders but he just had a knack for opening all the darkest rooms in my mind, rummaging through my stuff with a giant flashlight.

"You're super close. You don't need to worry about the clips. Just come on down. I'll catch you."

"Yep. Okay." I didn't move.

"New plan," he called up. "I'm gonna come and unclip you and then we'll climb the rest together."

"Honestly, I'm fine," I said.

"Sure you are. But I need to get this equipment returned, so can you help me out?"

"You should have brought your own."

"Weirdly, they weren't okay with that."

"Okay. I'll allow you to help me to help you," I said in a squeaky voice.

He chuckled. "Thanks."

The rungs weren't made for two people at a time. He had to balance a step higher and below me so that he was sort of bear hugging me from behind. My back was pressed tightly to his front. His warmth wrapped around me like a sun-dried towel after a dip in the pool.

"Just gonna do this one first." He unclipped me fast and confidently.

Everything about him was so assured. He moved through life as though he'd reviewed every step ahead of time and was just retracing a familiar path. I envied that poise but I knew the truth now. He was just as afraid as I was. But he didn't let that stop him. He leapt even when he was scared.

"Now, you're just gonna climb down. Just like a step ladder at work," he said.

My head shook even as I said, "Okay."

He laughed a little and it shuddered through my body.

"We're very close to the bottom. You could hop down from here. I promise."

"I know. This is humiliating."

"No. Totally normal. Post-adrenaline crash. Happens all the time."

"You just made that up."

"I'm sure it's a thing. But, Roxy." He lowered his head to whisper in my ear. Goose bumps trailed down my neck. "Are you ticklish?"

"Don't you dare!" I said.

I pushed back and threw him off me. He hopped off and landed on his feet with a chuckle.

"Trust fall!" I yelled.

"Roxy, wait!"

But it was too late. I fell, crashing into his arms. We both collapsed onto the ground, rolling in a heap of limbs and swearing. I elbowed him hard on the chest. He gasped out a loud "oomph."

I rolled off him and stood up. I unsnapped the helmet and the harness with shaking hands, feeling like I couldn't breathe again until all the gear was off. Shrugging out of them so fast you'd have thought spiders were crawling all over them. He did the same from his position on the ground, wincing a little from where I hit him.

"Sorry about that. Is your ankle okay?" I asked with a frown. We were lucky it didn't get more hurt the first time he fell.

He looked up at me with a soft smile as he watched me peel off the gear. "It's fine."

I worried my bottom lip. "You keep getting hurt around me."

"I'm just happy to be around you," he said earnestly.

This man who was infinitely patient with me. This man who pushed me outside my comfort zone while holding my hand so I wouldn't fall. What sort of person acted like that? How was he able to be so open, so sure and sexy and confident?

I'm sure my nerves were part of it. I'm sure the residual fear added to it. And I was positive that final look he gave me pushed me over the ledge.

I attacked him.

I threw myself on top of him and pushed him back into the dirt. I lowered my mouth to his. There was no thought. I had to kiss him again. He tasted better than I remembered from last night. Better than our first night in Denver. His body was on fire beneath me and I wanted to warm myself against him. My whole body shook but so did his. It amplified the heat burning through me. Our tongues rubbed. He sucked on my lower lip. I moaned embarrassingly loud. I pulled back to breathe. His hair was a mess. I guess I did that. My hands were still tangled in it.

He wasn't smiling. His eyes were ablaze.

"Was that okay?" I asked.

A second later, I was on my back and he was kissing me again. He spread my legs with his and pressed his rock-hard erection into me. It was jarring. How was he this hard this fast? I wasn't complaining. It was clear where his swagger came from.

"Yes," he breathed as I gasped for breath. His eyes flicked back and forth between mine. They roamed over my face, his nostrils flared. He seemed almost as surprised as I was. Gone was the charm, burned away by dark desire.

I pushed him up and over until I was on top of him again.

"Control freak," he said teasing.

His blue eyes were wide and sparkling with lust as they shifted to search my face. They lowered to my chest where my boobs were dangerously close to falling out of my sports bra and shirt.

Free the nip!

He must have had the same thought because his head lowered and he pressed his face into my cleavage.

I gripped his head closer. Balancing on one arm, he managed to wrangle a breast free because one was in his mouth a second later. He sucked at it, flicked my nipple with his tongue.

"Sanders," I gasped.

His hands roamed up my shirt. They gripped and moved frantically like he couldn't decide where to touch first or where to stay. I didn't mind.

This was madness. But I couldn't stop. I was on the forest floor. I had leaves in my hair and a branch sticking into my thigh. I hoped that was a branch, otherwise I was way out of my league here. I was about to take this man in the middle of nature.

"Wait," he said. His hand gently pushed me up.

I was still straddling him. His boner was placed perfectly so that I had to keep myself from grinding on it. God, I wanted to. So I did. He threw back his head and moaned. The strong tendons of his neck were so yummy I bent forward and bit into them. Mostly gentle.

He rocked against me.

"No, wait." He shook his head. "Not like this. Not here."

He was the picture of sexy. His eyes were hazy with desire. His lips were red and swollen from my kiss. He looked up at me like I was something to be desired.

Then his head seemed to clear as his words settled in. "You deserve so much more than this."

"Meh." I shrugged.

"No," he said foggily. "I'm sorry."

Reluctantly, I tucked my boob away and climbed off of him. He was probably right. People could walk up and I wouldn't want to traumatize a vacationing family. "Why can't I seem to control myself?" I asked myself out loud.

He looked up at me, his eyes burning. "I know why for me."

He got up on his knees and let out a long breath, arms akimbo at his sides. He looked up through his lashes, his head slightly bent. "I know we talked about going slow. Being professional. I'm just having a hard time remembering why at the moment."

"Me too," I said honestly. Then I shook my head. "That's part of the problem. Things go all haywire in my brain. Just now when you caught me … it's like the moment we touch I forget my priorities and I just want to smash my face against yours."

He chuckled. "Yeah. Same for me."

"Maybe we should wear those giant sumo suits, you know the kind for wrestling at parties, whenever we're around each other?" I suggested.

"You know, I'm weirdly into that. I don't think that would help."

I laughed, feeling at ease. He was so good at diffusing my embarrassment. He knew just what to say.

He was rubbing his chest with a pained expression.

"You okay?" I asked.

"Just a bit of heartburn," he said.

I scooted closer. "I have antacid back at the hotel."

His face scrunched. "I don't think that'll help."

We were kneeling face to face. Just a breath away. I wanted so badly to lean in and kiss him more.

He grabbed my hands and held them between us. "I want to be a person you can rely on, Roxy, truly. I'm not just saying that. I want you to think of me any time you have to work through a problem. I want to be a person you can call if you have a flat tire. I want you to trust me."

"I do," I whispered and realized I meant it wholeheartedly.

"So." He squeezed my hands. "If that means we have to leave all the physical stuff out of it, I'm willing to do that. If my attraction to you is complicating things, I can be better. I keep trying to be better."

"It's not just you." We needed to get through this week without our bodies getting in the way. We had a job to do and then he was leaving. "But you're right."

"I really hate being right," he said.

Our foreheads dropped to touch, our hands still clasped between us.

"We'll focus on this next week with MooreTek, so there's no worry or complications, and then ..."

"And then?" I couldn't help the eagerness in my voice.

"And then I'd like to take you on a date, Roxy Kincaid. A real date. Fancy restaurant, nice clothes. The whole shebang. We'll do this right."

"That sounds nice," I said.

Maybe I could manage this balancing act. Maybe I was enough.

CHAPTER 20

SANDERS

I skipped into the lobby with a smile on my face and a whistle on my lips. I stopped short when I discovered Skip pacing the lobby of the Lodge gnawing on his thumb. He'd clearly been waiting for me because the second he saw me, he walked to meet me.

"Skippo? What's up, mate?" I asked.

Skip pacing wasn't always an emergency, sometimes he just got caught up in his head a little too much and just needed me to talk him out of there. But it was never a great sign. He scratched at his hair.

"I've been trying to call," he said.

"I've been out showing Roxy the zip line. I told you I was going. I didn't have a missed call. Sorry, mate."

I led him to the couch where Roxy and I had held hands. I definitely wouldn't smile about that now but the reality of the progress we'd made settled fully on me. After this week, she was open to dating. She was into me. That fucking amazing kiss told me that and so much more. I daydreamed of a time where I'd be able to take her places and hold her hand it public. And what if we did decide to open a branch out here? I could live in the same city as her. We could see each other any time we wanted. What a gift that would be.

But I needed to focus on the here and now.

"Tell me what's going on," I said when we were settled.

He ran a hand through his hair. "Ford's Fosters wants to do a camping trip."

"Fantastic. How many kids?"

He shook his head like that wasn't important.

"Explain?" I asked calmly.

"They can only go this week," he said.

I understood immediately. "And did you tell Ford that it couldn't be this week because of a prior client?"

"He said that he understood but he was in a bind because the other volunteer vendor pulled out last minute and the kids were really looking forward to it. They had the buses reserved and everything. He said he knew it was a last-minute shot in the dark." Skip's leg was bouncing so much it shook the whole couch.

"Why don't you do the camping trip and I'll do the MooreTek event. Serendipity that you're here, then, hey?"

"I knew you were going to say that." His thumb immediately went back to his mouth to chew.

"What am I missing here, mate?" I gently pulled his hand from his mouth.

This happened a lot too. Re: the ten steps ahead. Skip sometimes forgot that the rest of us were still in the present while he mapped out every possible series of events like Dr. Strange.

"I talked to Ford today," he started. "I guess the company that cancelled heard that some of the kids had been in juvenile detention … which is just such bullshit. Kids like that need to experience the outdoors more than most. Statistics show that once a kid has—"

"It sounds like Ford needs help?"

He nodded. "I told him Outside the Box would help him."

"Which is great. You know I want to help. But since I am otherwise engaged, you agreed to help?"

He nodded.

"Okay, so tell me where things went south." I tried to meet his gaze but he wouldn't focus on me.

"Ford hadn't planned to go. He and Suzie are out of town for the week."

I let out a breath. "I understand. You don't want to take a bunch of kids you don't know into the forest. I totally understand. I'll talk to Roxy, there might be something else—"

He shook his head. "Jack is going. In Ford's place. He's—his friend Jack is going instead." He glanced at me and looked away.

Okay, this time I really understood. I remembered how Jack and Skip were at each other's throats. He didn't want to be trapped in the woods with him when they couldn't agree on anything.

"No worries, mate. You don't have to go. Like I said, I bet Roxy—"

"I want to go," he said. He looked at me and looked away. "It's just two nights."

"Okay. So what do you need from me?"

"Can you help me prepare? Maybe give me some topics to talk about?"

I kept my face serious. Was Skip worried about impressing Jack? Or did he not like him? Or maybe it was both. I needed to proceed with caution. "Of course. But you don't need me. Just show him what you know about camping. You can build a fire in seconds. That's *hot*."

His eyes went wide and I regretted my bad joke immediately.

"It's not like that," he growled. "No. I just don't know how to handle— you know, teenagers."

I was so late to this party, but this time I really understood. He was so comfortable around me that I sometimes forgot that his slight speech impediment made him feel self-conscious. He was great when he knew the topic but he got easily flustered when conversations went off script.

"Teenagers are easy, Skippo. Just treat them like people. That's all they want."

"I didn't understand them when I was one."

"Nobody feels comfortable in their skin as a teen. But you'll be great," I finished. "You show them how to start a fire or catch their own fish and they'll think you're a god. The past, the things that happened, they don't know any of that. You just walk in like you know shit and people will believe it. Plus, you have that sick beard. That instantly makes people believe anything you say."

He blushed. "I'll try. Maybe we can make flashcards before I go? So I don't get stuck on my words. I'd like to be better about the customer side of things."

"Of course. Whatever helps, mate. And if you need me at any point, I can leave and come get you. Okay?"

"Sounds good." He nodded and took in a full breath.

I put my arm around him. "I've got you, okay? We've got this. That's why we're partners."

He tensed under my arm but nodded.

"Also, we need to talk about OTB. Dev called and said he still hadn't talked to you. You said you were going to talk to the team."

My chest tightened and I frowned. I was feeling so good about Roxy and our kiss. I didn't want to think about this yet. I didn't want to feel the rainclouds building up behind me.

"I know, I just—"

My phone buzzed. I jumped on the distraction to see a notification of a voicemail. "That's weird. It didn't even ring." I slid the call log open. "Oh, it's from an hour ago."

My heart dropped. It was my dad's home. Or rather, his last home.

"Everything okay?" Skip asked.

"Of course." I smiled. "I've just gotta listen to this. We'll talk more in the morning. Make a whole game plan. Don't you worry, I won't leave you high and dry." I walked away as he opened his mouth to protest. I gave him a thumbs-up and he frowned. The world around me went silent as I listened to the message.

There was a shuffling sound and then the voice of the owner saying, "Hello, Mr. Olsson. This is Angelina Montoya from Sunrise Care Facility. I'm just calling to let you know that some of your father's belongings still haven't been picked up. I know this is an extremely difficult time but your father's room is needed for a new tenant. This is the third time I have called without hearing back from you. Please come pick up his things as soon as possible. Unfortunately, if I don't hear from you in the next week, we will have to move his things into storage at your cost. I'm so sorry for your loss, once again. Please call me back. Thank you."

Acid churned up in my throat instantly. I had been flying so high with Roxy and our plans for the future but this news brought me crashing back to earth. It reminded me that I had escaped an entire life back in Denver. I would have to go back and deal with it. I needed to be better for Roxy. I needed to be better for Skip and the team.

I barely made it to a back hallway before my smile fell off my face. The pain in my chest was so tight I couldn't catch my breath but I welcomed it. My dad had deserved so much more from me. I scrolled through my older voicemails, looking for one from a year ago when his condition had started to go downhill fast.

A second later my dad's voice came on.

"Sanders? Sanders, my boy? How's school? Taking it easy on those teachers, I hope?" His rich laugh rang in my ear. I closed my eyes tight against the pain. "Your mom says hi. We miss you, boy-o."

I was so glad I was nowhere near Skip because in that instant my face crumpled. I gripped the wall to keep from falling.

The message broke me the first time I heard it. I had been out with a client. When I came back into service, I had this message from him. He was already so lost by then. So confused. I couldn't bring myself to delete it. Now I listened to it as a reminder, like picking a scab off a wound to watch it bleed again.

The message ended with some shuffling. It was right before I put him in the home. I put a fist to my mouth and bit my finger so hard I thought the skin would break. I hoped it would. I'd give anything to take away from the pain in my heart. I'd break my own leg to distract myself.

Everything came crashing down around me at once. I came out here to help the business and to clean up my act. To prove to Skip that I could fix things. But what if that was all a flimsy facade to cover the fact that this entire trip was an act of complete selfishness? Wasn't I just running away? Always, unable to bear the real world. Look at the emotional turmoil I was putting Skip through. He'd travelled across states for me. He was putting himself so far outside his comfort zone. I caused this. He was on the verge of a breakdown again because of me.

And Roxy. What was I doing to her? She was trying to be better than her past all because I was pushing her to test her own boundaries. I was no good for anybody. I was selfish. I kicked the wall, relishing in the sharp pain in my toes.

I wanted to be better. I would protect those I cared about, even if it meant space from me. A storm was brewing outside but I would avoid the bridge this time. Hiking a trail was better than jumping out of a plane, right? I needed to just get away and figure out how to make everything right.

* * *

Roxy

I WENT BACK to my office in the Lodge after I dropped off Sanders to pick up a few things before I left for the night. I had a missed call on my cell from my mom. Was it already time for our monthly check-in? The back of my neck tingled with familiar daughter guilt as I debated returning her call. I let out a sigh and braced myself.

"Hey, Mama," I said when she answered. I let go a slow breath out the opposite side of my mouth away from the mouthpiece.

"My baby," her richly accented voice cooed. "How you doin', sugar?"

"I'm fine. How are you and Daddy?"

"Oh we're lovely. Just sitting out here listening to the crickets, thinking about you. Life is as good as it could get."

"I'm glad to hear it." I grabbed the pen and flicked it repeatedly against the desk.

Reminding myself that it could be much worse. Suzie and her father still struggled with his sloppy, embarrassing shows of alcoholism. His constant begging for money. Well, before. It did seem like going to AA was helping. But my mama and daddy were what I called quiet alcoholics or functioning alcoholics. They went to work, they paid their bills, and they never had the cops called on them. However, they rarely left the house and went through a couple handles of vodka every week. Still it could be worse.

"How's your man?" Mama asked, her voice was slurred which meant that they must have been at it a while already.

At this rate they wouldn't have livers by the time they turned sixty. But knowing them, they'd be alive until a hundred drinking vodka and Diet Pepsi every night just to prove everyone wrong. I pinched the area between my eyebrows.

It'd been over four years since I left the Wraiths and even longer since I was with Jethro. But that was when I'd sometimes go over and drink with them. I knew they loved it when they didn't drink alone.

"I'm not seeing anybody right now," I said.

Though for some reason a wild image popped into my head. Bringing Sanders around and brandishing him like a trophy. *See, Mom, he likes me.* I mentally shook away the unwanted thought.

"Oh, honey, but you're so pretty. Don't you worry, you'll find a man."

I used to say I don't need a man, now I didn't bother. She wouldn't remember this conversation anyway.

"Thanks, Mama."

"Why don't you pick up some vodka and come over. Just like the good ol' days. We miss you," she said.

I sucked my teeth. "Can't tonight."

"My beautiful, beautiful girl." She sniffed softly. Wow, she was all the way to maudlin. They must have started at noon. "You've grown up so fast. Your brother too. He never talks. Always too busy. We did our best, you know. We loved you as best we could. Our parents were never around. Grandpa used to leave the bar and—"

"It's okay, I know. And Rick is busy but he loves you," I lied through my teeth. I never talked to my brother, Rick. The last time we spoke, he said he couldn't care less what happened to our parents. Last I heard

THE ONE THAT I WANT

he ran with a different MC. It was hard not to think about his choices and feel like I wasn't meant for much more.

"He does? Did he say that?" Mama asked.

"Yeah, he did." I closed my eyes.

I knew they wouldn't remember anything from our conversation. I don't know why I tried or cared … and yet.

"I'm getting another promotion. At work." The words slipped out. My heart hammered in anticipation.

"A promotion! Good for you, honey," my mom said louder, probably leaning toward my father so he could hear.

Despite myself I sat up straighter.

"A promotion?" I heard my dad's deep, Southern drawl ask through the line. "What, now she's a dancer too? Not just a bartender?"

His laugh crackled through, wet and too long. He kept laughing even though there was no joke. His words shut down the small sliver of excitement I'd been feeling about sharing my news.

I slumped. "I don't work at the Dragon Bar anymore," I mumbled knowing she couldn't hear me over his raucous laugh. It wasn't even a strip club. It didn't matter. None of this mattered. I was doing fine on my own. I was going to be more than this.

"You shush. Be happy for your baby," my mom whispered but still loud enough to hear.

He belched.

I dug my nails into the palms of my hand. I could have been the president and they wouldn't remember. I told myself it didn't matter. I had people who cared. Though, currently I wasn't talking to some of them. My good mood officially evaporated.

"I gotta go," I said. "Have a good night."

"Oh already? Okay, sugar, you have a good night. We love you. Tell your man we said hi. Love you, baby girl."

"Love you." I could hardly get the words out for the tightness in my throat.

I hung up the phone and stared into space past my desk. No matter how I told myself it didn't matter, these conversations always hurt.

I felt so alone. I could call Gretchen. I missed her. She'd give me the reminder I needed. *Friends are family you chose.* But I couldn't bring myself to call. I felt too much … shame? Maybe kissing Sanders meant she was right all along. But that didn't excuse how she went about it.

I still needed more time. With a shake of my head, I grabbed my purse and phone and locked up my office. I stood outside the Lodge, doubting myself for the longest time. Debating what to do and where to go.

Then a man strode past me. So determined on his mission that he didn't even see me standing there. He was walking toward the forest.

Sometimes, people did need each other. Sometimes a person comes into your life for a reason. And then I knew what I had to do. Maybe I wanted to be done just existing. Maybe I wanted more. Even if it was temporary.

CHAPTER 21

SANDERS

I was just heading into the forest when my phone rang. If it wasn't for my residual guilt from earlier, I would have ignored it. When I saw who it was, I answered immediately.

"Roxy?"

"Hey." Her voice sounded shaky. "Remember when you said I could call if I ever needed to talk?"

"Where are you?" I stopped and turned on a heel to head back to the Lodge.

"Right here."

As she spoke, I heard her voice outside and on the phone. A shape stepped out of the shadow. We both hung up and walked toward each other, meeting halfway. I fought to reach out and scoop her into my arms.

"It's going to rain," she said with a frown. The heavy storm clouds blocked the setting sun, giving the impression it was much later. The wind kicked up and she rubbed her arms up and down. I shrugged out of my coat and gave it to her. "Thanks." It was too big for her but the sight of her in my coat warmed me up.

"Are you okay?" I asked.

She squinted into the horizon. "I don't think so. Are you?"

Fuck it. I stepped closer and pulled her into me for a hug. I wrapped my arms tight around her as she rested her head on my chest. Fuck the rules. If Skip was crying, I'd hug him too. When you see someone in pain, you help them. The soothing went both ways. The second she was in my arms, some of the pain in my chest released.

"No," I whispered.

Maybe I didn't need to throw myself into another pointless risk tonight. What would that solve anyway? At least with Roxy in my arms, I could try to fix some of the hurt I'd put there. I could make a little difference. And in return I would be honest. I knew Roxy, better than I should at this point, and whatever it had taken for her to call me had not been small.

"I was feeling all alone," she admitted.

"I was about to go rock climbing in the dark."

She didn't respond, just made this soft, sad little noise and wrapped her arms tighter around my middle and squeezed.

"I guess when I say it out loud, it sounds pretty silly," I said.

"How about tonight we keep each other from doing something we know is stupid?"

"Deal," I whispered.

I would try so hard to keep that promise. But talk about jumping out of the frying pan into the fire. I couldn't be around her and not want to do something stupid. Being around Roxy defaulted my brain to factory settings. Protect. Love. Hold.

"I have an idea," she said against my chest.

Ten minutes later, we pulled up to an elementary school.

"I'm pretty open-minded, but if I listed ten places I'd expected to go tonight, I wouldn't have even come close," I said.

"Trust me."

We walked through a large parking lot where a couple of buses were parked. It had grown dark but a few surrounding streetlights shone on the playground where we headed.

"If you wanted a playground, all you have to do is visit Outside the Box ... it's basically this but adult sized."

"Well, this is just a little closer, don't you think? Also, it's mostly cement, so the mosquitoes aren't as bad."

"Mozzies. Evil bastards." I swatted at my neck just thinking about them.

"Swing or spin?" she asked.

"Let's start with the swings."

That way if she felt like sharing, we wouldn't be facing each other. I found that Skip was more likely to open up that way.

"As teenagers we would come here, Gretchen and I, when things were shitty or we were bored. She'd stay with me when my parents forgot to pick me up." Her voice cracked. "I smoked my first cigarette over there when I was eleven." She pointed to a tunnel on the jungle gym. "We hid in there and thought we were so cool."

"When I was eleven, my dad was taking me on camping trips," I said not sure why. "Do you miss Gretchen?" I asked hoping to keep her as the topic of conversation.

She looked sad and distant. "Yeah. I'm remembering some of the things she did to distract me when my parents forgot about me."

215

"She's a good friend?"

"She is." Roxy slowed her swing and drifted back and forth. "I pushed her away when I should have just talked to her."

"It's a defense mechanism."

"I'm a walking defense mechanism."

"Can you call her?" I asked.

"I almost did. Still working through things."

"Is that what's got you down tonight?" I slowed my swing to move in tandem with her.

"No. I just talked to my parents and that always sets me off."

"I understand," I said honestly.

"I'm sorry. You just lost your dad. I shouldn't complain."

"You can be frustrated with your parents even though mine are dead. Want to talk about it?"

She glanced over at me. "There's not much to say. They don't know me. They never have. They liked me best when I brought booze from the bar and partied with them. Now, we're mostly strangers."

"It's hard when we realize our parents are just people."

She made a hum of agreement. "So why were you about to go hiking in the dark with another storm blowing in?"

As though hearing her question, the wind picked up and blew her fringe and hair all around her.

"Ah, no reason," I said.

"Hey." She kicked my foot. "I showed you mine," she said with a teasing smile.

I grabbed her feet with mine and gripped her so we faced each other, rocking a little. I couldn't meet her eyes though.

"Honestly, nothing happened. Not sure why I got so down. Skip was just telling me about this camping trip with Ford and then my dad's home called. I need to go get his stuff from the care facility."

"I'm sorry. That must be so hard."

I rubbed my chest. Above us, heavy gray shapes covered the stars.

"I'm just happy he's at peace now," I said. It was my canned answer. She must have sensed that.

"How are you really feeling?"

"I'm fine." I smiled and released her legs to face away. She didn't let me. She looped her legs around my thighs, bringing us closer.

The heat, as always, was there in an instant.

"Roxy, I don't want to talk about this. It's too ..."

Hard? Depressing? Pointless?

"Who do you talk to about it?" she asked ignoring me.

I rubbed the heartburn from my esophagus.

"I don't have anything to say. It won't change anything." My skin started to itch. Even feeling the weight of her legs on me wasn't distracting enough.

"It might help you process." Her legs tightened, not letting me move even an inch. I was being held captive and any other time I would have loved it but I didn't want to talk about this.

"I'm fine," I said.

"You keep saying that."

"Because I *am* fine. Why don't you or Skip seem to understand that? I'm glad he's not suffering anymore," I said feeling my voice rise despite my attempt to be cool.

"You can be upset. Nobody would blame you. You can feel what you feel."

The words were too close to the truth I clung to desperately. I couldn't do this anymore. I couldn't feel her body on mine. I couldn't talk about my dad for a second more. I couldn't sit here feeling like my chest was being pried open and she was gripping my heart in her hands.

I broke out from her grip and stood up.

"Sanders!" she said affronted.

"Roxy, I don't want to do this."

"That's bullshit!" she yelled and I stopped in my retreat and turned back to her.

"What?" I asked feeling sad and defeated.

"You pushed and pushed me. I opened up about things in my past I never wanted to share. I shared with you, Sanders. And you can't do the same for me? You can't let me help you?"

"There's nothing to help. I'm fine," I said, tossing out my arms. "I've had a charmed life. I've got nothing to complain about."

"That's bullshit. You can't even look at me."

"There's nothing to talk about. As far as I'm concerned, I'm glad my father is dead!"

Her face went blank. As soon as I said the words, a crushing wave of guilt crashed over me. I had felt that way for so long but to say it out loud made me feel like the lowest level of scum. I shook my head, furious at her. At myself. She pushed me too far. She couldn't relent.

"Fuck!" I yelled. "Why couldn't you just listen to me when I said I didn't want to talk about it."

The pain in my chest was so acute I had to stop talking and focus on my breathing. I stopped and bent forward and dropped my hands to my knees, half bent over.

She stepped closer until I could see her shoes in front of me. "I'm sorry," she said softly. "I know how you meant it."

It was too late though. I'd said it. I put it out there like an absolute piece of shit.

* * *

Roxy

SANDERS WAS HALF CRUMPLED in front of me. I had pushed him too far and I regretted hurting him.

"I'm sorry," I said again.

When I put my hand on his shoulder, he turned his head and shrugged me off. I withdrew my arm and balled my fist. I stepped back.

He mumbled something I couldn't understand. I dropped to my knees to see his face. "What?" I asked.

His eyes were shining and red-rimmed. "I'm fucking awful," he said.

"No. You are not," I said emphatically.

"I am." He dropped to his knees too and we faced each other, kneeling on the squishy plastic flooring of the playground. "I just said I was glad my father is dead."

"Explain what you mean," I said.

He bit his lip and looked up at the heavy clouds. "It was awful at the end. He was gone. All that was left was just this sad shape of a man that used to be my father." He glared at his clenched fists. "There were many years where he was still mostly lucid. There'd only be flashes where he'd get confused and angry. Paranoid. He'd go missing and a neighbor would find him wandering down the street."

He took a break to swallow. My own throat tightened in sadness.

"I can't imagine how hard that must have been for you," I said softly but his gaze was distant in memory.

"But at least there were times when he was still there. But at the end. That wasn't him at all. I just wanted him to be at peace. I wanted him to go be with Mom and stop suffering." His lip trembled and he took another breath. "He's gone. The man who raised me will never ... and I hate that I feel relieved."

I held his hands in mine and he let me. "You're not awful. I think most people would feel that way."

He stood up and paced. "I don't want to. Shouldn't I be grateful for the time that we had? Even at the end. Even when it was hard. I should have been there every moment holding his hand."

"You can love your father and be angry. You can feel sad and be thankful. You're a living, breathing person. Nobody expects you to be happy all the time."

"They don't?" he snapped. "Because isn't that who I'm supposed to be? Isn't that what people want from me? The 'good time' guy. The guy that makes choices and moves forward."

"I hardly think if you asked Skip what he liked most about you, it would have anything to do with you being happy all the time. People love you for you, not what you do for them. Isn't that what you told me?"

That stilled him.

"I'm just tired of feeling like this." He rubbed his chest one time with a fist. "This constant pain. I don't fucking want this. He would have been okay. He would've taken it in stride and handled it like a man."

"Your dad?" I asked.

"When my mom died, he kept it all together. He knew how to take care of me and be strong."

"I'm sure he struggled," I said desperate to soothe him. He was so hurt and fragile. This big, confident man so full of life was just as alone as the rest of us. My heart ached for him.

I stayed kneeling looking up at him as he walked in circles.

"You should be mad," I said.

He stilled and looked at me. "No. Anger is for the weak. Anger is a young man's emotion. For toddlers. That's what he would say."

"Emotions make you human," I said.

"They make me a coward. They make me run." He stopped and took me in. I saw myself in his eyes, kneeling in front of him, eyes wide, mouth open in wonder. "You have no idea how fucking weak I am. If you had any idea …" He tore his gaze away from me and paced.

"You can be angry." I threw out my arms. "Just be mad. Feel it. Accept it. It doesn't have to consume you. You can acknowledge it without letting it define you."

He shook his head.

"Be mad, Sanders. Feel it."

"At who?" he asked.

"The world. God. The universe. Me. Your dad. The situation. The air you breathe. It doesn't matter. You can be angry. And then you can move on. Take it in like a breath and then let it go. It's horrible and it is so not fair."

"I am angry. I'm so fucking angry." He kicked the swing but it must have not satisfied him enough.

He kicked the ground but the foam flooring just absorbed the impact. He punched the air. Finally, he went to the trees a few feet away and picked up a large branch. I wouldn't even be able to lift it above my head and yet he swung it around, flourishing it like a sword. His arms flexed in strength. He smacked it against the swing set, the metal rang out in response. The muscles of his back and shoulders pushed and pulled with the effort. He swung it again and again like a blacksmith shaping a sword.

He looked like a man finding truth. As though he was trying to cleanse himself. Breaking free of the invisible chains that had been holding him to the earth. If wings sprouted from his back and lifted him into the air, I wouldn't have been surprised.

When he finally stopped, his shoulders were hunched as he heaved in ragged breaths. Turning back to me, he dropped to the ground where I still knelt, pulling me into his lap and burying his head in my chest. I held him tight to me.

"It's not fair that you lost them both," I said.

"It's not fair. It's bullshit. He was everything to me. After my mom died, it was just me and him. And Skip," he said with a sad laugh.

"Tell me about him," I said.

"He had such a presence. Everybody loved him."

"Sounds familiar," I teased and I felt him smile against my chest.

"He was everything I wanted to be."

"He sounds amazing." I ran my fingers through Sanders' hair.

"He was. Fuck." He nuzzled deeper into me with a shuddering sigh.

"I know," I said.

He wrapped his arms around me and squeezed me closer. I had to wrap my legs around his waist to let him get as close as he needed.

He gasped as though he couldn't fight back the pain. "To go out like that …" His voice broke off again.

"He's still the same man he always was. How you and Skip remember him. That's who he is."

He nodded against me.

"Sometimes I think …"

"What?" I prompted.

"I sometimes think that it would be better to go off in some tragic accident than how he went. Or from suffering from cancer like my mom went."

I held still. I had wondered what caused his reckless behavior. I wondered how a man so confident and put together would go and do these things so clearly set on hurting himself. It made sense now. My poor, sweet man.

"Fuck. You're probably thinking how awful I am," he said when I didn't respond right away.

"I was thinking about how amazing you are." I grabbed his face and pulled it up until he could see how seriousness I was. I held his gaze and let the words flow out of me. "I was thinking how you've dealt with so much sadness, so much tragedy and you still treat everyone you meet like they're special. You make people feel wonderful just by giving them eye contact. I was thinking that your dad must have been the most amazing father to have raised a son who is as wonderful as you are."

His mouth crushed against mine. There was no hesitation. His tongue explored my mouth which opened as soon as he touched me. We kissed with the abandon we felt that first night in Denver. Every ounce of angst and pain were transformed in a minute to pure burning lust.

He pulled back, still holding my face. His eyes shifted back and forth between mine, full of something I'd never seen. "Roxy, I—"

Just then the sky opened with a crack of thunder and lightning so close it made my hair rise.

I yelled as the first drops of rain landed on our heads. Within moments the rain was pouring down in buckets.

"Oh, come on!" Sanders yelled over the crashing rain and another clap of thunder. Water was already collecting around him. His arms were spread out and he pretended to backstroke.

Water poured over me, making me shiver. "Let's go. This is dangerous!"

"The rain out here hates me," he yelled. He swung out his arms and legs like making a snow angel, splashing water in small waves over my ankles.

"Sanders!"

I watched him and realized he was laughing. It was like the rain was cleansing him. This man who had locked away so much was being reborn. He was beautiful and brave and he had my heart completely.

CHAPTER 22

SANDERS

*R*oxy tugged at my hands, slipping as she tried to grip them. "Get up," she shouted over the rain.

I groaned and rolled to standing, arms spread out, face toward the sky. The rain washed over me. I closed my eyes and felt every drop. Heard the sound of it slapping the ground around me. Smelled the dirt growing wet. I was alive.

Thunder cracked and I ducked. I intended to stay that way for a while.

"Come on!" Roxy yelled.

I let her pull me in a run back to her car. I didn't mind the rain. Wait, scratch that, I was starting to think Green Valley's weather was the ultimate cockblock. But the rain had cleansed me. I felt changed. I felt whole and more like myself than I had in years.

I never intended to share any of that with Roxy. But she pulled it from me. I was in awe of her for knowing exactly what I needed. Could it be possible that I could feel this way and it didn't make me a terrible person? Out loud, it sounded so obvious and ridiculous. But when it's only a dark thought in your head for so many years, it's hard to trust yourself. I thought I had to be something more than I was. But maybe I could just feel what I feel and it didn't make me a bad person.

She opened the back door of her little car and gestured me in. She dove in after me and closed it behind her.

I smiled at her, water dripped off her nose and had plastered down her hair. Under my flimsy coat, her thin T-shirt was soaked through, so her hard nipples were visible through the material. But it was her face that held my attention. She was smiling at me like I was something special.

"Hang on," she said, reaching over me to grab the bag on the floor by my feet. "I have some extra clothes in here in case I go to Stripped—"

"Go where now?"

"—and I think there's a towel ... here it is." She handed me one end of a large purple towel. It was fluffy and soft, and when I buried my face in it, it smelled as good as she did. I couldn't wait to spend a weekend between the sheets of her bed, knowing that they'd smell just like this.

"What sort of fabric softener is this?" I mumbled as I wiped my face.

"What?" she asked with a laugh, lowering the towel from my face. "You mumble a lot."

"I do no such thing."

Slightly dryer, we sat still, taking each other in. We had changed together. We had crossed a river and there was no going back. The bridge was flooded. She was where I needed to be.

She shivered. "Hang on. Again." She leaned forward to the front seat. Her wet jean shorts gave me a spectacular view of her thighs dripping with water and covered in goose bumps.

The car rumbled on and a blast of heat moved through the small space. An acoustic guitar strummed as a rich, deep voice sang quietly of orange skies and love. It was loud enough to be heard over the rain but soft enough to change the atmosphere inside the car from playful to romantic in an instant.

As she sat back, I grabbed her hips and pulled her onto my lap. She didn't shrink back. She didn't even blink. Her gaze went hazy as she studied me. She pushed her fingers through my hair and off my face. Her tongue slowly wet her lips.

I wrapped my fingers around her neck and into her wet hair, lowering her mouth to mine. She opened to me and her tongue slid in my mouth. I loved her tenacity. It might be one of my favorite things about her. I squeezed my eyes closed as relief washed over me. I would take whatever she would give me but I wanted it all.

We luxuriated in the taste of each other, taking turns to nip and suck and memorize. She shuddered in my arms. I ran my hand down an arm covered in goose bumps.

"You're wet," I said.

She raised an eyebrow. "Presumptuous."

"Take off your shirt," I demanded.

Her smile faded into a sultry pout. She sucked on a lip and kept her gaze locked on mine as she crossed her arms to pull the hem of her shirt up and off her head. It felt like the biggest test of will.

Will you hold my gaze when what you really want to see is inches below?

No sweat, I replied.

You just looked.

Shit.

I lifted a hand to fix her fringe as she always seemed very concerned it was in the right place. She smiled and nestled into my hand. My heart hammered in my chest. I held her against me. Her skin was damp and cool. I wrapped the towel around her, trapping the heat in until the car warmed and her shivering subsided. She was as content to luxuriate in this gift as I was. I kissed the top of her head and traced the art on her exposed shoulder with my hand.

"What's the story with this one?" I whispered. "You told me that you would show them all. If ever there was a time ..."

She hid her face into my chest.

"Are you ashamed of them?" I asked.

She pulled back and gave me a look of defiance. "No. I'm not."

I followed the line from her shoulder, down her arm, past her exposed, perfect breast and to her rib cage. I preened watching the skin prickle and hearing her soft sigh.

"I think they're beautiful. I love that they're a part of you. Everything about you is beautiful."

"You can't say stuff like that," she whispered, arching her back as I teased her. I grasped her lightly, gentle teasing as I weighed her breast and ran a thumb over the pebbled nipple.

"Why?" I asked before lowering to flick her with my tongue.

"Because when you talk like that, I forget that I can't be falling in love with you."

Roxy

SANDERS HELD me close in the small space of my car. I was falling for him. But I wouldn't worry about that now. I would only be here now.

"Roxy," he whispered and nuzzled my chest. He cupped my breast and sucked on me, sending fire through me. I threw my head back and luxuriated in this moment. No worrying about the future. Take his advice and just breathe. Feel him. Feel this moment and stop worrying so damn much.

"I'm not sure why you would ever hide these. They're beautiful."

"I want to say thank you but I didn't do them."

"Your breasts? You kind of did."

I threw my head back and laughed. "I thought you meant my tattoos."

He winked. "I did. But in this case, it's the medium that makes the art." He licked a flower stem that climbed up my rib cage.

My pulse hammered at my throat. To be completely exposed. To have him see every inch. I was equal parts terrified and aroused. Could he feel that?

"I don't know. I just associate them with a totally different life."

His hand went to my chest. He had to feel how my heart pounded against his palm. He had to. "This person," he said. "Dressed up. Dressed down. Young … old." He swallowed. My blush grew. "Nothing else matters but this. Who you are. It's you I—"

I kissed him. I wanted to hear the words but we weren't ready. It was too soon.

We finally stopped to breathe. Panting in the soft music.

"This one?" he asked.

His finger gently touched the edge of a tattoo that started at my throat just above my collarbone. Most shirts covered it. But totally exposed like this, he saw it all.

"That was a long session. Five hours. I barely made it."

"Jesus. Your pain threshold is insane."

He had no idea. "It only really smarts at the end. Most of the time I can play on my phone through them. One time I started falling asleep. I find the sounds soothing."

"Insane." He leaned closer looking over every detail. A soft puff of his breath tickled the hair at my neck.

His hands moved all over my body. When he reached the ones on my hips, he tugged my shorts down.

"They're beautiful. All of them."

"It's no butterfly tattoo," I teased.

I was sprawled out on the seat, completely naked in front of him.

"You're the most wonderful thing I have ever seen."

I felt so vulnerable lying there in front of him. He was completely dressed and I was in a position I once promised myself I would never be in, and I was okay. I was more than okay. I was terribly aroused and happy.

And then it got worse. Better?

He began to slowly explore my entire body. His face following his finger, hot breaths caressing all over my skin. Every touch was agony and ecstasy. When I was near the brink of orgasm just by his touch alone, when he lay on top of me. Our bodies folded to fit in the car. The scratch of his clothes against my exposed flesh was almost too much. I felt wicked and sexy. I loved every second of it.

He swallowed with effort. "I love this."

"Me too," I said.

I was so lost in the moment I couldn't stop him if I tried. His fingers explored me more. Goose bumps rose in his wake. He lowered his head and blew on my nipple.

It pulled tight, almost painful, with the desire for more contact.

I looked down to find him studying my body's reaction to his touch. I let out a long breath and looked up to the roof. I would let myself have this.

"So sexy." He moved to my hip to examine another flower that wrapped around my waist. "So responsive."

He kissed lower and lower. Neck to collarbone to breast. Then rib cage and belly. He reached the point where my hips arched off the seat, closer to his mouth. His mouth was on me in that instant. Licking, sucking, coaxing toward a peak I was desperate to reach.

He paused to kiss my inner thighs and the sensitive skin all around. Delaying the inevitable climax I was so close to.

"I'm crazy about you, Roxy. I'm crazy about every single inch of you. I'm dying to explore it all. Every glimpse feels like a gift. I'm devoted to you. I'm hopeless. You've made me this way."

"Sanders."

He lowered again and my hands gripped his head as he worked. Ever the gentleman. Licking and sucking as a finger slid in and curved just enough to have me arching up again.

My hands gripped tighter, he groaned a pleased sound and worked with more intention. I felt sexy and in control even though I was the naked one writhing against the mouth of this man. I couldn't sit still as he brought me closer and closer to the edge. My body tried to crawl back, the sensations were too much. He matched me inch for inch until he was kneeling between the seats.

As the orgasm took over, my arms flung out, and I rode the wave grinding on his face as he slowed and eventually withdrew.

Sanders sat up, licked his lips, and grinned at me. It was the cockiest of all his cocky grins. "Good?" he asked.

I rolled my eyes before grabbing his shirt and pulling him in for a kiss.

"Sanders, let's go back to my place," I said, holding his gaze.

His smile waned a little. "We don't have to. This was enough for me—"

"Sanders, I don't want to wait anymore. We've wasted enough time. Take me home."

He swallowed. "Okay."

I grabbed the extra shirt and workout pants from the gym bag and slid into them, sans underwear. As I climbed into the front seat, his hand smoothed over my bottom. A second later I felt a gentle bite on the meatiest part.

I squealed and fell forward.

"Sorry. I could only take so much," he said.

"Feel better?" I called over my shoulder.

"A little."

When he'd climbed to the front seat, I asked, "Ready?"

He swallowed and nodded. "You have no idea."

CHAPTER 23

SANDERS

*R*oxy drove us back to her apartment in what might be the longest car ride in the history of humankind. I wanted her. I was so tense it felt palpable in the air. I didn't want to be a regret to her. I didn't want her to hate me later. I wanted ... everything from her.

Then her hand crossed over the shifter to reach for mine. I grabbed it immediately and squeezed, rubbing my thumb over the back of hers.

"Sanders?" she asked as she put the car into park. "Is there something on your mind?"

"A thousand things," I answered honestly.

I wasn't the one to overthink. I was the one to jump in and run and run until I couldn't catch my breath. I didn't want to be like that anymore. I wouldn't screw this up.

"Do you want to come up still?" she asked.

"More than anything," I said. She turned to face me. "I just don't want to be a regret. I would rather have only a taste of you and nothing more for the rest of my life than have you look at me with regret."

"I want this. I trust you," she said simply. "And finally I trust myself to know what I want."

I leaned forward and kissed her deeply, anchoring her to me with a hand behind her head, so afraid to let go.

When we pulled apart a few minutes later, she blinked up at me with heavy eyes.

"Let's go up," I said.

She grinned at my demand, heat flaring behind her dark eyes. She wanted this. I had always wanted this. Now we were on the same page. I had been given a chance to show her all that I felt for her and I wasn't going to waste it.

It took a lifetime to climb the stairs to her place. It took a millennium for her to get the door open. The moment the door closed and dead bolted, she was on me. I smiled against her mouth.

"Hello," I mumbled against her in between breaths.

"Hi," she said.

"What do you need, Roxy?" I asked.

I wanted to make her happier than I'd ever made anyone. I was dying to be inside her. My body shook with the barely restrained desire coursing through my blood.

"Just you," she said.

She took me by the hand and led me down a short hall. The walls were probably covered with pictures. There were probably rooms with furniture. I didn't give a shit about any of it. I only saw Roxy as she glanced at me over her shoulder and led me to her bedroom.

I was the most important man in the world. I had to be, to deserve her. I wanted her to feel as cherished as she deserved, as perfect as she was in my eyes. No, not perfect, fully human and multifaceted and strong and beautiful. Better than perfection in her reality.

I would take my time with her. I would make her come over and over after hours of foreplay, worshiping every inch of her body as she was meant to be.

"Sanders?" I blinked up to find her sprawled out on the bed and beckoning. "Take off your pants and get over here."

That worked too.

I pulled off my shirt and pants and tossed them on to a chair in the corner.

She still wore the clothes from the car, and I intended to pull them off her like a candy wrapper. I couldn't wait to run my hands up her long legs. Her chest heaved, nipples hardening in the cool room. I was about to finish undressing when I caught her molten gaze as it took in my body. Her brown eyes darkened with desire as a tongue flicked out to lick her full lips.

"How are you so hot?" she asked.

"Funny. That's exactly what I was thinking."

I dropped my drawers. I was rock hard and jutted out proudly. I ran a hand down myself, used my thumb to wipe the pearl of moisture over the tip as she watched me. I almost came right then.

"Perfect," she said.

"Hardly. But I'm yours and that's all that matters."

Her lashes fluttered.

"And don't tell me I can't say things like that," I added. "Because I can say what I want here. I can tell you you are the most beautiful woman in every room. You're funny and clever even when you're trying to be cranky. You're amazing," I said as I walked to her. My words were in sweet opposition to the rough strokes on my cock.

Her gaze flicked between my face and the action of my palm. She crawled on her knees to meet me when I arrived at her bed. Her hand reached out to meet my cock. I hissed as she stroked me once. I was already too close. I held her wrist, stopping her.

"Turn around," I said.

She hesitated only a moment. Heat narrowed her eyes as she licked her lips. She liked being told what to do. In this safe space with only our mutual respect and desire, I could push her boundaries and tease her. Tell her what I wanted her to do and she would like it.

"Lift your arms," I said.

Slowly, she did as she was told. She complied with my demand but on her terms. I growled as I grabbed the hem of her shirt and lifted it off her. I gently brought her arms back down, pushing her long brown hair, thick and straight, off her shoulders. Her shoulders were tight with tension but she melted into me as I massaged them.

"That's nice," she said softly.

I rubbed my thumbs in circles down her back, focusing on the strong muscles of her spine until I reached the sweet little dimples just above her pants.

"Stand up," I said.

Her cheeks were flushed as she stood, glancing over her shoulder at me. I knelt behind her, slowly pushing down her bottoms as I went. She wore no underwear and all her beauty was revealed to me.

"Bend over," I said.

She leaned on to the bed as I ran my hands up her calves, the backs of her thighs. I took my time rubbing each tense muscle, exploring each piece of art up close. I wanted her as worked up as I was. I wanted her close to bursting. I dug my thumbs deep into the muscles of her glorious bottom. She moaned.

She was so beautiful.

"Sanders," she gasped out my name as I licked up her once, just a tease. She was so wet for me. My skin felt too small. My balls were so high and tight, my cock rock hard and ready to take her.

I stood up too fast, almost dizzy, and gently walked her back to kneel on the bed, still facing away from me.

I memorized the shape of her back as it curved into her waist and out to her ass, like a smooth, stringed instrument. I greedily took in the canvas of her body, memorizing the art. I stepped until there was no space between us, and gently pushed her hair over one shoulder. I kissed her shoulder and neck as my cock pressed between the cheeks of her ass. My fingers explored under her, tracing across her chest, watching the bumps form in my wake. I cupped her breasts, gently pinching her nipples, causing her to gasp. My hands ran down her stomach.

"Remember the night that I met you?" I asked, bringing her to my chest so I could whisper it in her ear.

"Hmm, no. Should I?" she said.

I gently slapped her bottom before rubbing it. She turned to look at me, fire in her eyes. Our mouths clashed.

When we broke apart, I said, "I wanted you so bad that night."

"Me too," she said. Her hands came up to gently scratch at my arms that held her.

"I could have waited longer, you know. I could wait forever for you."

She kissed me softly. "We've wasted enough time. Let's just be here, now."

I lifted a hand to her forehead. "Are you okay?"

She grabbed my palm and kissed it softly. "I'm following the advice of some crazy guy." She shrugged.

A sneaky grin spread on her lips. Her arm reached back between us and found me.

I hissed a breath and thrust into her gentle grip. She started slow, a thumb brushed over my tip, and then she stroked down the length. The action pushed her breasts forward as she arching away from me. I was wrong earlier, *this* was perfection.

She stroked faster despite the angle. I was too close to coming. If she touched me anymore, I was going to end the night way too soon.

I grabbed her wrists and gripped them both in my left hand, holding them behind her back. She squirmed and groaned. Her back arched even more. I ran my free hand up her whole body, starting at her knees and ending with a thumb dragging across her lips, dipping it into her mouth. She sucked it in deeper. I groaned and my hips thrust forward.

"What am I going to do with you?" I asked, taking out my thumb and gently turning her head to me.

"Everything," she said.

I continued my exploration of her as I stood behind her. With every stroke and kiss, she melted against me and I held her up. Sweat collected everywhere our bodies met. I positioned myself so I was pumping between her closed legs, a temporary substitute for the real thing. I dipped my fingers into her, felt her want for me. Let her feel mine for her. I teased her until she was flushed and panting, begging me.

I watched her closely as she came apart again for me. She was heart-achingly beautiful.

"Lie down," I whispered in her ear as I gentled my touch, pulling my fingers out of her pulsating body.

She moaned an acknowledgement and rolled onto her back, spread out in the most beautiful offering I'd ever seen. I was afraid of coming as I rolled on the condom. Especially as she watched me with fire in her eyes.

This time she beckoned me with a finger. I moved to cover her and slicked myself with her moisture as we kissed deeply.

When I finally slid into her, it was so easy, we both gasped. Her muscles gripped me and I had to stop moving to breathe in through my nose. Her nails scratched lazily up my back. She kissed my neck and shoulder as I counted my breaths.

This was what everything led to. This was what life was about. This was a miracle.

"I just decided," I said. "I don't think we can be just friends."

She threw her head back and laughed. I felt it through her whole body.

"Friends are overrated," she said.

* * *

Roxy

I SIGHED with a happy smile on my face. I would never look at the ceiling of my bedroom the same way again. Every time I looked up, I would think of this night. After the second round, we both lay on our backs panting. Our legs spread and tossed over each other, sliding with satisfying sweat. Soon I would get cold but right now I glowed with contented warmth.

"I can't move," I said.

"Moving is dumb."

I laughed and reluctantly got off him to go clean up.

When I came back to bed, he'd cleaned up too and flung back the blankets to let me in. I dove, snuggling up against his naked body. I didn't realize how cold I was until the heat of naked skin seared me back to warmth.

"Get closer," he demanded. "I need to touch as much of you as possible." His hands roamed me as I cuddled closer to him with a sigh.

My head rested on his chest. His heart still beat loudly at a quick tempo. I didn't need to see his face to know he was grinning.

"Why are you smiling?" I asked.

"I think my face is frozen like this now."

"Well, lucky for you, it suits you."

"You think I'm pretty," he said.

I laughed into his sparse chest hair. I bit his nipple gently to make up for when he bit my ass earlier. I was so weird. He growled. At least he liked my freaky ways.

"I knew it would be like this for us," I said.

He hummed a questioning sound.

"That night we danced. We were so perfectly in sync. I wanted you so bad. I knew when we came together—"

"Literally," he mumbled.

"—it would be this good. I never felt like that with anybody which sounds cliché but, I guess, I'm a cliché now."

He stilled under me as I started talking, but by the time I finished, his hands went back to exploring my body. I would never tire of the way he touched me, like I was the most fascinating thing he'd ever experienced.

"I knew the second I saw you that I would regret it the rest of my life if I didn't at least ask you to dance. Then when you left …" his voice rumbled under me.

"Sorry," I whispered.

"I felt fear like I never had. I thought, 'If I can't talk to her again, I will never be okay.'"

"I had never felt like that with a stranger either," I admitted. "I think I just freaked out."

"I was freaked out too. I couldn't let you go. And then we talked and I knew." He swallowed so audibly it made my heart start to race.

I wanted to ask what he knew. I wanted to hear the words. But I wasn't sure that we were ready for that. It didn't seem normal to feel so much so soon. This couldn't be normal.

"I just wish …" I said cutting off his unfinished thought.

He gently prodded my shoulder. "What?" he asked.

I moved up so I could look in his deep blue eyes. "Now I'm just thinking that we could have been doing this for weeks."

His smile faltered. "It had to be this way. I couldn't handle it if you had regretted me."

"Never," I said and leaned to kiss him.

"Everything worked out as it had to," he said and I believed him.

"So tomorrow …" I said not wanting to mention the elephant in the room but knowing that I wouldn't be able to sleep if we didn't have a plan.

"Tomorrow we will do our jobs," he said seriously.

I couldn't help the fear that made my palms sweaty. Was this his way of saying—

"And then in the evening I'm going to come back here and I'm going to kiss every inch of your body again and make you come until we lose track of the time. Because I don't think I can go even a full day without having you."

I chewed my cheek to keep from smiling and then wondered why I was hiding it. I unleashed a full smile on him saying, "That sounds like a very good plan."

Instead of laughing at my smile, his eyes grew dark. He pulled me back in for a kiss. Soon, he was inside me again. This time I rode him gently. Our hands clasped, as strongly connected as our gazes. In no time, we came apart together.

Though I was glad we had discussed a plan for the next day, it was obvious neither one of us was going to be sleeping much tonight.

Sleep was overrated too.

CHAPTER 24

ROXY

$\mathcal{M}$ ooreTek arrived and the next week passed in a blur of happiness. Whenever thoughts about our eventual expiration date would leak in, I pushed them aside with a simple, "Not now." Yes, Sanders would have to leave and go back to Denver, but those thoughts could wait. We were, as it turned out, a damn good team. My anal-retentive planning of every detail balanced out his laissez-faire attitude. And everything did work out. More impressive was that when something unexpected happened, I was able to handle it with almost no freak-out.

Like on the third day of the MooreTek retreat, when the kitchen ran out of gluten-free and vegetarian options. Normally, I would head out and grab the needed ingredients, scrambling to get back in time, sweaty and frazzled. Instead, I headed into the male-dominated kitchen and pointed to one of the sous-chefs.

"Can you run to the farmer's market and grab whatever the kitchen needs?" I asked.

He glanced to Johnny Delaney, the grumpy kitchen manager.

Whatever, Johnny, you take your broody good looks and shove it.

"Is that okay with you?" is what I actually said to him.

He crossed his arms and grunted what I guessed was consent. That guy needed some damn sunshine in his life.

Oh God, look at me. Since I'd started hooking up with Sanders every beautiful night, I was turning into Suzie, wishing love and happiness on other people. Gross. Soon I wouldn't even recognize myself anymore. And I could delegate like a boss now. Literally.

And wasn't that amazing.

I was still a professional. Of course. I still wanted my promotion, I wouldn't do anything stupid. But I was happy.

I couldn't help but smile as I walked back to the lobby. My face just did it all the time now. When I looked up, Sanders was watching from across the room where he was about to take the group out for a morning hike. His eyes met mine and he smiled with his whole body. I tucked my hair back and focused on the task at hand.

Each day went like that. We were professionals and we were badasses. We'd work all day, impressing the shit out of the customer and then at night … well, the nights were amazing. It was risqué and sexy to work as professional counterparts during the day only to lose ourselves in each other each night.

The same day as the kitchen shortage, I was walking down the hallway when a hand grabbed me and tugged me into the janitor closet. The room was dark, but the second a hard body pressed me up against the door, I melted into the kiss that met my lips.

Sanders kissed me in the darkness of the closet, grinding his erection against my thigh as he made me come against his fingers.

"A girl could get used to this," I said as we straightened ourselves back to sorts.

"You go out first. I need a minute," Sanders said breathing deeply and gripping a rack of supplies, slightly hunched.

THE ONE THAT I WANT

"I could help with that." I reached out and ran a finger along the length of him.

"Don't touch him. He gets confused. He's a simple creature. Plus, if I make him wait, the better tonight will be."

I flushed with the anticipation.

The days blurred together. Muscles I didn't even know I had ached throughout the day, bringing a smile to my face as I coordinated the events with a professional ease. I loved how bossy he was in the bedroom. I loved that I took the lead too. We'd already explored so much of each other but my mind drifted throughout the day imagining a hundred more ways to love his body with mine.

On Friday, Vincent found me double-checking the bus taking the group back to the airport.

"Roxy." Vincent smiled, standing coolly with one hand in the pocket of his dress pants, his blazer open slightly. Busy with the MooreTek crowd, I'd hardly seen him this last week except when he checked in a few times. The sight of him caused the same anxiety as before despite knowing the week had been a success.

We waited as Sanders finished helping the last MooreTek employees climb onto the buses. I watched him jog over to join us, nodding professionally at me before giving Vincent his entire focus.

Oh, we were so good at this.

Vincent glanced between the two of us. "Do you both have some time to chat?"

Sanders and I exchanged a nod before following him back to his office.

When the three of us were situated in his office, an unaccountable wave of nerves crashed over me. I longed to reach for Sanders but clasped my hands gently in my lap.

245

"I just spoke with the CEO of MooreTek," Vincent jumped right in as usual. "She could only say great things about the both of you. I think the term 'power duo' was thrown around more than once. Not only do they want to make this an annual event, they're happy to share their recommendation with other businesses."

"That's fantastic," I said, letting out a slow breath. I knew it, but hearing this review released some tension in my shoulders.

"Great news," Sanders said at the same time.

"Mr. Olsson, I hope this means you'll consider partnering with the Lodge on a more permanent basis," Vincent said. "We can all discuss the details. Maybe we can draft up some ideas before you leave. Things are a little crazy around here but I think it's an arrangement that would benefit us all."

I fought to keep myself as still as possible. A thousand thoughts flew through my brain. Sanders and I … it was only supposed to be temporary. Short-term I could handle. Short-term wouldn't derail me but even just looking at how obsessed we'd become with each other this last week … Could we sustain that momentum and focus on our careers?

Not now, I told the thoughts in my head. I kept my neutral expression on Vincent as Sanders responded.

"I think Outside the Box would very much like that. When Skip returns, I'll discuss the idea with him."

I stole a glance to see his big goofy grin.

Vincent turned to me. I sucked in my lips.

"Roxanne, I never had any doubt you'd be amazing. I've watched you all week. You've learned to trust and delegate. I've never seen two people so communicative. Next week let's discuss your transition into the lead events coordinator."

"Thank you," I said with a grin. "That would be great."

Vincent smiled back. Flicking his gaze back to Sanders, he added, "Now why don't you two go out and celebrate. You've both been working so hard all week, you're practically dead on your feet. You should really get some sleep." He glanced between us one last time with an unreadable expression.

I knew we hadn't been as discreet as we'd thought. My palms began to sweat. Things were happening too fast.

After we left Vincent's office, Sanders turned to me, his gaze far too intense to be appropriate for work. "Good work, Roxxo."

"Thanks, Colonel." I fought to keep my face neutral. "So are you thinking of partnering with the Lodge?"

"Of course," he said, his excitement growing more palpable with every step. "I think this could really work," he said. His eyes shone with a manic excitement.

"Well, as lead events coordinator we'd probably work together regularly," I said, flicking a glance to him, playing it cool.

Once we reached the lobby, he stopped in front of the fireplace, eyes bright and wide as they bounced around my face. "That's the best part. I could move out here and start a second location in Green Valley. Guaranteed business through the Lodge and maybe more throughout eastern Tennessee." He all but bounced on the balls of his feet. "Yes. Yes, this is perfect. I'll start looking for an apartment today."

"Today?" The shock of his words chilling me. I forced myself to think about the logistics. "Wait. Wait. You can't just—"

His smile faltered and I realized I had to be careful how I framed this. He was so quick to go after what he wanted. But he needed to do things the right way. *We* needed to.

"Okay. Before you do that. Let's think about a few things. You said you have to go handle your dad's estate."

He flinched. "I don't—"

"And what about your office in Denver? You should probably go talk to them before you do anything sudden."

"Don't you want me?" He frowned. "To stay?"

"Sanders," I said evenly. "Of course, I want that. This last week has been amazing but I just think you should slow down."

"Why slow down when I know what I want? I want you. I want to be here with you. What else is there to know? We're a great team. MooreTek said it. Vincent said it. You have a mind for the details. I handle the activities."

Wasn't that what he said about Skip? Was that how Sanders saw me? As Skip's replacement? His words weren't sitting right. He grabbed my hands as a growing panic sped up my heart. I glanced around.

I tried to pull my hands away but Sanders held me tighter. "What are you looking for?" he asked, his smile was gone.

I tugged my hands free. "We're at work."

"Well, they're going to need to know about us."

"No, I know. Just. Slow down." I pressed fingers to my forehead to fix my bangs. "I need to think."

Icy panic threatened to close my throat. This was all happening too fast. Buses were loading and unloading. A line had queued up at the front desk. The lobby was bustling for a Friday afternoon, guests checking out and new ones arriving.

Breaks squeaked loudly to a stop outside, drawing my attention. Skip stomped off a bus followed immediately by Jack.

I couldn't hear them but Skip was frowning, fists clenched and head down, as he entered the lobby. From behind him, Jack tossed out his arms and shook his head before turning and getting back on the bus.

"Hey, Skippo," Sanders called carefully to his partner.

Skip took in the pair of us, clearly noting my panicked gaze as he joined us. His scowl melted into concern. "What's going on?"

I'd never seen Skip so disheveled. Dirt smeared his cheeks, his flannel and hiking pants were wrinkled and dirty. The smell of campfire and male stung my nose.

"Whoa, mate, you need a shower," Sanders said.

"I know," Skip snapped. "That's where I was headed. You called me over. What's going on?"

"Geez, cranky. I've got great news."

I kept my face expressionless as Skip looked between us. "Okay?"

"The Lodge wants to partner with Outside the Box," Sanders said excitedly but faint lines of tension bracketed his eyes. He didn't like my concerns. He didn't like seeing his friend grumpy. His gaze flicked to the bus where Jack was presumably trying to get the kids settled to return home. Sanders focused on his best friend. "Is everything okay with Jack? How was the camping trip?"

"One thing at a time," Skip said. He ran his hand through wild hair.

"It's good news, mate. I can stay here. You can handle the Denver office."

"What?" Skip swallowed as a flush splotched up his neck.

"Yeah. I'll stay out here. Get a place and start a new branch."

"Wait," I started. "Vincent just threw out the idea," I clarified. "He still wants to talk to you both. The Lodge is in a state right now anyway. It could be months before the board approves anything," I emphasized. Couldn't he see this was too much for his best friend? Couldn't he understand that Skip needed him to go slow? Couldn't he see that *I* needed him to go slow?

Sanders looked at me like he couldn't understand why I'd said that.

When Skip spoke, his voice was slow and deliberate. "Dev and the team need to hear from you. You can't abandon the Denver office."

"I'm hardly abandoning anybody."

"You know, Dev and Callum told me they were thinking of starting their own business."

Sanders faltered for a minute, then shrugged. "So let them. Denver is over. Green Valley is where it's at."

Skip's face drained of color. "I spent the last ten years of my life building that business with you."

"So come here. Start over and move here with me."

Skip's nostrils flared. He glared at Sanders like he couldn't believe the words coming out of his mouth. "I have a life in Denver. I can't just drop everything to live here. I can't just run away from my problems."

Sanders flinched, the smile completely gone from his face. "Whoa, mate."

"Okay," I cut in. This was too much. I didn't need to be there while they worked through this. I would talk to Sanders later. "I think maybe you two need to talk."

Sanders threw out his arms. "I don't understand you. Either of you. This is great news. We're getting everything we wanted."

I started to back away.

"No," Skip said loudly enough that a few people looked over. Vincent looked up at us, his dark eyebrow rose behind his thick black frames. "You're getting what *you* want in this moment and you're forgetting about everything else. You're distracting yourself from real life." His hand gestured to me.

Heat burned my cheeks. "I have to go," I said.

"Roxy, wait," Sanders called but I couldn't hear any more. I wouldn't be the reason Sanders avoided his responsibilities. I wouldn't be a momentary distraction.

I walked away. I couldn't look at him anymore. I was too close to breaking. To falling into his arms and letting him use me as an excuse to avoid real life. When I looked up, Vincent's gaze followed me with a pinched expression that may have been disappointment but I didn't have the emotional energy to care.

* * *

Sanders

I RACED AFTER ROXY.

"Hang on, just stay here," I snapped to Skip. "I can't let her go."

Skip ground his teeth and shook his head.

I caught up with Roxy a few feet away. "You can't just run away from me again," I said to her.

She flinched. "Don't you say that to me, when that's exactly what you're doing."

My body went rigid.

She gentled her voice. "You need to deal with your dad's death, Sanders. You need to go home and take care of your office, your business, and all the other stuff. I'm not the one running."

"What about us?"

Her face was deliberately cool. "You need time. I need time too. Maybe the timing isn't right."

"We make it right, then. I think we have the potential to be something great."

"Sanders. We are something great … were … I dunno. But I do know that you can't be in two places at once."

"And us?" I asked as fear and anger warred in me.

"We were a summer fling."

Her words sliced me in half. Roxy was lying. She was lying, as sure as I knew when we played two truths and a lie that day. She was pushing me away. She was running. Not me. I saw the moment she left me in her mind. The moment a façade of ice formed over her heart again. One not even my sunshine could thaw.

"You're just scared," I said. "Your past is telling you that it won't work but that's not true."

"It is true. We haven't even slept this last week. We're lucky nothing messed up. We're lucky the client was happy. I've barely spoken to Gretchen since the moment you got to town. And I'm not saying that's your fault, of course, but my friendship has to come first. My job. I told you what it meant to me. How long could we keep this up?"

"We would find a way," I said through my teeth.

"I'm not saying we couldn't. I just—we just need time, okay?"

"I'm serious about us," I said.

"Let's not commit to things we can't promise. You go take care of what you need to. In a few months, we'll reevaluate." Her gaze moved over me one last time, shuttered and cold. She walked away leaving me numb and defeated.

"She's right," Skip said, snapping me back to the present.

I frowned at him, I didn't even hear him come up beside me. "What are you talking about? This fixes everything. I thought you'd be happy."

His fists were balled at his sides. "This fixes nothing. This is you escaping one problem and leaping into something else."

"I fixed my mistakes. I got us more steady business than we'd ever have in Denver." Now I was growing angry.

He shook his head at the ground, jaw tense. "What about the team? What about your father? I'm not going to go back there and clean up your mess. I'm done."

"What mess? It's fine. Everything is fine." I rubbed at my chest, acid burning up my throat. This wasn't how today was supposed to go. Our week with MooreTek had gone great. Roxy got her promotion. Outside the Box had gained new clients. Why was everyone freaking out?

"Sanders," he softened his voice. "You have to go home. You have to go say goodbye to your father. You have to get his things. You have to close your apartment, if you're serious about all this. You have to talk with our employees. You can't just leave people behind."

I didn't want to hear this. Why couldn't we all just move forward? Couldn't we just … pretend?

"Fine." I shook my head. "Fine. If everyone wants me to leave so bad, then I'll go."

"Sanders, you know we—"

But I waved him off and made my way to my room. I packed my bags and found a flight home. Twelve hours later, I finally walked into my apartment. Just like that, I'd left Green Valley.

My phone chirped with a voicemail from Roxy. I didn't want to hear it but I forced myself to listen anyway, just like my dad's messages.

"I heard that you left." Her voice was soft, making my insides feel shaky. "I'm not happy that you left without a goodbye. I know I was the one who told you to go but … I don't want you to think it's because … I loved our time together. I'm telling you this in voicemail because I don't think I could have said it to your face without breaking down and just asking you to stay." Her voice wobbled and I shut my eyes. "You had to leave. You said you want to be better, right? This is where you start.

"I have to be better too. You've made me want to be better. There's so much love just pouring out of you. You're so lovely and passionate and I'm so thankful for our time together. Take care of yourself, Sanders. Okay? Well, that's all I have to say. I didn't want to leave things where they were. I'm so thankful for our time together." Her voice went higher as she fought back emotion. "It's a lot more than I ever thought I deserved. It was everything to me. I miss you already. Goodbye."

The message ended. The silence rang out. I blinked around my empty, dark apartment as my heart thudded loudly against my chest. It was like everything came back at once. Being here, a million things I'd been pushing away came crashing down on me like a storm. There were no distractions or adventures anymore. I dropped my bags and fell to my knees. Then the tears came.

CHAPTER 25

ROXY

*S*anders left. I pushed him away because things were moving too fast. Now it was almost nine and I sat stroking the condensation off my beer outside the Lodge bar on the patio. My shift had ended hours ago but I couldn't force myself to go home where I would be accosted by memories of my time with Sanders. I stared at the sunset wondering how my life had gone from so perfect to unbearably wrong in just a few minutes.

"I'm leaving in the morning." Skip's voice pulled me from my wool-gathering.

I blinked back the burning in my eyes and looked up at him. "Okay," I said.

He held a beer and looked freshly showered but the sadness that radiated off him was almost too much. I gestured to the chair next to me. "Join me?"

We sat in silence for a long time. A new ache spread as I realized how much I would miss Skip too. I mourned the lost potential of what could be a really great friendship.

Without thinking, I reached out and squeezed his hand not taking my focus from the tall pines casting us in shadow.

"I can't do this anymore," he said into his beer.

He pursed his mouth and the gleam in his eyes reflected the reds and oranges of the sunset. I knew that he was referring to Sanders' behavior. "I can't keep being the one left behind. He does this. He leaves. He runs. He leaps without thinking ..."

I remained quiet as he collected himself.

"And I'm always right behind him. I'm always following him into the wreckage. I can't do it anymore," he whispered to himself mostly.

"Nobody should be treated that way," I said hollowly.

I was starting to see Sanders and Skip's relationship for what it was. A co-dependency. Both of them enabling and holding the other back. This was why I couldn't let Sanders stay for me. I didn't want to be his temporary Band-Aid. Sanders struggled with handling his emotions. He had this incessant need to keep everyone around him isolated from his pain. I'd witnessed the turmoil destroying him the night at the playground. I thought he'd cracked open to let it all out and let me in ... but he needed more than I could provide.

"He hides. He treats his pain like a wounded animal would. Only coming back out of hiding when he's better. Like he has to be this magnanimous presence or nothing at all," Skip said.

I nodded. My heart ached thinking of all the hours in bed we shared. The ways we loved each other's body. How open he seemed when I first met him. Only to learn later that he was far more shut down and fragile than I ever imagined. If I thought I was locked down, I had nothing on Sanders. It made me want to be more willing to explore emotions other than anger and retreat. It helped me understand that my actions weren't in a vacuum. I could hurt the ones I loved.

"You deserve better," I finally said.

"I'm starting to understand that I do." Skip smiled softly, that hidden, secret smile of someone falling in love and not really believing it. It was the smile I had worn all last week. I was happy for him. Lord knew, the man deserved to be happy. I hoped that the timing of this fallout with Sanders hadn't ruined that for Skip.

Sometimes you meet a person and you know they're meant to be in your life even if you aren't sure how yet. I had felt that way when I met Gretchen as a little girl. A different sort of regret added to my melancholy.

"You deserve all the happiness," I said holding up my beer to him.

"So do you," he said and gently tapped my bottle with his own.

"Thanks." We smiled at each other. "How are you? How are you feeling about the death of Sanders' Dad? I'm sorry, I never learned his name."

"His name was William too. Like me. When I moved in with them, they started calling me Skip. To avoid confusion." He smiled against the lip of his bottle. "And for other reasons, but that's a story for another time."

"William was like a father for you too," I said.

"Yeah." He thought for a minute. "I'm sad. So sad. But ... you know, it had sort of been coming for a while. I'm thankful for him in so many ways. He saved my life. He made me the man I am." Emotions tightened his throat. After a few breaths he continued, "But William as I knew him had been gone for a while. I think I accepted that on some level. It may sound terrible but I feel at peace. I'm glad he's finally with Eleanor again."

"Was that his wife? Sanders' mom?" I asked.

William and Eleanor. I ached for the couple I would never meet. Ached for their son. Ached for the bittersweet fact that they were reunited now.

"Yeah. I never met her but William talked about her a lot. More when it was just us two. I think, he was worried it would upset Sanders."

I frowned.

"What?" he asked me.

"Sanders just made it seem like his dad was okay or maybe not okay after his mom died, but that he handled it well."

Skip chewed his lip thoughtfully. "William? Yeah, I don't think he liked for Sanders to see his pain. I think he was so worried what losing his mom might do to Sanders that William fought to be the best dad and keep all that hurt at bay. But he never stopped loving Eleanor. He talked about her all the time."

"I wonder if Sanders knows this …" I said out loud but was thinking it mostly to myself. It didn't match the image of the man Sanders had built for me of his father. Would it help if Sanders knew how much his dad had been actually hurting?

"It was why they moved back to America. William couldn't handle being in Australia. He said it was too painful."

I raised my eyebrows. "Sanders told me he got a job out in Denver and wanted to be closer to his family," I told Skip.

Skip digested this information. "I guess in part. He needed family to help raise Sanders. But mostly it was because he missed her."

"Sanders doesn't know this," I realized. It explained why he felt the need to always be the life of the party. The strong one. Although while it did explain a lot, it didn't excuse his actions. Sanders needed to heal. He needed help that Skip and I couldn't give him. We would be there for him and love him as best we could, but he was the one who needed to *want* to change.

We fell quiet again. Eventually, he said, "It's not that I don't like it in Green Valley. I actually think it would be great to move here. For a few reasons. But I have a life in Denver and he does too—"

"And he needs to fix some things."

"He does," Skip finished. "He needs to face the music."

I realized that I might not ever see Sanders again. Wasn't that what I wanted? Maintaining control over my life had always been so important. I stared into the final sliver of light before it evaporated into dusk. I didn't know what I wanted anymore.

* * *

Sanders

THE BOXES STARED at me for over a week. Not that time mattered. Not that anything mattered. I was alone. My best friend was mad at me. The love of my life pushed me away. Yeah. I said that.

LOVE OF MY LIFE.

I glared at the boxes. The stack of old and worn ones. The stack of new and freshly taped ones. All of them sat staring at me, silently judging, waiting for me to make progress, from the corner of the downtown Denver loft I shared with Skip. The loft I used to share. The day he came back from Green Valley, he told me he was moving out.

I was growing to hate those boxes and everything they represented. A daunting task was ahead of me but I would open them. I would deal with my father's death once and for all. I would be okay. I had already scheduled my first therapy session for next week. I needed to learn how to stop running and start processing the deep pain the loss of both parents has left in me, no matter how I tried to hide it.

With a final bracing breath, I stepped toward the boxes of Dad's stuff. My hands shook as I opened the first few things. The first boxes contained old clothes that could be donated or thrown away and a few trinkets I would hold on to. I even found a few old newspapers that had featured about Outside the Box. Then came the pictures. Lots of pictures. Pictures that caused a pain to shoot into my chest with such

PIPER SHELDON

sudden force, it felt splintered and shattered, like a wrecking ball hitting a windshield.

I had no idea he had all of these. Mom and Dad. Dad holding me on his shoulders with the western coast of Perth behind us. The three of us grinning like fools at the camera. Another of Skip and me as non-smiling teens.

Pictures from a time I would never get back. Pictures of the pure, innocent love a child has for a parent that I would never feel again. Getting older was so hard. Growing up, you never knew you were living in the best moments until you looked back. Or maybe it was looking back on them through the lens of your current life that made them the best. The longing for something I could never have back hurt so physically, I thought I might never take a full breath again.

I loosed a shuddering sigh and sat back.

There was one last box. A small cigar box, completely worn on the edges so the cardboard layers showed. It was wrapped in dry-rotting rubber bands that crumbled away as it opened.

"What's this?" I asked the empty room.

Inside there were letters in dozens of unsealed envelopes simply addressed to "Eleanor." They weren't worn but they were yellowed with age.

I slowly unfold the first one, holding it with reverence that I instinctively understood it deserved.

The date at the top of letter was exactly one month after my mom died. Her birthday.

My hands shook as I read the first one.

Eleanor,
Happy Birthday, wherever you are. I never really put a lot of
thought into the afterlife but now I pray every night for a place

260

*where I will hold you again. I miss you so much. Every morning
I wake up and I have an instant where I wish I dreamt every-
thing. Then I remember the truth and I don't think I can even
breathe.*
*Then Sanders comes tumbling into the room and I smile for
you. For him.*
*I don't know if I can do this without you. I'm not strong enough.
I thought it would start to get easier but it hasn't. It hurts more
every day, in different ways. Sometimes I feel so angry I think
I'm going to burn something to the ground. Some days I'm sure
I won't be able to get out of bed ever again.*

I stopped reading when the words blurred in front of me. I wiped my
eyes on the sleeve of my shirt, feeling such intense pain. A physical
blade. Sharp enough to cut me into pieces.

I grabbed a different letter and forced myself to read on. No more
running. Just confronting this pain head-on. This one was dated a few
years later, also on her birthday.

*I know it's silly to write these letters to you. I look forward to it
now. It reminds me of when I was your Farmer Charmer trying
to court you and I had to sneak letters past your dad. I felt like I
was able to be myself more in those letters. Talk more freely
than I could in person. I hope Sanders isn't afraid to share his
feelings. I try to impress on him that it's okay to feel things and
not hold on to them. Sometimes he seems so okay and other
times I know he's hurting. He feels so deeply. He's such a sweet
and strong boy, that kiddo of ours. You wouldn't believe how
he's grown.*
*Skip lives with us now too. I couldn't see the bruises anymore
and stand by. That poor boy. I went to his good-for-nothing
father's house…*

I read on and on. Letter after letter as my body shook with sobs I tried to hold back. I had to stop several times to blow my nose and take a few deep breaths.

I never knew he felt so much. I never knew he hurt so bad. He had tried so hard to be strong for me. He loved her so much. It never weakened. It never stopped. I understood that he had been trying to teach me to accept the pain as it came, not to run from it.

Boy, was my new therapist going to have a lot to unpack with me next week.

> *I don't think I'll ever love again. At least now how I love you. I think a lot about the first time I saw you. You never believed me but I knew it the moment I saw you. I knew that if I didn't get your name, I'd go crazy. I was a stupid American and you were way too good for me but I took a chance. And then I never let you go. I wasn't the smartest. I wasn't the most handsome. But I had something none of those other fellas had: a secret weapon. I knew, without a doubt nobody would ever love you as much as I did. It was that simple for me.*
> *I know we fought. I know times were hard. Sanders never slept as a baby (already worrying about missing out on life probably) and we struggled to make ends meet sometimes. But God, what I wouldn't give to struggle through anything and everything with you at my side.*

I took a deep shaky breath and reread the paragraph again.

That was exactly how I felt about Roxy when I first saw her. It was like somebody shone a spotlight on her and a tiny voice in my head said, "You're gonna wanna talk to that one, mate."

I clenched my jaw so tight, my teeth ached. I'm not saying I would believe it if I heard it from anybody else, but I knew my father and I knew myself. Us Olsson men, when we fall, apparently, we know.

Nobody would ever love her like I would. I just needed to prove that. I needed to show her. It wasn't enough to just say it, not after a lifetime of running. Starting now, I vowed to change everything.

What I wouldn't give to struggle through anything and everything with you at my side.

I would give anything to be the person that struggled through life with her.

Fueled by my resolve, that week, I met with Dev and the rest of the team of Outside the Box and explained the situation. Of how I had screwed up and it cost the business but also of the potential in Green Valley. They were patient and understanding with me but had still decided to leave to join Callum and Dev, staying in Denver. I promised to send any remaining business in Denver their way. We departed on amicable terms even though it felt like the end of an era. That just left Skip and me. Skip, who wasn't talking to me at the moment.

After our meeting with the rest of the team, I stopped him in the hall.

"Can we please talk?" I asked him, knowing I didn't deserve the chance.

Reluctantly, he stayed and listened because Skip was nothing but a great guy. I explained that the Lodge had agreed to wait before signing anything official with OTB. I was done with rushing into situations and screwing things up. We had enough business here to get us through the end of the summer.

"Do you want to close down OTB? Tell me what I can do to show you I'm serious," I said.

"I need to think," he said. "I have a few more clients to wrap up over the summer. I'm not taking on anything new for fall. Let's reevaluate then."

Read: I'm still not ready to talk to you.

The days dragged by. Skip and I wrapped up the rest of our events in Denver, speaking only when necessary. Soon a whole month passed. I hadn't called Roxy back yet. No texts. No emails. Nothing. I was ashamed but I didn't know what to say. I didn't feel ready. She deserved me at my best, not the mess that I was. With every conversation I had with my therapist, the more I realized about myself. Let's just say I had a lot of work to do. She didn't need a partner that was so messed up or one that made her feel like she was nothing more than a passing distraction. No. When I came back to her, I would show her I meant business. And if she had moved on, well, I would cross that bridge then. I wanted us to be a team but I also knew I needed to be a better man for her first.

Green Valley felt so far away. Like I had dreamed this most perfect scenario but had since woken up to cold, harsh reality.

Roxy. She was in my mind all the time. She took up more real estate than anybody else. The longer I was away from her, the more I realized that maybe she had been right. Skip had been right. I had tried to drown myself in her rather than deal with my feelings. Now it was time to be better. I had to make things right. No more running.

I dug through a drawer to find a pen and paper. If Dad could pour his heart out fully on paper, then maybe I would try it too.

Dear Roxy ...

CHAPTER 26

ROXY

*M*onths passed. Weeks. Days. Seconds. The measurement of time didn't matter. I worked until I collapsed. I had my new office. My new title. I had the prestige that went along with it. At this point, everyone in Green Valley knew I was the events coordinator at the Lodge. Sure, maybe some narrow-minded individuals still saw me as a Wraith's girl. But you know what? I didn't care. They could see me however they wanted. Just like the calls with my parents, it didn't change what I knew about myself. I had worked hard to change my life. I had done it by myself with the help of a few people who had my best interests in mind. What others thought of me wasn't any of my business and I couldn't care less.

But I didn't have Gretchen. I'd still not been able to talk to her. Nor did I have Sanders because I pushed him to go. He needed to return to Denver but it still hurt to know that I had sent him away. I'd tried so hard to prove that I was living my life to its fullest and yet I worked every day until I passed out. I missed Sanders and our nights together. I missed the SWS and knowing what was happening in their lives. If only I could get over myself and reach out.

I was so alone.

I sighed as I watched a group of forty-something women chat happily about their upcoming girls' trip that weekend. They complained about their husbands and children in a way that said they couldn't be happier to have so much to miss back home. The ache in my chest sharpened to a point that jabbed my heart every time my lungs filled with air.

Maybe I should have gone with him. I used to think that one day I would know what the right thing was to do in every situation. But there was no right thing. There's what your head wants. And what your heart wants. Add in what you think the world wants for you and somehow none of it ever seemed to sync up. I fought the idea of flying out to be with him in Denver every day, but then what?

* * *

I NEEDED to talk to Gretchen. I realized that I had felt like a burden to her ever since she pulled me from the Dragon Bar. That I owed something to her, even though she was simply trying to give me a second chance.

"Hey, Roxy?" Vincent approached with one hand in his pocket and a cool look on his face.

"Hmm?" I asked straightening. I had been staring off into space. Just standing in the middle of the lobby without anything to do. Everything was taken care of. Everything was running smoothly. Which, unfortunately for me meant I had nothing to distract me.

"Are you okay?" he asked.

His handsome face showed a hint of concern. I hadn't thought he'd been paying attention. Now that I looked at him, really looked at him, I could see what a catch he was. Handsome, successful … here. Vincent had completely intimidated me at first but now we had become not friends exactly … but peers? The idea made me happy. I'd spent so long feeling like I needed to prove myself to him but he didn't care. He was never judging me. To be fair, he probably never thought about me at all. That's the secret I would pass on to all graduating classes from here out: *Hey, it's depressing but also majorly freeing once you realize nobody actually cares about you. Everybody is too busy worrying about themselves.*

I frowned. "I'm okay. How are you, Vincent? It's been a crazy last few months."

"It's been nuts. I tried my best to keep my side of the Lodge running smoothly, but I need to go back to the city."

"Oh," I said. I had grown to like working with Vincent.

"You've been doing a great job here. You earned that events coordinator title. But don't let it be your whole life. It's just work."

I gave him a look.

"I'm just saying that I recognize the sign of early-onset workaholism."

He had no idea. What else was there for me? Sanders had said I was worth more than what I did for other people but I still couldn't help but think if I had just done more, then I wouldn't be alone right now. If I had just …

But I was the one who pushed everyone away, determined to prove something.

"I'll have my doctor run some tests," I said.

He grinned at me.

"And I appreciate you allowing me time to get to know you more," he said. "When I read that initial recommendation email for your hire, I had some concerns. But I figured, if you could handle a biker bar—"

"I can handle pretty much anything," I finished. I didn't flush worrying what he thought. That was forever ago. It wasn't who I was now.

"It's a shame I never got to meet this Bethany Winston. It sounds like she was a major matriarch of this town."

I blinked at the random reference of Jet's mama, who I'd never met. "Bethany Winston?"

"She was the one who emailed Diane recommending you for hire. It was way down in the emails but I got the impression when Bethany suggested something, people listened."

I nodded dumbly. How had Gretchen convinced Bethany Winston to email Diane Donner about me back in the day? I didn't even know Jet's mom. None of this made any sense.

He went on but I was still focused on his last comment. "I've enjoyed working with you." He swallowed and I watched his Adam's apple move up and down. "I had hoped maybe we could get to know each other more."

I blinked in surprise. *Wait, what?* All these months of thinking he was judging me for being small-town trash and he'd actually been looking at me like I was a woman he was interested in? I replayed all our inter-actions in a new light. But there was nothing there. There were no zips and fizzes. He was a good guy but he wasn't mine.

When I didn't say anything fast enough, he sighed. "But I suspect that you're interested in getting to know Mr. Olsson better?"

I made a sound that came out like a groan and a growl.

Vincent scratched at his eyebrow under his glasses. "Yeah, I had a feel-ing. Had I known I was pushing you two together …" He shook his head and cleared his throat. "I lost my wife a few years back."

"I'm so sorry. I had no idea." I watched his face closely.

"I don't like to talk about it but I'm just bringing it up because well, if you have strong feelings for someone, you should give yourself a chance to explore them."

"Oh—okay." I straightened my bangs, wondering where he was going with this.

"I know it's weird for me to say this to you. I'm not trying to be unprofessional. But since I'm leaving anyway." He shrugged. "I witnessed the way you two looked at each other when you thought nobody was looking and … it made me think of my wife."

Emotion tightened my throat. I had no idea what to say. This was by far the longest and weirdest conversation the two of us had in all our months working together. Not that it was his fault, I didn't exactly scream "people person."

He cleared his throat and went on, "Also, I was organizing some files and found these mail slots in the back office." He reached into the breast pocket of his jacket. "The mail cubbies look like they've been long forgotten but I found these. Addressed to you."

He handed me a stack of letters.

"These were in the cubby with your name on it," he explained. "That kid at the front desk said he'd been putting them there instead of bringing them to you." He made a face that shared my opinion of the kid. "I assumed you didn't know they were there."

I shook my head dumbfounded. The shocks kept coming with this one. I recognized Sanders' all-caps scrawl on each one. My heart hammered. Letters. At least a dozen of them, addressed to the Lodge, care of me.

"People use email … since like the nineties," I said numbly.

What had Sanders been thinking? Nobody had used those mail cubbies since the construction started. That room was for storage mostly.

"Not everybody," Vincent said and I remembered he still stood there.

"I can't believe this," I said mostly to myself.

"Seems like maybe he realized it was a mistake to leave you," Vincent said and his strong gaze held mine.

Not quite, but it was nice of him to think that.

"Thank you for bringing them to me," I said.

"Good luck, Roxanne," Vincent said.

"Roxy. Please." I smiled.

"I hope everything works out, Roxy," he added with a demure smile. He started to walk away.

"Wait, Vincent. Are you coming back to Green Valley?"

"Maybe." He shrugged one shoulder. "For the right reasons."

He gave me a wave and walked away.

I stared down at the letters. With shaking hands, I brought them back to my new office. I wasn't sure what this meant. What could it mean? All I knew was that Sanders hadn't been ignoring me at all.

* * *

THE LETTERS WEREN'T what I expected. They were updates, casual conversations about what was happening in Sanders' life. Though it was nice just to hear from him, I wasn't sure how to reply, if at all. He had been mailing them for weeks at this point without my response, I doubted he expected any.

I needed to talk to somebody. I needed to clear the air with Gretchen. The longer the time passed between us, the more excuses I made. And I knew they were just that. But as I tried to think of the perfect way to broach the hard conversation with Gretchen, the universe decided to step in.

One text from Kim and I was moved to action. I was at Gretchen's apartment above Stripped within minutes.

"Did you see that bullshit?" I said as way of greeting when Gretchen opened the door.

Gretchen's eyes widened for a fraction before her face slid into neutral. "Come on in. Suzie's already here."

"She must know it's not right if she's texting us," I said as I walked into the room.

I dropped my coat on the side of the chair as I entered the living room where Suzie sat. She looked up at my proclamation.

"I agree. Something's as wrong as a feathered armadillo," Suzie said. "We should have tried harder to convince her to stay."

"You know us. An SWS member won't change her mind until she is ready to," Gretchen said pointedly.

I let out a sigh, fidgeting with my bangs.

"I've fucked up. I know I've been a bad SWS member and I'm really sorry. But we need to help Kim," I said. "I'm not here because of me."

They seemed to accept this before looking back at their phones. Kim had sent a text to the SWS group chat. It was a picture of a pill that was definitely not a placebo or an herbal supplement.

"I'm googling," Suzie said from the corner scrolling on her phone furiously.

"I knew it was a bad idea when she agreed to do this tour with Roddy. She never seemed excited," Gretchen said.

"That Instagram account is like watching a stranger. That's nobody we know," I said. My words weren't an outright agreement with Gretchen but hopefully she'd take it as a small white flag. Recently she'd accepted to go on tour playing her cello with her sort of ex-boyfriend, now business manager, Roderick Chagny. None of us had a good feeling about him but wanted her to be happy.

Gretchen looked up at me and nodded. "I didn't know you were paying attention."

"I was upset and needed space. I didn't stop being a friend," I said.

Gretchen raised her eyebrow in disagreement.

"Blithe texted about the drug too," Suzie said, reading her phone. I wanted to ask where she was, but I didn't feel like I had the right to.

I'd forgotten my phone at home, I'd left so fast. "Tell Kim to 'stay the fuck away from those pills!'" I said.

Gretchen, who'd been texting furiously, nodded and I heard the swoop of another text being sent.

"She's not responding." Suzie chewed her lip.

I glanced at the microwave clock in the kitchen. "She's probably on stage."

"You don't just text someone something like that and go MIA," Suzie said.

"Just like you don't fall off the map and stop seeing your friends," Gretchen said with no shortage of salt.

Okay, so we were doing this now.

"I need to go lock up the studio. I'll be right back," Suzie said before leaving Gretchen and me to a long overdue "come to Jesus" chat.

Sitting at the kitchen counter alone with Gretch's animosity, I was more nervous than I thought I would be. I had so much anger for so long about the night at the drive-in and then after everything with Sanders it all morphed into regret. But pride was a dangerous thing and I wasn't the only one who needed to apologize.

"You can't just stop talking to people. That's not okay," Gretchen finally said.

"I needed time to think. I'm not like you. You refuse to understand that people handle things differently," I snapped, her words putting me on the defensive.

"That's not true." Her arms were tight around her crop top.

"It is."

"Then why are you here? If I'm such a terrible friend, why not just stay away?" Red traveled up her neck.

"Gretch. You're not a terrible friend. That's not what I'm saying … I didn't mean to start on this foot. With us both getting worked up," I said.

She threw out her arms but I could see through her bluster. Her hands shook and it cracked my proud shell. "We've been friends for most of our lives. When you shut me out, it felt like my family abandoned me," she admitted.

That cut me to the quick. I knew some of Gretchen's pain. I knew what it must have cost her to admit that. "I know. I'm sorry. I felt bombarded. I was so mad at you and confused about what I wanted," I explained.

She sighed. "We probably both could have talked more that night. When I care about someone, I know that I can be a little …"

"Controlling," I finished.

"I was going to say overly concerned. But I've missed you, Roxy. I have wanted to call you a hundred times."

We couldn't quite look at each other, the stubborn-ass women that we were. "I've missed you too. You've always been there for me over the years."

"You have too. Even if you don't admit it," she said.

I shrugged. "You're a great friend. I'm just asking you to understand that people need to do things their own way sometimes."

"I just know what's best," she said, her voice high and innocent.

"Gretch." I looked at her.

"I was right though, wasn't I? You and Sanders clearly had a connection."

I sighed. "You're missing the point."

She straightened her spine and then relaxed. "Do you really think I'm so nosey because I don't want to deal with my own shit?"

"Sometimes," I said honestly. "But I know you're also one of the most caring, fiercest, loyal, and loving women there is. I'm honored to be a person that you give all that to. You'd do anything for the people you care about."

She didn't say anything but her chin wobbled.

"The crazy part is, I'd been doing all this for you," I said.

"What do you mean?" she frowned.

"I've worked so hard to show you that I was worth saving."

"Worth saving? What're you talking about?"

I gave her a look. It was the night we never talked about.

Realization set in and her mouth fell open before she said, "*You* saved my life that night at the Dragon Bar. I was set on murder." She sounded genuinely baffled. "*You* got me out of there." Her words were high and tight.

"You got *me* out," I said, shaking my head, disbelieving her point of view on that night.

"We saved each other," she said with a firm nod.

She was right. I'd spent so long feeling like a burden but the saving went both ways. The truth settled in and made me feel warm and valued. I let out a breath and nodded in return. "You're right. We did."

"But listen, that doesn't mean that you have to be somebody you aren't. It doesn't mean that you constantly have to prove yourself worthy of love. You exist and therefore are worthy of being loved."

"Sanders said something along those lines." My heart squeezed in my chest thinking of him. Two of the most important people in my life felt the same way when I couldn't see it myself. That's what loved ones do; they love you when you can't love yourself.

Gretchen's gaze drifted; she was putting pieces together. "I thought you and him could just hook up and have fun. I didn't know how deep your feelings went. You didn't tell me."

"He got under my skin that first night in Denver. I was shook up."

"It's not a bad thing to meet someone like that."

"And then what? He'd be here and I'd be consumed by him. I'd lose myself to him. I'd lose you."

She smacked me upside my head. "Ow," I winced.

"No you wouldn't, you doofus. You think I'd let that happen?" She shook her head like I'd just insulted her outfit. "Real Love is complicated. You don't get lost in someone, you help each other find who they're meant to be."

I studied Gretch's retro Formica table. Sanders and I had done that. We'd known how to push each other.

"I just didn't want you to think I didn't appreciate what you did for me. Getting me the job at the Lodge and—"

"Hold up. *I* didn't get you that job."

I rolled my eyes. "Well, I mean, I know I interviewed and stuff but I wouldn't have even gotten that if you didn't somehow get me that recommendation."

She shook her head, placing a hand on my shoulder to look at her. "No. Listen. I didn't get you the interview at the Lodge. Diane Donner and I weren't friends. Why would she listen to me?"

"You didn't get Bethany Winston to email her?"

Now she looked at me like I set fire to her whole wardrobe. "No."

"The links to the community college night classes? None of that was you?"

She shook her head. I stared into space trying to wrap my mind around all this new information. All these years I just assumed it was Gretchen and her meddling that got me into the Lodge. But if not her …

"Even if I had, you still would've had to prove yourself," she reminded me. "I just want you to be happy. That's why I push. You seemed stuck. You wear those suits and work so damn hard. Is that what you want?"

"I do like my job. I like working hard. I like being part of something bigger. I don't love the suits," I joked. Turning serious, I added, "I don't want you to regret what happened that night."

"I'll only regret it if you don't live the life that makes you happy."

The revelations were coming so fast, I couldn't process. I spoke the first thing that came to my mind. "If I don't do anything for you, why do you even want me around?"

"Because you're my friend and I love you. Oh my God, do you not understand that? Do you think that love is determined by what you can do for people? You're worthy of love all on your own."

"Thank you." Emotion stung my eyes. It was like a huge knot in my chest finally started to unravel. All these weeks apart. I missed her so much. Friendship like any relationship took time and dedication. I wouldn't lose her again. I wouldn't shut her out because I was scared. I took a deep breath. "I love you, Gretchen."

If Sanders could say it so easily to Skip, I could say it to her.

"And I love you, Roxy. Nothing will change that. Unless you stop talking to me. I can't stand that shit."

"Deal," I said.

"I'm pouring shots. The SWS is getting too fucking soft. These men infiltrating are making us weak and confused."

I rolled my eyes at her but happily accepted the booze. As we drank, I explained everything that happened with Sanders including his absence these last weeks until Vincent had given me the letters.

"Letters? Lame," she said.

"Well. To be fair. They're very sweet. It feels very old school."

"Like pagers?"

"No like ink pots and quill pens."

"Again, I say, lame," she said with a teasing lightness.

My smile melted as I sighed. "He just shares what he's been up to. His father's funeral. What's going on with him and Skip."

"Aww, how is Skip?" she asked.

"Good I think. He's actually here in Green Valley, we're gonna meet up for a drink."

"Why's he in Green Valley again?"

I frowned in thought. "I assumed it was for work but I'm not exactly sure."

"Hmm. Interesting. You know that night at the bar I could have sworn …"

"Gretchen. No. Down, girl. Let him figure it out," I said.

"Ugh. Fine. This is going to be hard."

"Time for you to maybe—" I started.

"I'm just gonna stop you right there." She held up a hand. "I'm good as I am. Okay, sorry I interrupted. You were saying about the letters. Tell me there are at least thinly veiled hints to sex."

"No. Not at all." I shook my head. "They're sweet but left me feeling like I wanted more, I guess. It's weird. When we met that first night in Denver … I wouldn't have expected all these months to pass only to be getting letters as a friend. It's like we're going in reverse."

"Nothing worth having is easy. It's a cliché for a reason. Look at what Kim and masked boy are going through. Look at the hoops Suzie and Ford jumped through. Love is a fucking mess."

"Yeah," I said sadly.

"We have to stick together," she said.

"I agree. I don't want you out of my life again." I grabbed her hand and squeezed.

She squeezed my hand back. "No ex left behind."

"Damn straight," I said and leaned in for a hug. God, I had missed her. It was like I could relax my shoulders after months of having them up to my ears.

When we pulled apart, she wiped at her face quickly and I pretended not to notice.

"Sanders has got to work through some things," she explained. "If I had known he'd be so emotionally unavailable, I would have never tried to set you up. Do you miss him?" she asked without judgment.

I chewed my lip. My throat was too tight to talk. I nodded.

"Such an idiot," she repeated.

I shrugged. "I agree." Then I cleared my throat because I was an idiot too. "What're we going to do about Kim?"

"I'll call Suzie back up. I have a plan."

"Of course you do," I said.

"We'll talk to her when she gets back, but whatever it is she needs, we'll be there for her."

I nodded. I missed this. This devotion to friendship.

"She needs to decide for herself," Gretchen said. "No more controlling. When she's ready for us, we'll be there."

I grabbed her hand and squeezed. "Good plan."

"But also, I might have to take a bat to that dipshit Roddy's precious car."

CHAPTER 27

SANDERS

I hadn't expected to return to Green Valley until I had a plan. I sure as hell hadn't expected to be back at a hospital so soon. The smell of disinfectant made my stomach sour. The squeak of shoes in the halls brought me back to those final moments with my father. My skin itched to leave, my palms sweated. But I was done making decisions for me. Or rather, I was done making decisions based on fear. I took a breath and pushed into the hospital room.

My throat tightened at the sight of him. His leg was in a cast, rigged to balance a foot off his bed using some sort of medieval-looking device. His color was not great and his beard and hair were more than a little unkempt, even for him.

My face must have betrayed the pain I felt seeing Skip like this. Seeing him off his feet took me by surprise. He was the one that was strong and steady.

"I'm going to be fine," Skip said. "You didn't have to come all the way down here." He faced the window and didn't turn to look at me when he spoke.

"Come on, mate," I spoke softly.

Skip and I had hardly seen each other most of July and August. With September coming to an end, I realized how far we'd grown apart. Once he moved out, I focused on wrapping up any other loose ends with Outside the Box. When we had spoken, it was brief and only about the crumbling business. We didn't talk about partnering with the Lodge. We didn't talk about the future of the business in Green Valley at all. I didn't even know he had come back here until I got the call from Ford of all people to tell me.

I'd fucked up so big I didn't even know how I was going to salvage our friendship. Or if I could. All this time I had felt like I had to deal with my suffering alone, so I pushed everyone away. Now that I really was alone, I realized that I'd been an idiot.

"Of course, I'm here," I said.

He glared at me. Finally. I was happy to see the anger. Anger was better than neutrality. Apathy scared me more than hatred.

I pulled the uncomfortable wooden chair next to his bed and sat down. "I hate this. I hate everything I've done. I hate seeing you like this," I said. Emotion made my throat tight. I wouldn't try to hide it though. I spent enough time pretending to be fine when I was suffering.

"Sucks, doesn't it?" Skip asked. "Seeing somebody you care about in a hospital bed?"

I held his gaze and nodded. I knew were this was going.

"Imagine seeing it all the time. Imagine seeing the most important person to you in the world, constantly putting themselves in danger, making stupid choices and not giving a shit how it impacted those around them," he said.

"I know. I've been so selfish. I'm sorry. I've been talking to a therapist. I know I was putting myself at risk because I—I didn't want to go out like my father. And losing my mom so suddenly. I guess it messed with me in ways I didn't even recognize. But I never did it to hurt you."

"Yeah, but you did," he said.

"I'm so sorry."

"You didn't care," he said. "You never cared enough to call before you left. To say where you were going. But I was always there, wasn't I? Walking behind you, sweeping up the pieces all too eagerly. You let me." It was the most vehement I'd seen Skip. It seemed he had changed as much as I had while we were apart.

I swallowed. Nothing he said was a lie.

"We're done with this, Sanders," he said. His arms were crossed and he was focused on the blank screen of the television.

"What?" I asked with a dry, cracking voice.

"This enabling of each other." His ears and cheeks reddened.

"I'm sorry," I said.

He wouldn't look at me. His chest was heaving with anger and his chin quivered. "I deserve better," he said.

"Fuck yes, you do. I want you to be happy. You deserve everything."

He sniffed once and looked at me tentatively.

"I needed you when Dad died. And you left."

I balled my fists until it hurt. "I've been so selfish."

"I know you were in pain. I was hurting too," he said.

"I'm not gonna do it again, mate. I'll show you in a hundred ways. Whatever you need."

Skip sighed. "I think it's time to close down OTB." He gathered his breath. "No. I know that I don't want to do OTB anymore. It was always your passion and not mine."

"Okay." I sensed it was coming but it still stung. It really was the end of an era. "We will work out the details when you're better. There aren't any clients right now anyway."

We sat in silence until, after a few minutes, he asked, "You're talking to someone?"

"Yeah. They're helping me work through some shit."

"Good. You're allowed to be more than one thing, Sanders. I'm your best friend for who you are, not because you can charm a car salesman out of his coat."

I fought to keep my features smooth when he said "best friend" but the relief was so immense that I couldn't hide a tremor in my lip. "I'm glad I haven't fucked it up so bad."

"You have a lot of making up to do. Not just to me." He held my gaze.

"Oh yeah, I know."

"Strength comes from living through the pain, not ignoring it. Your father told me that."

I squeezed his hand.

"Skip!" Roxy gasped out behind me, as if summoned on cue from the heavens.

My head snapped to the door where she stood, her hand to her mouth, face ashen. She was dressed head to toe in black. If she saw me sitting in the chair, she didn't acknowledge it.

"What are you wearing?" Skip asked, as he opened his arms for a hug without moving his lower body.

"It's a long story." She came forward and hugged him hesitantly. A waft of her sweet coconut shampoo reached me and I inhaled her deeply. "I was supposed to go to this thing with the SWS and—"

"Are you talking to the girls again?" I cut in.

She shot me a glance, faltering briefly as she took me in but quickly brought her focus back to Skip. "But I left as soon as I heard. Are you okay?"

"Yeah. Honestly, it's nothing. I'm just gonna be off my leg for eight weeks. You didn't need to come."

"I'd rather be here with you," she said with a wave of her hand.

"I'm glad you are."

They clasped hands and smiled at each other. Two months was a long time. I'd missed so much of my life by falling off the map. For a slight second, hand in hand, I thought the worst. I assumed the worst. Had my absence drove them into each other's arms? But Skip would never, not if he thought I had feelings ... not with—

"Skip?" another voice said from the door.

"Jack?" I asked, automatically looking for Ford who was nowhere to be seen. "What are you doing here?

Once again, the room ignored me. I deserved that.

Jack's usually dimpled cheeks were tight with tension. "Are you okay?" He walked toward Skip. His hands lifted and then dropped and eventually settled in the pockets of his coat.

Skip scooted up higher in the bed and tucked some stray hairs back. I looked to Jack. I looked to Skip. Jack and Skip looked nowhere but each other.

"I feel ridiculous. It's just a broken bone. I'm going to be fine." Color rose in Skip's cheeks.

What the hell had I missed in two months?

"We'll just go and see if we can find some coffee." Roxy dragged me to the exit as she spoke.

We came to a stop in the waiting area and she dropped my hand.

"That's a look." Her voice was neutral as she pointed to my beard.

Had she gotten my letters? Had she missed me? I had so many questions but found her so hard to read with this mask up. I kept my hands clasped behind my back.

"It wasn't on purpose. It just sort of happened."

My hair was long enough to be tied back. Curly in some patches and straight in other, it was a mess and super hard to manage. I needed to get it cut but hadn't cared at all until I sat here under her scrutiny.

"You look like you teach yoga on weekends off from your startup company and drink kombucha," she said without revealing any emotions.

I held back a smile.

"Really?" I looked down to examine my outfit of fitness shorts and sneakers. "I was going more for European-soccer-player exotic." I flexed my bicep and she smiled before she could catch herself.

"I've missed you," she said on an exhale and then frowned at her shoes.

"I've missed you," I responded immediately. Hope made my voice high and tight. "Can we talk?"

She glanced at her watch and chewed her bottom lip. "I have to go. It's a whole thing with Kim and her guy Devlin. But let's chat before you head back to Denver, okay?"

"I'd like that," I said.

I wanted to hug her. I wanted to scoop her up and handcuff her to me. But I could be patient. I wasn't going to give up. I was going to fight for her.

"See ya around, Colonel." She walked away, glancing one last time to flash a grin over her shoulder. As soon as she was out of sight, I clapped my hands and shouted "Woo!" causing a few nearby nurses to stare at me.

I pushed back into the room. Jack stepped back quickly from the side of the bed. Skip flushed and adjusted the blankets. Then he took in my face.

"Oh no," Skip said.

"What?" Jack asked, his face drawn with worry.

"Sanders has crazy-idea eyes."

"Oh boy, do I!" I rubbed my hands eagerly.

"Did you and Roxy figure things out?" Skip asked.

"Not even a little," I said grinning.

"So you're not happy?" Jack asked in clear confusion, looking between the two of us.

"No. Not really. But I think I can be," I said. "But I'm going to need help."

It was officially time to say goodbye to the Sanders I had been and start my new life.

CHAPTER 28

SANDERS

*T*wo nights later I found myself in an ultra-modern cabin nestled in the Smokies. Actually, scratch that, it was totally a mansion that looked like it had been pulled straight from the pages of a fancy home interior magazine. Did conducting really make this sort of money? I was in the wrong business. I would have loved to go exploring more but the owner was currently staring at me with daggers in his eyes and arms crossed. I looked around and behind me. Yep, definitely glaring at me.

"Devlin, he's cool," this came from Ford, who shot the big guy a skeptical glance. "He just messed up. You and I can't throw stones for that."

Devlin's frown deepened and he uncrossed his arms. He looked familiar but scowled every time I tried to place his face. Apparently, while I'd been away, all these guys had grown close in their proximity to the women of the SWS. Devlin, the scary one, had recently connected with his longtime love, Kim Dae. Ford Rutledge and Suzie Samuels were engaged. Ford and Devlin had worked together with Ford's Fosters, much like Jack and Skip had volunteered their time.

Interestingly enough, it was Devlin who invited us all to his mansion to make a game plan, but despite the invite, I didn't exactly feel welcomed.

"I didn't leave for two months," Devlin defended.

As I paced a living room the size of my entire apartment, Skip and Jack brought beers over from the kitchen. Well, Skip just scooted on his wheeled stool thing and Jack carried the beers.

"But you did let her leave," Jack said.

Devlin asked me in a deep, rumbling voice, "Two months and you didn't do anything to win her back? No wonder she's protected herself against you."

"I wrote her letters. The whole time," I said. "I don't know if she got them but the idea was there."

"Letters?" Ford asked with obvious skepticism.

"What's wrong with that?" The big, scary man glared at Ford.

Ford's eyebrows shot up. "No. Nothing. Very romantic." He cleared his throat and turned back to me. "What are you going to do, Sanders?" Ford asked.

"I'm not sure. I need to do something big."

"What does she want more than anything?" Ford asked.

"Could you write her a song?" Devlin said at the same time.

"I think she just wants to be loved for who she is. What we all want," I said to Ford. Then I turned to Devlin. "Unless I changed the words to 'Twinkle, Twinkle Little Star,' I got nothing."

"Well, what do you bring to the table?" Jack asked. There was a definite defensiveness to his tone. He'd not exactly warmed up to me. Hopefully he would in time.

Skip looked from Jack to me with a frown and then added, "Meaning what can you do for her that no other person in the world could?"

The three men looked at me expectantly. The reality of my situation hit me. Then I remembered my father's letters.

"I know without a doubt nobody will ever love her as much as I do." I slumped into a massive leather couch next to a fireplace the size of a car. "But that's not enough, is it? Roxy doesn't need me. She's totally fine without me."

Devlin and Ford exchanged a look.

"Well, he's not as dumb as I thought," Devlin said and moved to a chair to my left. The man was huge. No wonder he needed a house this size.

Ford sat across from me. He leaned in seriously. "Here's the thing. None of these women need us. They are all more than capable of handling life on their own. But that doesn't mean that they want to."

Jack helped Skip sit down before joining him on a smaller couch.

"I just want her happy," I said on an exhale. "I think I fucked up too much to get her back."

"So don't get her back. Just show up. Every day. Be there when she is sad. Hold her hand when she feels alone," Skip said.

"Believe in her when she can't believe in herself," Ford said.

"Tell her that you need her. That she makes you a better person," Devlin said gruffly, then cleared his throat.

I looked to each man, swallowing down a lump. "It's all true."

"Just tell her everything you feel. Don't hold back," Jack said. "The only way to receive real love is to open yourself to it. To become vulnerable to it and risk pain like you never felt."

Skip stilled, his gaze piercing the floor.

"Sounds awesome," I said dryly.

"It's everything," Ford said at the same time Devlin said, "It is."

Skip held my gaze. "It's the only thing that makes it all worth it. Having people. We could go through life alone. We would survive but we aren't meant to. We're meant to need people and to lift each other up."

"It's what this is all about, as far as I have been able to figure out. It's the whole point of life," Ford said to himself, looking at his hands.

"What?" I asked.

"To love. And to be loved," he said.

The room went silent. I would have never thought in a million years that I would be in a room full of men discussing the power of love. And yet here in this moment, it felt like the most important thing. We all studied our shoes. After a few sniffs and grunts, Devlin stood up.

"Okay. I'm getting another round."

"Yeah, sounds good."

"I gotta piss."

"I'm going to chop some wood."

We all spoke at once.

When we came back together, Devlin asked, "Okay. So what does she like in a guy?"

I thought back on our conversations. I thought of what she said about her ex, the biker. I thought about her parents who had no idea what a treasure they had made. Finally, I said, "Stability, I think."

"We've established that showing up and sticking around are a must," Jack said.

Ford was frowning. "I have a thought. Suzie really seemed to like it when I cleaned up." Color rose high in his cheeks. "Finessed my looks."

"Kim likes a little wildness," Devlin said, glaring around as though any of us would challenge him. "She likes my bike."

"I'm not a biker. I don't even know how to ride one," I said.

"I could teach you," Devlin said.

"Wait," Jack said. We all looked at him expectantly. "Oh. I have an idea."

"I don't like that look," I whispered to Skip.

When I looked to my best friend, he was watching Jack with a smile on his lips.

"Trust him," Skip said.

"How do you feel about sideburns?" Jack asked.

* * *

Roxy

"MOTHER NATURE APPROVED," Gretchen said as we all looked up and warmed our faces in the unseasonably warm fall day.

The SWS had just arrived at the Autumn Carnival just outside Green Valley, celebrating the start of my favorite season. A traveling carnival had arrived to town. The once abandoned mall parking lot now housed a carousel, a few sketchy rides, and food trucks. The delicious smell of fried Twinkies and cotton candy filled the air. This year's theme for the Autumn Carnival was 1950s and Gretchen of course had taken the theme and run with it. Earlier in the day we were invited to her closet and she dressed us accordingly from the wardrobe that could double as a store.

"It's a shame we look so damn cute," Kim said. "I'm about to eat my weight in fair foods."

"Don't worry, boo, I'll roll you out on one of those roller-coaster carts," I said lightly but inside I was a bundle of nerves.

"You're a good friend." She nudged me with her shoulder.

Kim wore white linen shorts that highlighted her fantastic legs. Her chestnut brown hair was rolled in pin curls and tucked neatly under a maroon ribbon. Her shirt was a long-sleeved crop top that wrapped around her to show just a smidge of her midriff. It was a patterned plaid of browns, yellows, and oranges, with a starched collar.

I wore simple pedal pushers in a retro pattern in a rainbow of golden-rod, hazelnut, and pea green. I wore a turtleneck of a solid goldenrod and a thick brown belt that cinched my waist to unrealistic proportions. I finished my look off with black and white saddle shoes and a high ponytail with ringlets. Gretchen even gave me a cat eye on point with hers and curled my usual straight bangs to fit the style.

"I'm glad you came out," Suzie said to me. "You've been working so much."

Suzie wore black capris and ballet flats with a fuzzy pink, cap-sleeved crop top. Her hair was reminiscent of Audrey Hepburn in her pixie phase … but with a body strong enough to hang perpendicular off a pole.

"I didn't really have a choice. Gretchen made me," I teased.

"Hey! I am not so pushy these days. I'm getting better," she added when I gave her a look. "Listen, people don't change overnight."

"Ain't that the truth," I said. "No. I really did need a night out. Seeing Skip at the hospital was a wake-up call." I didn't mention the other person I saw there nor my big plans for the day. Only Gretchen knew and helped me ensure it would happen. "I'm going to be cutting back a little at work."

"Glad to hear it. Did he seem better?" Kim asked.

"Yeah, he'll just be in crutches for a while. But they gave him one of those cool scooty things so he can still get around."

"That's good," Kim said patiently. "But I was referring to Sanders."

"Oh." I let out air. He looked tired that night at the hospital. His preppy look had grown out. The beard had been surprisingly dark and thick for his light coloring. His longer hair showed that he was more of a dirty blond, sun-bleached and saltwater-textured. Like he'd been captaining a ship especially wearing that damn knit sweater. I said, "He seemed sad. Better and worse. Haggard? Skip said he's talking to a therapist though. I'm glad."

"Therapy is so necessary," Kim said.

Suzie nodded. "We need to treat mental health like a priority and not emergency aftercare. If it was up to me, we'd have therapy as often as haircuts."

"Agreed," Gretch said sucking on a red lollipop that she had produced out of nowhere. Of all of us, she looked the most at home at the carnival. Her fiery red hair was wrapped in a silk polka-dot scarf paired with oversized white sunglasses so big her fire-engine red lips popped even more. Her outfit was a simple white and cherry halter dress with a sweetheart-cut top and a flared skirt.

"Does he love you?" Gretchen asked.

I shrugged. "He hasn't said so."

"Maybe the timing wasn't right?" Kim said.

She and Devlin finally reunited and they were in a very happy honeymoon period. Her cheeks glowed perpetually with joy. I was only a tiny bit jealous. Only because I had tasted joy like that once and now life seemed bland.

"Yeah, but I'm not the same. I think we've both changed," I said.

"You're still Roxy. And if he loved you, then that didn't change."

Let's hope, I thought. Instead, I said, "Can we eat fried food until I bust out of this ridiculous girdle? Thank God girdles died."

"Cheers to that," the girls said in unison.

We clinked our plastic cups of cherry soda.

After I swallowed, I said, "Damn, y'all. We seriously look good. Check out all the looks we're getting."

Kim blushed and Suzie blew a kiss at a passing teenage boy who then tripped over the flat ground.

"Everyone else here barely made an effort," Gretchen said.

"Everyone else here is wearing cheesy costumes from those Halloween superstores," Kim said. "We look like we stepped out of a black-and-white film."

"Seriously, Gretchen. You should dress people for a living," I said.

She shrugged. "I just popped around some vintage shops. No big deal."

Gretch was weirdly modest about her multitude of talents. But we did all look fantastic. We all had outfits that perfectly accentuated our different figures and most importantly we all felt beautiful.

"You could open a shop from your closet alone," Kim said.

She took a long sip of her soda. "When are the fellas coming?" she asked, effectively shifting the focus off herself.

"Ford is on his way." Suzie examined the crowd.

"Devlin too," Kim said.

"Oh, did you ask him about an autograph—" I asked.

"No," Kim said. "We just got back together. I'm not about to scare him off with your intensity."

"Fine," I said. "I can wait a couple days."

I was so happy for her. And Suzie. I knew their relationships wouldn't always be so easy but I figured since they had survived a rocky start to their relationships, together they'd be able to handle whatever came next. I couldn't wait to watch.

I blinked at the setting sun, feeling a new sort of hope.

"Are you thinking about him?" Gretchen asked softly at my side.

"Yeah," I answered honestly.

She put her arm around me. "He'll be here soon."

I rubbed my palms on the thick fabric of my pants. "What if he doesn't come? What if I've pushed him away too many times?" I asked.

"Then you'll be okay. Time makes it better." Something about the way she said it made me believe she herself had experienced the pain. I'd known Gretchen her whole life but she had so many secrets. "But also don't forget who you're dealing with here. He'll be here." She winked at me. Lord knows what strings she pulled.

"Okay," I said and rested my head on her shoulder. I was so glad to have my SWS back. No ex left behind. It was okay to miss the connection with these amazing women. It didn't make me weak.

A rumble in the distance made all of us turn our heads. All the SWS girls had a bit of instinctual reaction when we heard the growl of a bike engine, for good or bad.

"Oh, there's Devlin," Kim said. "Wait. That's his bike but that's not …" She trailed off.

"Oh my God." Heat burned my cheeks.

That was not Devlin. The man on the bike struggled to maintain control, jerking the handlebars trying to overcorrect. That blond head of hair shone like a beacon in the pink light of the setting sun. He coasted into the space in front of us, coming to a stop. Sanders' legs shot out to stop the bike from falling over.

"What is even happening?" Suzie asked next to me.

"I have no idea," I mumbled.

I imagined all four of us mirrored the same shocked face, jaws hanging open. Kim's shocked laughter broke the silence. It wasn't long until Suzie and Gretchen joined.

Sanders finally wrangled the bike into a standing position and hopped off with his usual cool confidence. He shook out his wind-blown hair. If there had been any wind. Or if he'd been really riding and not just pushed into the parking lot by Devlin who waved to Kim from a few yards back.

"Oh my God," I repeated, hiding my face in my hands.

At my side, the girls oohed and awwed.

"Look at those pants. I need those pants," Suzie said.

Above black and white Chucks, Sanders wore black leather pants. *Tight*, black leather pants. In fact I would argue that "wore" wasn't the right word because he clearly had been painted into them. They left very little to the imagination.

"Okay, well, now I get it," Gretchen said and I elbowed an "oof" out of her.

I was vaguely aware of Ford, Jack, Devlin, and Skip on his crutches approaching the scene. My friends and I continued to stare as Sanders put on his show. He chewed on a toothpick, as he shrugged out of his leather coat, and laid it on Devlin's bike. He squinted out to the horizon as he took a black fine-tooth comb from his back pocket. His arms flicked out with gusto.

"Lord help us," I said.

Carefully, he brought the comb up to the side of his now trimmed hair to run the comb through the gelled sides. Slicked back with what must have been copious amounts of gel, he smoothed it out with the comb. His beard was gone but sideburns were halfway down his cheeks. Without the leather jacket, the white shirt he wore was fully on display. I had to admit the biceps flexing under the tightly rolled T-shirt did very good things to my insides.

He finished his dramatic hair comb and tucked it back into his leather pants. Honestly, I was astounded there was even room for it in those pants.

He made his way over to us and my heart beat faster.

"Hi, Roxxo," he said.

"Hi, Sanders. I like your pants," I said thoroughly examining them.

"They're great, eh? I may not be able to have children now. But I'd say it was worth it."

I bit back a smile.

"Are you grand-gesturing me, Sanders?" I asked.

"I'm here to ask you out on a date," he said.

"I don't want to date you," I said.

"Lie," he said, the charming smile sliding from his face replaced with heated intensity. I was vaguely aware that my friends had begun drifting off to give us privacy.

"I don't want to talk to you, Sanders," I said.

"Lie." He stepped closer.

When we were only a few inches away from each other, he stopped. He didn't reach for me but his body burned brighter than the midday sun had. Now that it was almost set, his body glowed in the perfect light. He actually glowed. I so badly wanted to lean into him.

"I don't want you to hurt me again," I said.

"Truth."

I leaned in and kissed his cheek before I whispered, "This wasn't how this was supposed to go."

He frowned. "What do you mean?"

I turned and walked away.

CHAPTER 29

SANDERS

*O*nce again I watched Roxy's retreating form. I went to chase after her when a hand stopped me.

"Give her a minute," Gretchen LaRoe said.

"I thought you weren't getting involved," I said.

She bit into the sucker in her mouth. It cracked loudly. "Not unless I'm asked."

I thought of what Roxy said before she walked away. I squinted in suspicion. "What is she going to do?"

Gretchen raised an auburn brow and shrugged with a secretive smile. "Nothing more ridiculous than this." She gestured to the pants that were currently strangling my legs into numbness.

Suddenly, the music playing over the loudspeaker screeched to a stop and a monotone voice filled the air. *Sanders Olsson, please meet your party at the Big Jump.*

I glanced to Gretchen, wide-eyed. "Better hurry," she said.

I walked as fast as these horrible torture-device pants would allow. Once I started looking, it was easy to find the Big Jump. Probably because it was a one-hundred-and-fifty-foot bungee jump rig that reached farther into the sky than any other attraction at the fair. By the time I reached the front of the line, the sun was already down. The bright lights of the traveling fair clicked on loudly and drenched us in light. I caught sight of Roxy's pale face as a man strapped her into a harness with a thick green bungee. My heart dropped into my stomach.

"Roxy!" I called.

She looked up to me. "Hi, Sanders."

The man checked the harness by tugging on it. My own eyes studied every hook and latch to make sure they were in place. Her body shook as she gripped the edge of a red, boxy cage designed to lift her into the sky.

"What are you doing?" I asked her.

I reached for her but she couldn't seem to let go of the flimsy metal walls.

"I'm showing you that I'm not afraid. I'm grand-gesturing *you*."

Despite how terrified she looked, I couldn't help my smile. "I didn't think you were the type," I said coyly.

"And I didn't think you would ever paint yourself into leather pants," she teased despite her quaking.

"Roxy, trust me, you don't have to do this."

"Yes. I do. I am tired of being afraid all the time. I want to show you that I'm literally and figuratively ready to leap. This would have been far more dramatic if you showed up like you were supposed to. Instead of on a motorcycle." She shook her head with a laugh. "What were you even thinking?"

Pushing forward, I finally managed to grab her hands. They were ice cold and clammy. "I wanted to show you that I could be what you need me to be. I wanted to show you that I could be a biker. I dunno. It was Jack's idea. He could be fucking with me, now that I think about it." I shook my head to stay focused. "I'm serious about us. I'm not running anymore either. You can run and I will chase you. That sounded a lot more stalker-like than I meant it to."

She huffed out a nervous laugh.

"I can be here and provide for you. I can give you whatever you need," I said. I'd have to figure out the logistics but I never wanted her to feel alone.

"I don't want you to do that. I just want you. You're the one that I want."

"You're the one that I want," I repeated back to her.

"Alright, now or never," the bungee jump operator said stepping in between us and starting to close the door. "Going up with her or not?"

"Yes," I said and jumped in before they could close the door. There was another ride operator in the cage, checking his phone, not at all listening to us.

"Here we go," the first operator said, showing no emotion as he locked us in. Apparently our personal drama wasn't unique. He signaled something to the second man and the whole box lurched.

"Why am I up here. Oh my God, why am I up here?" Roxy chanted to herself.

The cage stuttered as it slowly started to rise. A familiar rush of adrenaline hit me as the ground moved further away.

"You don't have to do this. I don't want you to do something that scares you."

"Oh my God, oh my God," she said. She looked down as we lifted slowly before tightly shutting her eyes. The higher we climbed, the fainter the sounds of the carnival became.

"It's okay, Roxxo. You don't have to do it. We can go back down. Hey, man, how do we take it back down?" I asked the guy on his phone.

He glanced to Roxy in question.

Roxy said, "No. I'm doing this. I want to." The cart came to a stop and swayed lightly in the wind. "Oh my God."

The operator checked her harness and opened a door that transformed into a little plank for her to jump from.

He brushed past me to illustrate how she needed to keep her arms crossed in front of her chest. "Make sure you keep your hands tight to your body when you jump. Try not to flail," the guy said not caring at all that she was freaking out.

"Jesus," I mumbled.

Roxy was stone silent. Her eyes were wide open now and her whole body shook.

"When you're ready, walk forward and jump," he said and slunk back to the corner. Apparently, he was used to customers taking some time.

I shuffled to the edge to look over as Roxy mumbled to herself. Down below I saw our friends waving.

"Just jump!" Gretchen yelled, her voice barely carrying all the way up to us.

"Not helping," I yelled back down. Turning to Roxy, I said, "Let's just go down and talk. I know you have no reason to trust me—"

Roxy finally looked at me. "I trust you more than anyone." She shook her head. "It makes no sense. From day one, I've felt like I've known exactly who you are."

"There is no one else for me," I said, all silliness dissipated.

She watched me closely.

"The moment we met, I knew you were the one. I knew that every stupid, impulsive choice, every bad thing that had ever happened, had led me to that moment so I could meet you."

"So grandiose," she said but her eyelashes fluttered.

"Tell me you didn't feel it too. Tell me that when we talked, you didn't feel a connection unlike you have ever felt with someone. Because the more time I spent with you, the more I realized that what we have is the real thing. It was not fleeting. It was everything. These weeks apart have made me understand that I don't want to waste another minute." I brought her to me, trying to get as close as possible with a giant green harness in the way. "Life is too short to waste this. I love you, Roxy Kincaid."

Something smoothed the fear from her face. She leaned into me and kissed me softly. "I love you too," she said.

When I leaned in to deepen the kiss, I found only air. I opened my eyes to find her turning away. My hand shot out but it was too late. Without another word, she took two steps forward and tumbled over the side.

She screamed the entire time. People on the ground watched in mixed humor and horror. I covered my smile.

"Damn, I love that woman," I said.

BY THE TIME the operator and I came back down, everyone had gathered around Roxy. Her face was flushed and her friends complimented her bravery.

"You're gonna lose your street rep if you keep smiling like that," Gretchen teased to a grinning Roxy.

Roxy glared at her friend before sticking out her tongue.

"There she is." Gretchen hugged her friend and they laughed.

I tugged on Roxy's hand. "I need her," I said to the group without waiting for a response. I pulled her to a more silent alcove between two food trucks.

"Let's play again." I didn't have to clarify.

She looked away. I tugged her hands closer and bent until she held my gaze.

"I've been too scared to understand the gift that your trust was," I said.

"True," she said immediately.

"I've missed you so fucking much."

She looked up and to the side as her eyes shone in the setting sun. "True."

"I love you."

"True." She sniffed. "It's two truths and a lie."

"No. No more lies." I brought her closer, gripping her elbows. "I want to grow old with you."

"True," she said.

"No matter what happens. No matter what life throws at us, I will always understand that you don't need me. That you could walk away at any time."

She frowned but I went on.

"You could. You are a whole person as you are, Roxy. I don't want to ever complete you. I want to complement you. I want to be there when you need me. I want to go away when you need space and return when you're ready for a hug."

Her chin wobbled.

"It's okay to want a person to lean on. You would be fine on your own but some days you'll be tired. Some days you won't believe in yourself and I'll be there for you. I'll be your cheer section and you masseur and … your sex slave …" I wiggled my eyebrows and she rolled her eyes.

She quickly wiped away a tear that leaked out. My own eyes stung with emotion.

"The good news," I said moving my arms higher and bringing her closer. "Is that there is no rush. Just like a tattoo, you're on my soul forever. The good times or bad, you're a piece of me and we have nothing but time. My life goal is to grow very, very old with you. Until you have to change my diapers."

"Lovely." She smiled.

I pulled out my metaphorical trump card.

"I have something else to show you." My hand went to the button of the birth-control pants.

"Sanders! Nothing in there can help right now," she said with a laugh.

I winked. I turned around and shook my booty just a little.

She groaned. I watched her over my shoulder as I lowered my pants just a little and lifted my shirt.

"Oh my God. Sanders! Is that my name?"

"It is."

Her soft finger brushed over the area my tattoo was, not the newly inked letters, but the gothic butterfly I got when I was eighteen.

"The lines are amazing and detailed. The skull pattern in the wings is so delicate you almost don't see it at first. Amazing," she whispered. Her hot breath on my skin made me shudder.

I quickly zipped up my pants and turned around. There was no room for growth in these pants. I brought my focus back to Roxy's incredulous face.

"You tattooed my name," she said with a shake of her head.

"I know I said they're a jinx. But that doesn't matter anymore. You will always be a part of me."

"You're insane. And this was supposed to be my grand gesture." She shoved me lightly before grabbing my shirt and pulling me back. She kissed me softly on the lips before saying, "No more leaving anybody behind. No more disappearing. I couldn't fucking stand that. Stay and have the fight but don't leave."

"I promise. Always. I'll always fight for you."

She shook her head. "Fine."

"Fine?"

"You better shape up," she said with an arched eyebrow.

"I will. Because you don't need a man."

"I know. But my heart seems to be set on you," she said.

I whooped and punched the sky. "I'll take it."

"I'll need to be satisfied." Her gaze dropped to my mouth and then took in my whole appearance again.

"Chills." I shuddered

"It won't be easy," she said.

"I'm up for the challenge."

I lowered my head hesitantly and she closed the kiss. When we broke to breathe deeply, I kept my head pressed to hers. "You're the one that I want."

She let out a sigh. "You are the only one for me."

I gripped her so tight. I was never letting her go again. "Let me share your burdens. And I'll share mine with you. Good or bad. beautiful or ugly."

"Together?" she asked.

"Every step of the way, no matter where."

"I think I'd love that."

"I love you so, *so* much, Roxy Kincaid. Every single inch of you. Inside and out. From here on out, you are not alone."

"And neither are you," she said. "I love you, Sanders Olsson."

Our lips met again. This beautiful, wonderful, amazing woman was mine. All mine. When we finally stopped kissing, the sky had almost completely darkened. The lights of the rides and stands glittered all around us.

I adjusted myself with a wince. "We can't do that anymore until I get out of these pants."

"Promises, promises," she said. "Let's drive off into the sunset on the bike."

"You're a little daredevil now. But I'm not risking your life or mine. We can take a car."

"Ah, so afraid to take risks. Live a little."

I held her seriously. "No more unnecessary risks. No more covering the pain with adrenaline. I'm going to show up every day and be with you."

She let loose a breath. "Me too."

CHAPTER 30

ROXY

The club thrummed around me. I danced free and without thought. I let the pulsing lights and the shaking beat of the music drive my body. I rocked and shook and raised my arms above my head.

A chill started just behind my ear and tickled down my arm, alerting me that I was being watched.

I glanced over my shoulder and found the source. A man with a piercing blue gaze watched me from across the dance floor. Chin tucked, he studied my movements like he couldn't see anything else. My breath came out in a gasp as his sexy glare penetrated me. He made me tighten with desire.

I pretended not to see him. But I liked how sexy it made me feel to be the only one he focused on in a room full of beautiful people. I moved with purpose. I let my instant lust for this man rock my hips and arch my back. My hands tangled in my hair before sliding down, sticking to my sweaty body. I thought about him licking me clean.

When I glanced back, he was gone. Until a second later a hard body pressed against my back. I sucked in a breath as a large calloused hand spanned from hip to hip under my shirt, bringing me close to his solid form. I threw my head back.

"Let's dance," he grumbled in my ear.

"So pushy." I arched my backside into the hard length of him. "I think we already are dancing."

He growled in my ear, and chills prickled my skin. "I couldn't stop watching you. I have to have you."

I turned my head as our bodies moved side to side, forward and back, swirled. His fingers gripped the flesh of my hip and he brought me closer yet.

"How presumptuous," I said. "I like your accent," I added.

He chuckled in my ear. "I like yours," he shot back. "I've wanted to hear it calling my name since the moment we met."

"My boyfriend wouldn't like you touching me like this."

"Your boyfriend is an idiot to ever leave your side," he growled.

"Fair point."

Sanders turned me in his arms so I could face him. This new little game was doing very good things to me. He brought a hand up to cup my cheek and pull me in for a kiss. "He won't be making that mistake ever again."

"Dance with me," I said. "Kiss me. Make me feel whole."

"You're already whole." He slid his leg between mine until I was obscenely straddling his solid thigh. "But I can make you feel full." He bit at my lip. "Cherished." He licked up the column of my neck. He rubbed himself against me. "And completely satisfied."

His thigh between mine, a hot spike of desire shot to my core. I fought to keep from grinding too provocatively against the hard muscles. One arm wrapped me close. My breasts pressed into his chest and he grunted. We were sort of still dancing as our mouths met. We kissed on the dance floor in front of God and everyone. Our tongues clashed and our hands tried to remember we were in public. I cupped his ass and squeezed roughly. He broke our kiss to growl in my ear and then gently bite my neck.

All at once the teasing became too much and I realized I couldn't hang at this level of role-play teasing. I was about to strip on this dance floor. He must have seen that fact in my gaze. His eyes went dark with want. His usual light blue eyes were almost black. His hands squeezed impatiently at my waist, bottom, thigh, and shoulders. He sneakily reached up between us to run a thumb across my nipple. I glared at him and licked my lips. He watched my tongue and bent to suck on my lips.

"Get a room," Gretchen yelled, dancing up next to us.

"Okay." Sanders shrugged and made to pull me from the dance floor. I dug my heels into the ground to stop him, laughing as Gretchen rolled her eyes and danced away.

I straightened my shirt and pulled my hair off my neck, fanning myself. Kim and Devlin danced a few feet away. Well, dancing was a stretch. They had their foreheads pressed together, Devlin lifting her slightly off the ground in his linebacker arms. Swaying to a tempo that nobody else heard. Their gazes were so intense, I had to look away.

I grabbed Sanders' hand and tugged him toward our VIP section at the club in Knoxville. Above the main floor, it was still loud but easier to talk. Suzie sat on a red couch with her strong legs thrown over Ford's lap. His hand slid up and down her legs as though he couldn't help himself. Whispering in her ear as she bit her lip and smiled. The mini, fake white veil slipped from her hair as she threw her head back to laugh.

I sat down and reached for a water as Sanders moved next to me, close enough that the entire side of my body was pressed against him. He kissed my neck and nuzzled into me as I gulped it down. I took a deep breath and wiped off my mouth, handing the bottle back to him.

A minute later, Kim, Devlin, Gretchen, Jack, and Skip joined us.

"A toast," Gretchen announced and lifted her glass.

We all lifted our various drinks into the air.

"To the happy couple, Ford and Suzie. May they grow old and wrinkled together."

"Cheers," we all said in unison and then clinked glasses across the low table.

Gretchen threw back her shoot and yelled, "Hot damn! Also—" She picked up another shot glass and held it into the air.

Sanders squeezed my side and I gave him a questioning look. I had no idea what she was on about but Suzie and Ford seemed happy enough to let her lead the show.

"Another toast. To Jethro Winston."

Suzie, Kim, and I exchanged a wide-eyed look. Sanders stiffened at my side. Devlin and Ford looked downright grumpy.

"Uhh, what the cluck?" Suzie said.

"Hear me out." Gretchen held up her free hand. "Romeo Jr. was a dumpster fire of a person. We can all agree he was on the path to become his father. But Jethro Winston … well, he tried to make things better, didn't he?"

Kim and Suzie exchanged a look I couldn't read. And I wondered if there was more to their Jethro story than I knew.

I thought about Jethro's proposal all those years ago and what he was trying to do. His heart had been in the right place. He had loved me in his way. Young love. First love maybe, but not real love. We would have never worked out. I had to admit he had been trying to rescue me from the Wraiths. I was just too damn stubborn to let anybody save me.

Looking around the table, Gretchen sighed in resignation, "And if we aren't even able to agree on that, we have to concede that he had fan-fucking-tastic taste in women."

"Well, that's true," Sanders said loudly with a shrug. He winked at Gretch and she rolled her eyes at him.

"Everything happened as it had to," I said loudly, finding my voice as I spoke. "I don't regret our pasts. Everything we have been through made us who we are. But that doesn't define us, right?" My voice grew stronger as I spoke. "We all have shit that we don't want to think about, but what we do now, how we act and love and all that shit. That's what matters, doesn't it?"

"I'll drink to that," Gretchen said and the rest chimed in with similar sentiments.

Heat burned my cheeks, but looking around the table, I knew I meant everything I said. And all the people at this table understood it too. We all have a story. We all have a life and things that make us strive to live better. We're all just trying to get by. These people brought joy to my life. But more than that, they made me feel like I was part of something bigger than myself. I needed people and that was okay. The SWS, and the men that love us, they made me a well-rounded person. It wouldn't always be easy … but I was happy, dammit.

After another few shots and a few more hours of dancing, we were all slouched along the couches of the VIP area again to continue Suzie and Ford's engagement party.

"Have you guys decided when the wedding is?" I asked Suzie.

"Next summer, we think," she answered.

"Where at?" Kim asked.

"I'm fine with the courthouse. Maybe Vegas. Oh, or a destination wedding! Unlimited drinks on white sandy beaches. What do you think, babe?" she asked Ford.

He smiled slowly, his salt-and-pepper hair disheveled and Suzie ran a hand through it to sweep it off his face. "I don't care. I just want to marry her. I want to let the whole world know I snagged the best woman."

"Aww," we all chorused and Suzie blushed deeply, happiness seeping out of her.

"Seriously, how did we all get so damn lucky?" Sanders asked.

"You're welcome," Gretchen chirped and I just shook my head. "I have a gift."

"You sure do. Well, let's see …" Kim said. "Devlin and me." She pointed to Suzie.

"Me and Ford," Suzie said.

"You led me to my Roxy," Sanders jumped in seeing where Kim was going.

"Don't." Gretchen warned as she straightened in the couch. Her red hair was a mess from dancing. "Do not even go there. We know this isn't happening for me."

"Why?" I asked.

She gave me a look like I of anyone should know why.

"Please. This isn't about me. Let's just be happy for the engaged couple. Okay? Soon, you all will be shacking up and popping out babies and I'll be cool Aunt Gretchen who helps them buy booze for parties."

"Wait, what?" Kim said.

I laughed. "Oh, Gretchen." I leaned forward to squeeze her leg. "Sweet, sweet Gretchen. All these years of meddling and you think you're just gonna get off the hook?"

"I don't need a man." She lifted her chin.

"And we do?" I asked.

Sanders was fuzzy with drink and winked sloppily at me. "Nope," he said.

"I just mean. I know—" She started but it was my turn to cut her off.

"None of us *need* these men." I looked to the grumpy faces of Devlin and Ford. "Sorry," I added not meaning it. Ford just nodded like it was true but Devlin shot me a look that made me flinch. "But we are certainly much better for having you all in our lives."

I turned in Sanders' lap, to look in his eyes. "You've made me believe in myself. You made me realize that love is not weakness. Love is the opposite. Fear is easy. Fear protects you. Love makes you vulnerable and scared. However, the reward is so much higher. I see that now, thanks to you."

"I love you," he said holding my gaze with somber intensity.

"I love you too." I looked to the others feeling embarrassing moisture in my eyes. "I love you all. And apparently I'm a sappy drunk." I sniffed and everybody shared their love in return.

I looked around the table and felt so much for each and every one of these people in my life.

"Time to go," Sanders said unceremoniously. He scooped me up and threw me over his shoulder like a fireman. I squealed and tried to keep my skirt from flashing all my friends. "We gotta go. See ya," Sanders said and started walking me to the front.

"Wait, we all took a limo!" I called.

He set me down but the others were coupling up and collecting their things too. They all seemed to have the same idea. Skip and Jack shared a look that brought heat to my cheeks.

"Alright, I'll tell the driver we're ready," Gretchen said as she brought her phone out. "Couples, blah." She stuck out her tongue dramatically but was smiling.

"You only have yourself to blame," I said and put my arm around her. I kissed her cheek.

"Yeah. Yeah." She smiled but there was just a hint of sadness that I vowed to take away, no matter what it took.

A few hours later, Sanders and I lay in bed at my apartment, sweaty and sated.

"We have to get up in four hours," he mumbled, glancing at the alarm clock.

I ran a hand over my face. "Whose genius idea was it to take those shots?" I asked even though I loved the heat from the love bites Sanders had left all over my body. I stretched, languid with satisfaction.

He pulled me closer to spoon, drawing the duvet up to cover us.

"I hope we don't smell like tequila in the morning. Someone will smell it on me."

Sanders groaned. "Don't say that word."

"Tequila?" I asked and he groaned again. I laughed and said, "Aren't you taking that group zip-lining today?" I teased.

He fake sobbed against my back. "Well, it may be me that loses my cookies this time." He yawned. "Is this the group from the Florida company?"

"No, that's next week. This is the one from Texas."

"Oh yeah. I did know that," he said.

"I know." I shimmied and turned until we were face to face. "Are you happy?" I asked him.

"So much. I love working with the Lodge."

"And you're glad you moved out here? It's very different than Denver."

"Mm-hmm." He nodded sleepily. His eyes were already closed.

"I think Skip is going to move out here soon. All these trips back and forth for 'work' have to be draining on him." I emphasized work because he clearly wasn't flying out to only help Sanders establish OTB in Green Valley.

"Hmm, hope so," Sanders slurred, almost asleep.

I traced a finger over his relaxed face. I loved him so much my chest ached with it. I deserved this happiness, I reminded myself. His light lashes fluttered under my perusal.

"I love you, Roxy." His eyes opened and held mine. "You have made me the happiest person alive. No matter what the future brings for us, I want you to know that you've made me a better person."

"I love you," I said back. "We're going to make each other great."

His eyes flicked back and forth between mine. "I think so too." Then he groaned.

"What's wrong?" I asked.

"I was just falling asleep." He sighed dramatically and pulled back the blanket. "Now, I have to have you again."

I giggled as he climbed on top of me.

I was complete. I was happy. I trusted in this. From now on, I wasn't alone at all.

ACKNOWLEDGMENTS

Like so many, 2020 was a struggle for countless reasons and there were many times, as with most authors I'm sure you follow, I wasn't sure if writing was something I could even do in a time of so much uncertainty. Eventually, Roxy and Sanders found their way back to me and their love gave me hope once again. Isn't that the whole point? That love conquers all. My love of writing and the love I felt from my friends and family did just that.

As always, this book would not be possible without many, many people (this year especially).

Tracy, thank you as always for picking me up and dusting me off to remind me that I could do this.

Kelly, Shan, and Layla, thank you for the reads, the company, the countless conversations and words of encouragement. This book would NOT exist without you.

Elaine, thanks for letting me blatantly steal an Aussie joke from you.

My fellow Smartypants authors and Fi for endless advice, support and laughter.

Browhiski, the MVP of my heart, thank you for all that you do.

Lynsey, thanks for telling the truth and making this book so much better. You think you are a storm cloud but you are often a ray of light when I need to see the sun.

My betas - your comments SAVED THIS BOOK.

Penny, for letting me live in your world as though it were my own. Your kindness knows no bounds.

Thanks to Pipe's Peeps. I cannot emphasize this enough, YOU ALL kept me afloat this year. Thanks for those who waited patiently, who checked in, who sent me thoughts and love. I am so grateful for you all. To the VIPeeps of my heart, thank you so much for sticking with me.

To JR, just…I can't even begin to thank you for saving me this last year and making me do hard things. We can do hard things.

To mini P, for keeping me going, making me laugh and astounding me every day.

Finally, Tina. May you never read this but know if not for you, I may have never returned from the darkness.

ABOUT THE AUTHOR

Piper Sheldon writes Contemporary Romance and Magical Realism books that hope to be NYT bestsellers when they grow up. For now, she works as a technical writer during the day and writes about love the rest of the time. Of course she also makes room for her husband, toddler, and two needy dogs at home in the Desert Southwest.

Find Piper Sheldon online:
Facebook: http://bit.ly/2lAvr8A
Twitter: http://bit.ly/2kxkioK
Amazon: https://amzn.to/2kx2RVn
Instagram: http://bit.ly/2lxxV7H
Website: http://bit.ly/2kitH3H

Find Smartypants Romance online:
Website: www.smartypantsromance.com
Facebook: https://www.facebook.com/smartypantsromance
Twitter: @smartypantsrom
Instagram: @smartypantsromance
Newsletter: https://smartypantsromance.com/newsletter/

ALSO BY PIPER SHELDON

Other Books by Piper Sheldon

The Unseen Series

The Unseen (Unseen Book #1)

The Untouched (Unseen Book #2) Coming 2021

The Scorned Women's Society Series

My Bare Lady (Book #1)

The Treble With Men (Book #2)

The One That I Want (Book #3)

Star Crossed Lovers series with Nora Everly

Midnight Clear (Book #1 Novella)

If The Fates Allow (Book #2) Coming 2021

ALSO BY SMARTYPANTS ROMANCE

Green Valley Chronicles

The Love at First Sight Series

Baking Me Crazy by Karla Sorensen (#1)

Batter of Wits by Karla Sorensen (#2)

Steal My Magnolia by Karla Sorensen(#3)

Fighting For Love Series

Stud Muffin by Jiffy Kate (#1)

Beef Cake by Jiffy Kate (#2)

Eye Candy by Jiffy Kate (#3)

The Donner Bakery Series

No Whisk, No Reward by Ellie Kay (#1)

The Green Valley Library Series

Love in Due Time by L.B. Dunbar (#1)

Crime and Periodicals by Nora Everly (#2)

Prose Before Bros by Cathy Yardley (#3)

Shelf Awareness by Katie Ashley (#4)

Carpentry and Cocktails by Nora Everly (#5)

Love in Deed by L.B. Dunbar (#6)

Scorned Women's Society Series

My Bare Lady by Piper Sheldon (#1)

The Treble with Men by Piper Sheldon (#2)

The One That I Want by Piper Sheldon (#3)

Park Ranger Series

Happy Trail by Daisy Prescott (#1)

Stranger Ranger by Daisy Prescott (#2)

The Leffersbee Series

Been There Done That by Hope Ellis (#1)

The Higher Learning Series

Upsy Daisy by Chelsie Edwards (#1)

Seduction in the City

Cipher Security Series

Code of Conduct by April White (#1)

Code of Honor by April White (#2)

Cipher Office Series

Weight Expectations by M.E. Carter (#1)

Sticking to the Script by Stella Weaver (#2)

Cutie and the Beast by M.E. Carter (#3)

Weights of Wrath by M.E. Carter (#4)

Common Threads Series

Mad About Ewe by Susannah Nix (#1)

Give Love a Chai by Nanxi Wen (#2)

Educated Romance

Work For It Series

Street Smart by Aly Stiles (#1)

Heart Smart by Emma Lee Jayne (#2)

Lessons Learned Series

Under Pressure by Allie Winters (#1)